# TREES
# AND
# WEEDS

by
Eric Carlton Neperud

ERIC CARLTON NEPERUD

For Judy,
Mother and Inspiration

By Eric Carlton Neperud

THE LIMBO CHRONICLES
     Trees And Weeds
     Limbo
     The Octagonal Knight
     Dragons And Golems
     The Brotherhood Of Giants
     Wizards And Druids

THE YELLOWSONE TRILOGY
     Wonders Of The Wilderness
     Fleas Upon Snow
     The Periphery Of Sorrow

Copyright © 2016 by Eric Carlton Neperud
All rights reserved.
ISBN: 0-9983838-0-5
ISBN-13: 978-0-9983838-0-4
Published by Valhalla Books

Cover Illustration by Amy Lorraine Silenieks-Rogers
Map on back cover by Eric Carlton Neperud
Map on page 229 by Eric Carlton Neperud

My name is Marvin Tinker, but you'll probably forget it. I almost have. When a person changes his environment he often becomes another person. It's only fitting that his name also changes.

# Chapter 1

## GUILTY

"A jury of your hypothetical peers has found you guilty of murder, forfeiting all rights and privileges of citizenship. Your name and history has been deleted from public record. You are to spend the remainder of your days at Dartmoor Penal Colony."

No longer being a citizen, I wasn't allowed to respond to the verdict. I was taken away immediately. I wasn't the only person to be tried and sentenced today. The court had a perpetually full docket. It ran around the clock, the only deviations in routine being the ebb and flow of attorneys, accused and proctors (token human liaisons/facilitators). Judges/juries consisted of algorithms that weighed evidence for and against the accused, balancing both local and universal norms, taking into account the dissimilar interpretation of laws of diverse racial, economic, and political groups.

I was escorted to a processing center. Transfixed in shock, I did so peacefully. Murder. Loss of freedom---forever. It was too much to take.  There were witnesses.  Many witnesses.  Virtual and human.  But I didn't do it.  I don't remember doing it.  Traumatic events cause amnesia.  The insanity defense?  It's been more than a century since the root of evil mattered.  Dead was dead.  A mental illness wasn't going to return a son to a mother, a husband to a wife, or a father to a son.

The room I now stood in alone was, essentially, a metal box.  Seamless.  No deviation in texture or color.  After my escort left, the aperture we entered from closed.  Molecular manipulation was expensive, but provided nearly flawless security.

"Strip."  I did what I was told, not having the emotional energy to become stubborn or throw a tantrum.  I understood the symbolism.  Leaving the same way we entered.  But couldn't there have been a better way to get the point across?  Or was it a new beginning?  Is being marooned on a penitentiary world a curse or an opportunity?

My life---as a pampered citizen---was over.  Not only will I have to cook my own food, I'll have to procure it:  gather, kill, scavenge, whatever it took.  Clothing, shelter, possibly none at first, then a struggle after that.  So many hours complaining about the government, but it did provide.  Citizens may have lived in cages, but they were gilded.

The room smelled funny, a combination of disinfectant and metal polish.  The lighting was subdued.  Like that was going to put me more at ease.

A hole opened beneath the pile of clothes I instinctively folded.  It immediately filled back in after collecting the synthetic linen.

Gas began to fill the room, smelling strongly like that disinfectant.  It burned as it made contract with my skin.  About the time the room was permeated the gas began to dissipate.

A transport portal glowed in the far side of the room.  Visionaries believed achieving faster-than-light speeds would conquer the universe.  Decreasing efficiency made such travel impractical.  Multi-dimensional bridging was the breakthrough. Originally a military project to create a non-permeably shield, rifts were found to not only warp space, but to circumvent it, as conduits.  The problem was sending something to a location you wanted it to go.  And for it to return.  That's where portals came in. Using a roundabout triangulation---involving many complex computer calculations---rifts could be connected.  With energy consumption being exponentially proportional to the diameter of a rift, portals were small, rarely larger than a man.

The portal's interior spun, colors shifting and transitioning, like oil in water.  "Step through the portal."  I hesitated.  So unlike me.  I was one of those people that confronted unpleasant situations to expedite their termination.  That was assuming there was something more affable to follow.  Those few seconds in front of the portal might be the highlight of my day.

It tingled as I passed through the electromagnetic curtain, like hundreds of insects crawling over my body.  Then it felt like I was being torn apart, from a thousand different directions.  I dreamed, recalling all memories in condensed form, a ten year documentary taking....

# Chapter 2

# HORNET

I stumbled.  There was usually solid footing on the other side of a portal.  Never grass and dirt.   Where was everyone? Thousands of convicts were sentenced to Dartmoor every year.  I expected a processing center. Some kind of orientation. Nothing. Where was everyone? I turned around. No portal. That WAS expected. A one-way device prevented inmates from circumventing activation barriers.

I looked down at my body. Yes, it still looked the same. Transport portals sometimes mutated people. Most of the time it was accidental. Intentional modifications were casualties of experimentation, received by people willing to sacrifice themselves for minimal monetary gain.

I was in the middle of a prairie. Mountains were on the horizon, the tops of the taller ones snowcapped. On the other side of me was a forest, kays away. That's where I needed to head. Better shelter there. And hopefully food. Water was more crucial for survival, but I was hungry. I haven't had an appetite since I was incarcerated. Now that there was some resolution---I was here and there was no turning back---it had returned with a vengeance.

It took minutes for my feet to be ripped to shreds and bleed. From grass? Technically, but it wasn't the kind you find in a park. It was gray, very dry, and brittle. I could hear myself move. It sounded like I was stumbling through the woods. I was being too loud. I was aware of that. Predators were going to hear me. Assuming they didn't see me first. I needed to reach that forest.

There were antelope here, and bison. I still may become prey, but after deliberation. If I had a weapon…. I had seen holographs of hunting, and read about it, so I knew the general concept, but I hadn't actually shot a bullet, or released an arrow, or sent an electrical discharge at an animal.

It wasn't that I was opposed to killing animals, if they were used for food. It was too expensive. The elite golfed and hunted. Both took up a lot of space, and land was expensive. Doctors, lawyers, entertainers, politicians, and CEOs spent thousands of dollars each week to locate and slaughter animals in hunting parks. The most addictive hunted on their lunch breaks. Many a marriage was broken up after a husband spent more time hunting game than his wife.  The sport really took off when the NORTHERN CONSTELLATIONS HUNTING LEAGUE began to broadcast its competitions.  All ages, genders, creeds, races, and social-economic classes watched, but it was evident from the onslaught of business commercials who the league catered to.  Someone living in the slums couldn't buy a firearm and begin shooting things.

I think I could force myself to eat raw meat if I had to.  And I could make my own clothes from the hides.  If I skinned enough animals I might even be able to make a shelter.  Again, I understood the principle, but I hadn't actually done it.

A few years back there was a popular reality holograph called ROUGHING IT, about teams of average people trying to survive in a park without any tools or outside assistance.  Very few did.  Participants had to sign a waiver, eliminating liability.  The tales of average people overcoming incredible odds was the premise, but people mainly tuned-in to see the deaths.  People falling off cliffs and being attacked by wild animals was extremely popular.  Watching someone starve to death, not so much.  It took too long.  The public eventually got bored with the show.  It was cancelled after three seasons.

If I was going to hunt I needed a weapon.  That was the first thing contestants did on Roughing It.  Some made spears out of sticks.  Overachievers attached stones to them.  Others used a more simplistic approach.  They collected rocks and threw them, usually not very accurately or with enough force.  Retaliatory episodes were the most popular.

There was a time when nudity was a broadcasting taboo--- not even an ankle could be shown for a decade or two---but violence was always a staple.  The pendulum had recently swung.  Nudity was commonplace now, but done in a tasteful manner.  Participants had to be of legal age, but not too legal, and extremely attractive and fit.  To adhere to the pledge of excellence, most actors and models had to be surgically modified.  In the second season of Roughing It someone used their clothes to make tools.

Participants were often fans of the show, resulting in mimicking behavior. Multiple layers of clothing were worn, creatively transformed, from sling shots to shelters. Some of the contestants went so far as completely stripping, breaking the code of conduct. It was such a scandalous thing that ratings went up, briefly. After realizing a 150 kilo middle aged man wasn't that titillating, ratings dropped, lower than they had been before the bump. Precursor to the inevitable. The maulings and broken legs would be missed. The show's replacement, COLORING WITH THE STARS, although better scripted, wasn't able to create as great a fervor.

I was knocked to the ground. Six black legs held me down as a cylindrical dagger attempted to pierce my hide. Looking up, I saw yellow and black stripes. I initially thought it was a tiger. But nothing constructed like that could be a mammal. It had a multi-segmented body, legs, and wings. It hovered above me like a hummingbird. It plunged the claw at the tip of its lower torso into my side. The searing agony spread. Before the pain became debilitating, it dispersed, a universal dull ache replacing the acute discomfort at the source of the injury.

Before the claw was able to commit additional injury, I seized it with both of my hands, hoping to control it at least as much as the monster on the other end of it. It became agitated. I was frantically shaken as its feet tried to dislodge me. It smashed its body against me, attempting to crush and impale. One thrust was so strong the dagger imbedded itself into the ground, with my hands still attached. If it had struck half-a-meter closer I would have been crushed beneath it. As it pulled upward I also pulled. SNAP! The claw broke free. A yellowish cream oozed from the wound. I hastily flipped the claw dagger, returning it to its owner. The first three thrusts were the most difficult. The thing squirmed before, and oozed after, each attack. Later it just shuddered, the ooze pearling on the new wounds being slung away like water on a dog. I stabbed it a few more times, even after the shuddering stopped. I didn't want to risk that thing reviving and attacking me again.

I pushed myself away from the carcass, the dagger still in my hand. I sat up, my elbows behind me, supporting. I felt my side with my free hand. I grimaced, then looked at my hand. It was crimson. I dropped the dagger: a stinger most likely. I put pressure against the wound with the heel of my hand. I had to stop the bleeding. I was already light headed.

I examined the monster in front of me. It was definitely an insect, maybe a bee. No, bees lose their stingers except for the queen. A wasp? A hornet. Hornets are the largest species of wasp. Maybe the portal didn't change me, but it definitely changed some things. Or contamination from terra-forming did. Or large insects were indigenous to this world.

I attempted to construct a bandage out of the creature's hide. Using the stinger dagger I cut a strip out of its epidermis. I tied it snuggly around my waste, using an additional piece of hide at the wound. That ought to stop the bleeding. I was more likely to die from infection, but that was days away, if not weeks. I also made a loin cloth. How could I be squeamish about a decaying carcass pocketing my genitals after placing it next to my gaping wound? I surprised even myself by using what remained of the hide to make a scabbard for my dagger. Almost a fair trade. Clothes and a weapon for the wound. If I was hungry enough, maybe even an insect steak to close the deal. No, hopefully I'll never be that hungry.

# Chapter 3

# SCREAM

Why was I here?  I was sentenced for a crime I...don't remember committing.  I don't remember anything that day.  Could I have actually done it, and my mind hid it from me, as a defense mechanism?  I've never done anything like that before.  I wasn't a violent man.  I was a teacher.  Do teachers murder people?  Sometimes we wished some of our students would...go away, but not to die.  I didn't even know the man I allegedly killed.

What was I going to do here, if---when---I found other people?  It would have been too expensive to isolate us.  There has to be settlements, towns, maybe even cities.  The only thing I've done since college is teach.  Children weren't sentenced to penal colonies, directly or inadvertently.  Sterilization assured that.  Was that one of things the mist did to me?

What did people do on a penal colony?  What kind of work was available?  Without anyone supplying us with food and clothes we would have to become self-sufficient.  The inefficiencies of making one's own tools, or building one's own home, would encourage specialization.  There had to be some people, like myself, who didn't want to hunt and gather indefinitely.

If I had to, I think I could survive on my own.  That might be better than associating with criminals.  I still couldn't think of myself as a convict.  Intellectually, I understood that maybe I HAD killed someone, accidentally, or in a rage, and that amnesia had concealed it from me.  What might real criminals do to me?  There were real murderers here, and rapists.  I didn't believe those stories of men being taken advantage of by other men in prison---not entirely. It couldn't be that rampant, but there were probably some men who did that. With few women here would some men change their sexual preference? Was that even possible? Men who might be leaning in that direction already might be swayed, but....no. There were SOME women here. Even if there weren't any women I didn't think I could force such a change in myself.

If someone attacked me would my instincts kick in? Would I be able to attack back? If I had killed someone, would I be able to kill again. Maybe my memory would return in time for me to defend myself. No, I hoped it never did. I got nauseous just thinking about killing someone. Whatever I may have done in the past, I couldn't kill now. How could anyone do that?

My stomach growled and my side ached. It became a competition, which affliction bothered me the most. I couldn't do anything about the wound, but I might be able to alleviate the hunger. If I didn't find anything substantial in another day I was going to assault one of those antelopes. I had a weapon now.

I couldn't walk as fast as I did before my wound, but I was still moving. A gulch, with some very unhealthy looking brush at its base, blocked my route. A wet-weather creek perhaps. I climbed down to investigate. The likelihood of animals increased in and around vegetation. I didn't find food, but there was a pool, nearly evaporated. It didn't look THAT dirty. I bent over. Cupping my hands I scooped up some of the water and ravenously consumed it, not caring if I got giardia. Getting a bad case of the runs was the least of my worries. I imbibed too much water at first, forcing the liquid back to the surface. I was careful after that to just take a sip. I washed away dry blood and dust, then took a final sip.

I heard a scream. For me to be able to hear it, the woman had to be close, within a couple of kays. An inherent reflex propelled my legs towards the voice.

After a couple of minutes of running I saw the woman, at the base of a small hill. She was naked. Five dogs surrounded her.

She was bleeding in a dozen places. The largest of the dogs finally brought her down. They began ripping pieces of flesh, devouring her.

She was already dead, but I still felt compelled to eradicate her assailants. I ran down the hill, yelling, the hornet dagger in one hand, while holding my wounded side with the other. The dogs were so focused on eating they didn't look up. My momentum carried me and the dagger into one of the dogs. After a surprised yelp, it toppled over. The other dogs fled.

Why did she have to die while I lived? If I had arrived an hour earlier, or she an hour later, would I have been the one attacked to death by those dogs? Did I deserve to live more than that woman? Had I not yet done what I was born to do? Or was I just lucky, not being in the wrong place at the wrong time? I survived the hornet attack, so maybe there was more to it.

Another two bodies, or what had been many days ago, laid next the woman's. Very little of their flesh remained. Even some of their bones were missing. They wore clothes, or did before the dogs or other animals had chewed through them to get to the tender flesh they had protected. A leather vest was the only piece that looked salvageable. I rolled the bodies over and found a small leather pouch under one of them, and a sword and dagger under the other. I contemplated replacing the hornet dagger with the metal one, but I had become too attached to the prior to abandon it. I could make another scabbard, but not now. I squeezed the new dagger beside the hornet stinger. The sword was too long for the scabbard, so I carried it in my right hand.

I loosened the cord puckering the pouch's aperture. I was careful to keep the pouch upright so nothing would fall out. Coins sparkled, but what caught my eyes were the two iridescent stones lying on top of them. I took one out to study it. It pulsated dimly, with every color of the rainbow represented. It felt concurrently warm and cool. Soothing and invigorating. Foolishly I brought it to my lips to taste. I knew immediately after doing so that I could have poisoned myself. Some substances were so toxic just a drop could kill. But it didn't feel like poison---whatever that was supposed to mean. I didn't die. The stone had the same taste and texture as unflavored gelatin, the firm kind, used for medication. Uncontrollably, my mouth sucked in the stone. Within seconds the object melted away, my body consuming its substance before I could swallow it. The wound at my side tingled and itched. I tore away the bandage covering it. Only a scar remained, and within seconds it also disappeared. All my aches and pains evaporated, even the blisters on my bare feet. The rush of wellness that flowed through me felt like it was still searching, but had to retreat, repeatedly, after hitting dead ends. After three minutes it ceased. Why couldn't I have been hurt more? I had wasted some of the medication. But could I have taken more damage and still lived? I was determined to only use the other stone as a last resort.

I now took time to inventory the coins in the pouch: three gold ones, eighteen silver, and three copper. But how much were each worth? They were two sims in diameter and weighed, the lot of them, about half a kilo. If I could buy some clothes with them, a night's lodging, and some food, I'd be satisfied. I felt bad for their previous owner, but he, or she---I hoped another woman hadn't died---wouldn't be needing them anymore.

Something wasn't right with the sun. It hadn't moved in...I don't know when. I'm aware the length of a day varies---dependent on how fast a planet rotates---but shouldn't I have noticed SOME movement? It was in the same spot it was the first time I saw it--- this morning, and yesterday. I shivered. The moon I saw last night had also been there. Was I on a synthetic world? Or was just the sun synthetic? I felt trapped before, but I at least had some autonomy. It was my will and ability to adapt that would determine whether I lived or died. Did it matter now, with someone else controlling my environment?

I began to run. Panic. Adrenaline. It wasn't my feet that bothered me, but my gender. The oscillation was unnerving, but

13

ultimately, my psyche adapted. Before I reached the forest, the sky darkened. Transitional, but at a more rapid pace than I was accustomed to. I looked up at the sun. As expected, it dimmed, transitioning into a full moon.

With the darkness came dark thoughts. I no longer thought in terms of WISH LISTS or BEST CASE SCENARIOS. How was I going to survive? I had been a teacher, not a pioneer. In some ways being sent here was worse than being executed. Perpetually afraid, not yet dead, but not being able to live either, not in a manner one wished to.

My energy was in freefall. Those healing stones must have been used to just heal, not to replenish. I felt I might be crawling before I reached those trees.

A LIGHT! Straight ahead, at the edge of the forest. It flickered, so it must be a camp fire. If I could push myself harder I might reach the light in...five minutes. But could I push myself anymore? I felt I might fall into a coma when I did stop. The only thing keeping me going was the routine my legs were following.

It might be a mistake dropping in like this. This was a prison, an entire world populated by criminals. But I was here, and I didn't feel like hurting anyone. There had to be others like me.

At the edge of the forest a voice shouted, "WHAT ARE YOU RUNNING FROM?!" I continued to run until I entered the forest. Instantly I was surrounded by five men wearing brown leather vests over gray shirts and pants. A silhouette of a tree, blue, was attached to the vests, over their hearts. One of the men had an acorn on the opposite side of his chest. They all wore leather boots up to their knees, and floppy camouflage hats. Swords were at their sides and bows drawn, each cocked with an arrow.

# Chapter 4

## INFANT

The man with the acorn maneuvered to stand in front of me, as the others sternly perused my arrival. "I asked you a question. What are you running from?"

I was scared, but also angry. HOW DARE THEY DETAIN ME! However, I wasn't stupid. I kept those thoughts to myself. I might not only jeopardize food and shelter, but also my life. The men surrounding me were criminals, likely having a history of harming others. "My name is Marvin Tinker. I arrived yesterday."

The men backed away from me as they pulled back on their bows. "I will ask you one final time," said the man with the acorn. "If you don't respond satisfactorily you won't have time to correct yourself." What have I gotten myself into? "What are you running from?"

I looked at the bows aimed at me. I spoke slowly, in an attempt to appear calm. I also wanted the words to come out precisely. Uttering something unintentionally derogatory would---very likely---get me killed. "I'm running because I don't want to spend another night unprotected." I wasn't dead yet, but they weren't responding. "I was attacked by a bee, a giant hornet, then some wild dogs. The dogs didn't actually attack me. I was able to scare them off."

"You look like you survived the encounters, unharmed. Remarkable for an infant. Half are killed their first day. And those that aren't show some...confirmation...of their tribulations. You are either very lucky, or not who you say you are."

"Why would I lie about who I am?  Who would participate in such an elaborate hoax, covering themselves with hornet hide and using the hornet's stinger as a dagger?"  I meticulously removed the weapon from its scabbard.  I slowly rotated it, allowing it to be seen from all sides.  The stoic men looked impressed, but they pulled back on their arrows a bit more.  Maybe that wasn't the wisest thing to do.  I returned the dagger to the scabbard.  "Wouldn't wearing ragged clothing, or no clothing, and carrying a stick be more convincing?"

"Sometimes ghouls inhabit the bodies of the dead.  Sometimes even the living.  Limbo is a hazardous world.  Men don't usually travel alone.  The only people who do are those who don't know any better, and those who are pretending to be those people.  You don't smell like a ghoul, so you must be who you say you are."  Bows were lowered, but not put away.

"What do ghouls smell like?"  For most of us that would have been a superfluous question, but I was very analytical.  I wanted to know how the world worked.  Did A cause B or B cause A?  Did the refrigerator light turn off when the door was closed?  When I was young, very young, I attempted to answer that question.  I was substantially chilled by the time my mother found me a quarter later.  The first few minutes of my imprisonment were fun.  Getting trapped in a refrigerator didn't happen every day.  Then I got scared.  The insulation that kept the cold in also kept most of my screaming from leaking out.  After awhile I wore myself out.  The only thing left to do was eat.  I was in a refrigerator, what else was I going to do?  It might be my last meal, so I didn't want to waste it by filling up on carrots or a piece of cheese.  Cheesecake I didn't have such disdain for, especially when it had cherries on top of it.  When I was finally freed, my mother gave me a bear hug, then began to cry.  The warmth of her body felt great.  Then she became upset.  Women's emotions had a tendency to change that quickly.  She yelled at me for eating the evening's dessert, spanked me, then sent me to my room.  I became sick.  I wasn't sure if it was the dark

16

or the cold that did it. I mainly blamed my mother. If she didn't spank me and yelled my stomach would have stayed settled. The possibility of getting a belly ache from eating an entire cheesecake never crossed my mind. Something that tasted that good would never let me down.

"Ghouls smell like death."

"When you say ghouls, you are speaking metaphorically? When resources are limited, it's not unheard for men---some men---to resort to cannibalism."

"Metaphors kill you on Limbo. Exaggerations? Possibly. But still deadly. There are things here that consume the dead. The rotting flesh that covers them---their own or their victims---is irrelevant when one is attempting to add you to their diet."

"Is there somewhere I can get a bite to eat?" Trust me, those last two thoughts were completely unrelated. "And maybe a place to wash up and sleep? And to buy some clothes?"

"So you got your hands on some gold?"

"I found some silver and copper coins on someone who wasn't going to need them anymore." I didn't really lie. I found silver and copper coins, in addition to the gold ones. If they knew I had gold, how likely would it be for me to have it in the morning? Maybe I shouldn't have mentioned the money at all, but I needed help from someone to survive, at least until I got acclimated. Police took an oath to serve and protect didn't they?

"It shouldn't surprise me. You obviously found that vest and sword somewhere too. Infants arrive ill-equipped. They sometimes unintentionally steal."

"Those men were dead, and no one was around to claim their gear."

"But for how long?"

I didn't know how to respond. Either I didn't hear him correctly...or I did.

"No one really dies on Limbo. It has something to do with the terra-forming. Our bodies die, but our spirits are remembered.

Limbo creates another body for us, and when it is completed, our spirit re-inhabits. I believe it's compensation for us not being able to have children."

"So if I had been killed by that hornet, I would have been reincarnated?" I studied religions in college, old and new. There were almost as many of them as there were people. That proved to me there either wasn't a God...or...he/she/it hadn't been discovered, yet. One of the older religions believed in reincarnation. It made as much sense as anything else.

One of the most popular contemporary religions, the CHURCH OF EVERYDAY ANGELS, or HEAVENISTS, as they wished to be called, believe God lives on an undiscovered planet. Our goal, as children of God, was to find Him. The Heavenists consider space heaven. When we left our planet of origin we entered heaven, becoming angels. There are so many Heavenists in Parliament a majority of legislation involves bills encouraging space exploration.

"Not quite."

I lost my train of thought. Had I missed anything? Not wanting to embarrass myself, or irritate the patrolman, I didn't ask?

"You don't start over as a baby. You are re-created as an adult, at the age you died---the age you were when you were imprisoned. We don't age here."

"So we never change?" The men shuddered. It sounded like cloning. Most food was grown that way. Choice cuts of meat were grown from cells in factories. Those parts of the chicken no one wanted didn't have to be wasted. For those people who prefer to eat an entire animal, stock was still raised, with most of the animals beginning their life as an adult, immediately ready for slaughter. Most go mad, the animals not being able to cope, psychologically. It became common practice to sedate them, until they're transported to market. How would instantaneous adulthood affect humans? It didn't sound like that happened here. Memories of childhood would exist, creating transition. Are people that are re-created the same people they were before they died? How can they be?

"Eventually we do change. Mutations occur---when we are re-created. The more we are re-created, the more we are mutated. Ghouls were once like you and me. All sentient species. Even some plants."

"That's crazy." Wasn't it? There are plants that can snatch a fly from the air, but a person evolving into one? They don't even belong to the same kingdom.

"It is crazy. Our wardens never knew how well they punished us. We never die, so there is no way to end the cycle of progressively becoming more insane as we mutate more extremely."

"These changes aren't just physical, are they? You said ghouls were once like us."

"We all are evil to some extent. That's why we were sent here. But our mutations are heavily influenced by our moral growth, negatively...or...positively. Those of us who become more evil will eventually mutate into a lower life form. Those of us who become more noble, into something superior. The problem is our core morality is low. More of us mutate negatively."

"You mentioned mutations being progressive. The more often someone dies the more extreme their mutations." How extreme might some of these mutations be? Dartmoor has existed for more than a century.

"Generally. Major changes sometimes occur after one re-creation, and minor ones, or none, after many."

"You haven't been here very long, have you?"

"The question is permitted. The implication behind it isn't. It's considered rude to ask someone about their mutations."

"I apologize. I'm...."

"An infant. Because you are, I will answer your question, and the implied one. I was imprisoned five years ago, and died just once. Have I been mutated? Nothing another person would notice. If I was someplace else I would have considered it a casualty of aging.  On Limbo, though, we don't age, we mutate.   Most believe there is a connection between mutations and how we lived our life."

That was the second time Raisin mentioned the relationship between behavior and transformation.  Sweat began to bead on my forehead.  If I was wearing clothes they would have been drenched. I was the type of person who never cut in front of someone in a line.  I opened doors for people, and not just for the elderly or mothers with babies in their arms.  "Those people whose money, clothes, and weapons I took, I REALLY did steal from them, because they'll be re-created---they'll return.  I'm already on my way to being damned."

"Don't be so hard on yourself.  It takes a while for someone's body to be re-created.  The more damaged the body, the more traumatic the death, the longer it takes, unless the body is completely obliterated.  Sometimes the body isn't even returned to the same area."

The woman attacked by the dogs wasn't in nearly as bad of shape as those men.  It would be interesting to talk to someone who had arrived on the same day as I.

The men who died did so days ago.  Those bodies were just bodies.  The people who inhabited them were probably already re-created, hundreds of kays from that gulch.

My stomach growled.  I had been so tired I wasn't able to allocate enough energy for its protest.  The break I had taken---was taking---had revitalized my organs.  "What about that food?"

The four men without acorns returned to the edge of the forest, watching for more travelers, human and non.  The man with the acorn threw a pack at me.  "There's some dried meat in there, and some water."  The patrolman sat on the ground, leaning against a tree.  "Bluewood City is five kays to the west.  We'll escort you there at dawn."

I found the dried meat and ravenously consumed half of it before I realized what I had done.  What animal was it from?  It was probably better I didn't find out. Some of the animals here were once people. I pulled a silver coin from the pouch I found and handed it to the patrolman. "Thanks for the food." The meat tasted like beef, but gamier. It was tasty, and filling.

The patrolman shook his head, then smiled as he pocketed the coin. "By the way, the name is Raisin Bluewood."

"My name---."

"You've already given it, but the point is moot. Everyone receives a new name on Limbo. You're in a different environment. You'll eventually become a different person, even a different species. It's tradition for the person who finds an infant to name him. Your surname designates your arrival, the location you were deposited: Polygulch Prairie. Your common name must be unique, and represent you. I was found eating withered grapes. You conquered a giant hornet. Hornet Polygulch. I'm envious. Some of us aren't honored with such fierce a name. But for us to evolve into a higher life form we must rid ourselves of such fierceness. Raisin doesn't sound too fierce does it?" So Hornet Polygulch it became. I was no longer known as Marvin Tinker. Few people learned what I had been called. It wasn't considered good manners to ask.

I was fighting a losing battle. I wanted to stay awake, so I could learn more about this fascinating world I was to spend the remainder of my life on, but I had already shut my eyes. Limbo. The name fit for this planet. People never die here, but they don't feel alive either. A prison doesn't make a home.

I opened my eyes. Raisin was still leaning against the tree, staring in the direction his men faced. I shut them again. "If you don't mind, I think I'll take a nap before we travel to Bluewood City." As soon as I lay my head down, or maybe a second before, I lost consciousness.

21

# Chapter 5

## PARTIALLY DEAD

Minutes later, or so it seemed, Raisin Bluewood shook me awake. "Just five more minutes." I always had trouble getting out of bed, first as a child, then as a college student, and finally as an adult. My mother assisted in my extraction when I lived at home, but when I left for college no one in my dorm, or later, in my apartment, cared enough to do the same. Some of my roommates didn't want to enable me. Others were just apathetic. At first I skipped breakfast---that would give me an extra ten minutes. And did I really need to take a shower in the morning? Another ten. And nothing really happened in the first five minutes of class. Sometimes I didn't make it to class at all. Most lectures consisted of professors regurgitating textbooks. When I missed the first hour of one of my finals---fortunately, I was able to finish the test in the remaining hour---I resolved that I wouldn't put off getting up again. That lasted about a week, about the time my jogging resolution also expired. I wasn't late to any more exams, but I did miss a few more classes. When I began teaching I forced myself to get up early every morning. I was one of those people who couldn't function in an unorganized world. That meant doing supplemental preparation every morning before I had my first interaction. As teaching became more routine I didn't need as much time to prepare. By my third year of teaching I hit the snooze alarm three times before getting up. Limbo didn't look like the kind of place that had clocks. It definitely didn't have patience for people not able to look after themselves.

Raisin and his crew were almost lost from sight by the time I was able to push myself off the ground. The too sudden attack on gravity made me dizzy. I stumbled to the end of the line of men following a wide trail through the forest. I had difficulty keeping up. I couldn't blame them for their rapid pace. The end of the journey likely meant a warm, soft bed. I looked up at the sun. It was in the same location it was when it dimmed yesterday and turned into a moon.

By the time I fully woke, a quarter later, we were already there. I had been so focused on keeping up I didn't have time to examine my environment, until now. Most of the trees we passed were oak, but they didn't look quite right. They were blue. So subtle it was possibly an optical illusion, a reflection of a synthetic sky. The leaves looked normal. They were green, with that characteristic scalloping at their edges, but the trunks.... If there could be redwoods, why couldn't there be bluewoods?

The settlement was shocking. Not the structures or people---they fit within the context of experiences and expectations---it was the suddenness of it. There wasn't a transition from forest to city. No signs. No outlying buildings. It was small, just a kay from where I stood to where the forest filled back in. A crudely built palisades surrounded it. The sharpened poles weren't particularly long or sturdy. The trail the patrolmen and I arrived on continued into the village, through a gap in its defenses. Trees and brush were cleared from the exterior of the palisades, but for only 20 meters.

A man wearing the same uniform as the patrolmen stood on a wooden platform beside the gap. He was four meters off the ground, twice as high as the palisades. He stepped down after noticing someone accompanying the patrolmen. He examined me, visually. "Another one? It used to be months between arrivals. Now weeks. What's happening out there, for there to be so many sentenced here?"

"At least this one can pay his way," said Raisin.

The guard looked skeptical. And who could blame him?

Men of means didn't wear rotting loin cloths.

Raisin turned towards me. "There's a toll for entering the city, Hornet. Defending our citizens from harm isn't cheap. It's a silver to enter, and a copper per day after that."

I didn't argue. I had the money, and if the village guards could keep me alive and safe from mutation it was worth every cent. I pulled out the leather pouch. Hastily I dug out a silver and a copper coin and handed them to the guard. It wouldn't have surprised me if he pocketed the money. I was relieved when he placed them in a large pouch with the Bluewood City logo on it. It was a good sign. If the cops were crooked what hope was there that the common man was honest. "What happens if someone can't afford the protection tax?"

Raisin answered. "We don't prevent anyone from entering the city, if that's what you're asking. Infants, or those down on their luck, find sponsors. In return they work for them, as indentured servants. The city has a sponsoring program. The duration of service is longer, but safer."

The guard opened a ledger. "Name?"

"Marvin...Hornet Polygulch."

"How many days do you intend to stay in Bluewood City?"

I had no idea. Forever or a day. There had to be someplace better to go. But where? And when? I had to get my bearings first. I needed to establish myself. I was wearing a loin cloth. My most cherished possession was an insect's stinger. I looked at Raisin.

"He's an infant, Brush. What did you do your first week? Probably run around like a chicken with its head cut off. Pissing your pants whenever you heard a sound."

"I couldn't afford pants my first week. I'll write TO BE DETERMINED. You see anything last night?"

Raisin dismissed his crew. They entered the city, stepping onto a boardwalk, the beginning of a complex wooden lattice that kept the Bluewoodians relatively clean and dry. "Nothing unusual. Dogs in the prairie. Tracks of a cat in the woods. Eight-legged. Not

24

sure if that makes it more dangerous. Four legs is more efficient, but the greater the mutation the more cranky. You might want to post that, instead of just putting it in the log. Buffalo continue to wander into the fringes, but they still haven't come within three kays of the city. I don't think we need to worry about them damaging the wall."

"How about the coons? Have they ransacked any more camps?"

I had to interrupt. "Raccoons? With this talk of corpses attacking, I thought I would have to be constantly looking over my shoulder, and beneath my feet. But considering how much time you're spending discussing cats and dogs, and buffalo and raccoons, maybe living on Limbo won't be that bad."

"There are raccoons, and RACCOONS," Brush responded tersely. "The raccoons we're talking about are as large as you or I, and nearly as intelligent."

"That's a bit of an exaggeration," Raisin responded. "Coons only come up to your waist."

"I once saw one that came up to here." Brush brought a hand to the bottom of his ribcage.

"That high on you is only up to my belly."

"You said these RACCOONS were intelligent," I interrupted again. "So they were once human, before they mutated?"

"Humans aren't the only species to mutate," said Raisin.

"So, if humans are becoming more like animals, and animals more like humans, how can tell what something originally was?"

"Does it matter?" asked Brush.

"Generally, the mutes that look more like animals were animals, and the ones that look more human were human. The same with intelligence. The more human looking ones are usually more intelligent."

"But not always. These coons we're talking about are smarter than half the people I know."

"I would say they're more devious and cunning than

intelligent. Most of that's innate, characteristic of their species, but enhanced. You might want to consider hanging out with a more intellectual crowd."

"So I'm going to have to not only look out for ghouls and packs of wild dogs, and gigantic insects, but also raccoons and squirrels and...."

"We haven't found any mutated squirrels," said Raisin.

"Yet," Brush added.

"I wouldn't worry too much about the coons, Hornet. They have only stolen from unoccupied camps, or after the people in them have fallen asleep."

"Yet. Like any wild animal, after they make their first kill they'll get a taste for human blood."

"They've never attacked anyone."

"It's inevitable. And when they do we'll have to exterminate them."

Raisin turned towards me. "Before I write my report, I'll walk you to one of the city's better inns. Good night, Brush. If nothing comes up I'll be snoring within the hour."

"Poker this afternoon?"

"If I wake up in time. I have to be back on the road by seven."

"Metric?" I was referring to second-based chronology. Not very practical upon planets with varying rotations, axial and solar.

Raisin nodded. "Days are slightly shorter. Without contact that's as precise as we can be."

I followed him onto the boardwalk. One and two-story buildings cradled the main thoroughfare. Most were businesses, with signs nailed to exteriors announcing goods and services for sale. Smaller spur boardwalks led to clusters of smaller buildings, a majority of them residences.

Something looked odd. It felt more like walking through a mall than down a street. There weren't any automobiles. Or the pre-combustion engine equivalent: horses and wagons. "How do you move goods from one place to another?"

Raisin stopped to answer. It would have been difficult to have a conversation at the pace we were moving. Completing his moral duty of delivering an infant to safety brought him closer to clocking out. "For the most part, we do it. Limbo's greatest resource is manpower. Freight-hauling, its most important profession. The genetic engineers believed convicts didn't deserve assistance in their daily activities. In most parts of Limbo humans are the only beasts of burden. Closer to the Frontier animals are exploited. An abomination to those of us in central Limbo who believe it's immoral to enslave something that may have once been human."

"Some people have mutated into horses?"

"You'll see, sooner than you wish to."

I wasn't worried about horses. Ghouls, I was scared to death of. I wish I could stop thinking about them. "Will I recognize a ghoul when I see one? They look human, don't they?"

"Humans that have been decomposing. You'll smell them before you see them. The partially dead don't have a particularly pleasant odor."

"Partially dead?"

"When they were re-created something went wrong. You might call it a mutation's mutation. Either their new flesh died as the soul reattached, or the soul returned to the corpse."

"What would it feel like to be living in a shell of rotting flesh?"

"You would probably be in a foul mood most of the time. And from everything I've heard about them, they are."

"So you actually haven't seen a ghoul?"

"Most live in the Frontier...but not all. Generally, those with the most extreme mutations live the farthest from the center of Limbo."

"The center of the planet?"

"The penal colony occupies a small portion of the planet."

27

"How small?"

"A circular area with a diameter of one thousand kays."

"How far are we from the center?"

"About 350 kays."

"So we're pretty close to it?"

"Not close enough. That's why we have this city watch---that diligently monitors the forest and prairie, protecting Bluewoodians from ghouls and other...monsters."

Monsters? So there might be things worse than ghouls out there. What had I gotten myself in for? Oh, yeah. I killed someone---allegedly. I had almost made peace with my...situation. Not about me being wrongly convicted, but of spending the rest of my life here. But this talk of new obstacles rekindled my anger. I was initially more shocked than upset. About the time it sunk in I was already beginning to cope. Those repressed feelings were coming to the surface. I needed to hit something, or someone. Or pull another stinger from a hornet.

By the time I had calmed down, Raisin had begun moving again. He was already a dozen paces in front of me. I jogged to catch up. He stopped in front of the BEETLE'S LAIR, a two-story wooden structure, small windows, without panes, above, and a large, open doorway below.

"A bit of monetary advice before I send you off into the world. Currency is simple on Limbo. Copper coins may look like pennies, but their value is closer to a dollar. One copper will buy you a basic need, like a loaf of bread or a half-liter of beer. Ten coppers can be exchanged for one silver, but the reverse isn't always guaranteed. Everyone is trying to make a buck on Limbo. Some business owners supplement their income by becoming money changers. A ten percent fee, or more, is not unheard of. It's beneficial to have exact change."

"Can a gold coin be exchanged for ten silvers?" I risked that gold was the logical currency progression. Announcing to the world you had the equivalent of a hundred dollars on you, or more, wasn't

28

the safest thing to do.

Raisin nodded. "For people who deal in large amounts of currency, gems are used. Diamonds, being the most common, have the least value."

"I heard of people shaving the edges of coins to get more value out of their money. How do I know I have legitimate coins? I don't want to get arrested for paying with underweight coins."

"Most merchants have measurement devices. The consequence of false payment can be severe. Criminals don't take kindly to others stealing from them. If you think you might have shaved coins, ask the merchant to test them before you make a purchase. They'll consider it doing them a favor as much as doing one for yourself. I wouldn't be too concerned. The risk of getting caught far exceeds the minimal monetary gain. Limbo is a greedy world. You receive nothing for free. Most merchants, and innkeepers, will attempt to overcharge. Your first lesson was giving me that silver coin. The food was worth a copper. At most, two. Never pay what is first demanded. The quicker someone drops the price the more inflated the original. Because people are greedy on Limbo, they'll eventually sell to you for a fair price, because even a fair price will provide a profit. A small profit is better than no profit. One last piece of advice. A room at a decent inn should cost a silver. The innkeeper will start at three times that when he recognizes you're an infant."

"Why are you helping me? What you are doing, I imagine, is beyond what a patrolman is required to do. Isn't everyone on a penal colony suppose to be greedy and corrupt?"

"Almost everyone. Some of us strive to become something...more. Most of us in the patrol believe in justice. I could earn more as a merchant, but wouldn't feel as good about myself. Good luck, Hornet Polygulch. May good fortune find you before your first mutation."

I watched as Raisin walked a couple of blocks, then entered the village's single three-story building. It had a blue deciduous tree painted on it.  The central boardwalk split at the structure, one route continuing forward, the other turning left.  What might I experience in each direction?  A fork usually meant a choice.  On Limbo it would likely be the last thing I would see before entering the mouth of a large monster.  At least I would have a bit to eat, a hot bath, and a place to sleep, before it happened.


# Chapter 6


# A FREE BATH


    I stepped towards the inn, stopping abruptly when I remembered how I was attired.  The inn may not have had a dress code, but I would still feel conspicuous, wearing a rotting loincloth.  Next to the inn was the POTPOURRI MERCANTILE.  A skunk with an angel's halo was painted beside its entry.

    I was immediately scrutinized upon entering the establishment.  The proprietor placed a large axe on the counter in front of him.  I couldn't fault his trepidation.  I must appear destitute.  How could someone dressed as poorly as I afford to buy anything?  It was common practice for stores in slums to bar their windows.   I wouldn't want to run a business in the middle of a prison.  I gathered two of everything:  shirts, pants, underwear, socks, but just one pair of boots, sturdiness being more essential than style.  The boots were the most expensive, but also the most vital, since they would protect my only form of transportation.  I spent more than a gold.  A third of my stash was already gone, and I still needed to eat and sleep.

The wooden cockroach above the BEETLE LAIR'S door reminded me of the vermin I saw daily as a child.  I never got used to stepping on them, especially barefoot.  I love the taste of crab, but was never able to consume it in its natural form.  The sound the cracking carapace made was like listening to someone snoring while they scratched their fingernails on a chalkboard.  Sometimes I even got the heebie-jeebies when I ate crisp fries.

There were a dozen tables in the inn's dimly lit great room.  Too many for a room that size.  Two young men---younger than me---and a man about my age, sat at one of the tables.  They drank beer.  From their demeanor it was unlikely their first.

The tallest man, one of the younger ones, was particularly enthusiastic in his boasting.  "You see how I cut it in two?  It didn't stand a chance."

"It was just a snake," spoke the oldest man.  He wasn't as tall as his companion, but he outweighed him by 20 kilos, and none of it was fat.  He was more subdued, more stoic, than the first man, who exuded emotion.

The third man threw a piece of the aforementioned snake onto the table.  He was shorter than either of his companions.  He was wiry, with a pointed nose that made him look like a weasel, or a rat.  He had a perpetual grin on his face, like he was up to something.  "So how much was the reward for this thing, again?"  I assumed the fragment was most of the snake, until I saw its head.  It was larger than my fist.  How long had it been before it was chopped to pieces?

The innkeeper entered the room, from what was probably the kitchen.  I tuned out the remainder of the men's conversation, focusing on renting a room.  I've been to hotels before where no one manned the desk.  For the owner to jump out like that from another room meant the inn was located in an often bypassed corner of the world.  Any business he received would be cherished.  He was stout, bordering on portly.  His muscular neck indicated he may have once been an athlete, either in school or professionally, before a desk job in the real world had taken its toll.

The innkeeper smiled, another sign of desperation. "I'm nearly full." Possible, but more likely the only rooms he had rented out so far were for the three men at the table, and they likely shared one. He paused for dramatic effect. "Don't worry. I think I can squeeze you in somewhere. Four silvers...."

"That seems a bit steep."

"Three silvers, five."

"I don't----."

"Three silvers flat, and a breakfast of biscuits and gravy thrown in. The good kind, with some meat in it."

The innkeeper was definitely coming down quickly. The way he was going, he might be paying me to stay by the time the deal was made. We settled for a silver, two coppers, with the free meal. The three men at the table looked displeased. They apparently paid more. I handed him the money. The innkeeper pocketed it. "Aren't you going to check it?"

"For what?"

"To make sure the coins are the right size and weight."

"Any innkeeper worth his weight has a good idea if the coins don't feel right."

I was looking forward to taking a bath. I was shocked to see only a wash basin in my room. It was filled with tepid water of questionable cleanliness.

I examined my room more closely. The mattress was down filled, as was the comforter. The sheets looked clean. An oil lamp was on the night stand beside the bed. A fireplace occupied an entire wall. There wasn't any wood, but I was confident I could have all I wanted for the right price.

I walked back downstairs. "How might I arrange a bath?"

"For one copper we'll fill a tub with water. For two more we'll heat it." It wasn't just the cold water that was influencing my decision, my muscles needed soothing. I handed over three coppers to the innkeeper. He pocketed them, like he did the initial

32

coins I gave him. He had to have some other place to store his money, but unlikely within view of his patrons. On a penal colony it was best to assume everyone would steal from you. "It will take a few minutes for Moss to heat up your water. He'll find you when it's ready. MOSS!"

The individual who burst from the kitchen was more child than man. He had the emaciated look teenager boys had who weren't able to satiate their hurried metabolism. "Heat some water for the tub." The innkeeper turned to me. "Where do you plan to be?"

"I guess I'll stay down here until my bath is ready."

"Find this gentleman when the water is hot and escort him to the tub room."

"Yes, sir." Moss darted back into the kitchen.

I sat down at one of the vacant tables. The only people in the room other than the innkeeper were the three who killed that snake. The innkeeper refilled their empty mugs, then stopped at my table. "Beer?"

It was still morning, much too early for me to start drinking. "Just some water please." The innkeeper frowned, but returned with a mug of nearly clear liquid. It tasted like the container hadn't been washed---in a very long time. Should I be drinking the water? I drank some water in the prairie, but I now had options. "Is this water going to make me sick?"

I intended for the innkeeper to answer, but instead the rat-faced man did. "It's going to make me sick if I have to listen to you whine about it. Just drink the bloody water. If you die you'll come back to life soon anyway, probably with a better appreciation for not complaining about the little things."

I didn't know how to respond. Would it be safer to ignore the man, or would that just make me seem weak, an easy target? Animals sensed fear, and some of the men sent to prison acted no better than animals.

"Leave the infant alone, Pebble," spoke his older

33

companion. "It wasn't too long ago that we cared if we ate from clean dishes, or slept in a clean bed." The innkeeper frowned. If was likely the next round of drinks would have more than dirt in them. The older man turned to me. "I wouldn't be too concerned. I haven't heard of anyone being sick in the four years I've been here. In addition to being sterile and immortal, we appear to be immune to disease."

"The bigger buggers are the one's we need to watch out for," said the tallest man. "Not that I've ever had any problems with them, but an infant might."

Moss tapped me on the shoulder, startling me. "Where did you come from?" If I was this inattentive in a pub how long was I going to survive in the wild? I wasn't looking forward to mutating. Would I grow six fingers or an extra leg? Would I become exceedingly hairy, or completely bald? Would my mind also change, and something as monotonous as chasing a stick make me feel giddy? With dying no longer being a terminal condition, dread diminished, but it would still hurt. Would my first thought after being re-created be a memory of that instant my soul fled my body as I was burned alive or my skull smashed in?

"The water for your bath is ready."

"Thanks." I emptied the water in my mug in one gulp, circumventing my taste buds. I had to run to catch up to Moss, who was already rushing up the stairs. Did the boy ever do anything at a leisurely pace?

Moss opened an unmarked door at the end of the hallway. The room was small, being slightly larger than the single tub in it. A bamboo pipe dripped into the already full 150 sim long oval basin. At the bottom of the tub a bung held in the water. A second bamboo pipe led away from the tub, evacuating the room through a hole in the wall. A small table had a brush, a wash cloth, and cakes of lye soap on it. It was of great internal debate which was the dirtiest. Two towels hung on wall pegs. They may have been white at one time, but were now dingy gray, with darkened smudges I

34

didn't want to think about.

"How much for a clean towel?" Moss gave me a blank look. Hadn't anyone asked him that before? "Drying myself with one of these will probably make me dirtier than I was before stepping into the tub."

"I think those are just for show, Sir."

"Do you just rub yourself against a wall then?"

"I just stand there until the water falls off me. Sometimes I get impatient and put on my clothes before I'm completely dry. On hot days it feels good to not be completely dry."

"If I wanted a clean towel bad enough was there some way to get one?"

Moss stood blank-faced for a long minute. A light bulb didn't exactly go on, but at least the door was cracked enough to allow the light from the next room to leak in. "I'll ask Mr. Splinter." Moss rushed off, closing the door behind him.

I dipped a finger in the tub to test the water. I snapped it back, being unprepared for how hot it was. I searched for a way to add cold water. There was just the single pipe above the tub, and there didn't appear to be any way to start the water flowing. How long would it be before it was cool enough to get in?

Moss returned with a slightly less stained towel. "Mr. Splinter said you can rent this towel for a copper."

I almost refused. Drip drying wasn't that bad. I weighed using a vaguely soft towel with questionable cleanliness with whisking water away from my body with my hands. Next time I went to a market I intended to buy my own towel. My once fat purse was becoming exceedingly fit. I handed a copper to Moss. Before closing my purse I pulled out another one. "This is for you." Moss smiled. The manner in which he clutched the metal disc indicated how rare it was for him to receive a tip. I always bought things for my students. Nothing expensive, just pencils, erasers, paper, occasionally one of those cheap pocket computers. It added up by the end of the term to a couple of weeks of pay.

Moss rushed out of the tub room again. I caught him before he shut the door. "If I wanted to add some more water to the tub, how do I do that?"

"You can't, sir, not from up here. Mr. Splinter doesn't want me to waste water, or for someone to flood the rooms below." Moss looked at the water in the tub. "After someone gets in the tub the water gets higher."

"No, that's not what I meant. The water will scald me if I get in now. I wanted to add some cold water."

"Oh. I can do that, even without asking Mr. Splinter first. I'll just add a bit, though. I don't want the tub to overflow. If the water looks like it's getting too high can you drain some of it for me? If the floor gets wet I won't eat for a day. If water drips downstairs I'll be beat. Release the plug if the water gets too high. Don't forget to put it back in. Mr. Splinter will charge you again if I have to re-fill the tub."

"I'll be sure to drain some of the water if the water gets too high. Does the drain water go into some sewer system? I was kind of surprised you had indoor plumbing."

"Most places don't. Some people who stay in inns want baths. The water from the tub empties behind the inn."

"Just out in the open?"

"It's not like its toilet water, sir. Sometimes people who walk by do get wet. Haven't you ever heard the expression FREE BATH? I guess not, you being new. Depending on how clean the water is, a free bath is either a gift or a curse."

Moss shut the door behind him. A minute later cold water began to pour out of the bamboo pipe. After a few seconds I tested the water in the tub. It was much cooler. Water continued to flow. It wouldn't be too long before the water was too cool. It stopped before it got to that point. Water continued to drip into the tub, but completely stopped by the time I stripped off my clothes. Should I drain the tub a bit before stepping in? I didn't want Moss to get into trouble. No, if I was careful the water shouldn't slosh over the sides. If I removed the bung I wasn't sure I would be able to replace it properly.

I oozed into the tub. "Ahhhh." It was that perfect temperature, a few degrees warmer than your body, for it to soothe you, but not too warm that it made you sweat. I leaned my head against the back of the tub and shut my eyes. I needed to clean myself, but it felt so good just to relax. It was worth the three coppers I paid, five counting the towel and the tip. I couldn't afford to do that every day, but I could pamper myself just this once, before I had to assimilate into the real world again.

What was it like for a boy Moss's age to be sentenced for life, on Limbo, to never experience life as an adult? Does the poor decisions a person makes when they are a juvenile, someone without enough maturity to make valued decisions, warrant them forfeiting their freedom forever? Maybe if what they did was so heinous, so un-redeeming. I couldn't imagine Moss doing anything like that, but he was here, so he had to have done something. Should one mistake ruin a person's life forever?

When I woke, the water was cold. Not cold enough to cause hypothermia, but cooler than my body temperature. Pieces of ash floated on the water, some of them being washed ashore onto my chest. I hadn't noticed them when I stepped into the tub. Maybe they had floated to the surface while I napped. How strange for tub water to be heated over a fire, and not by electric coils.

Before draining the tub I washed. I had to wash the soap before washing myself. There were things stuck in the cake I didn't want to think about. When the soap was free of sediment I lathered my body the best I could without using a wash cloth or brush. I splashed water on myself to rid me of the suds, then yanked the bung out. The water sounded strange leaving the tub. I was accustomed to it flowing through a series of interconnected plastic pipes. It was a straight shot from the bottom of the tub to the hole in the wall.

I dried with the towel Moss gave me. It wasn't particularly soft, but it smelled much cleaner than it looked. The coloring must have just been stains it had picked up through the years.

The clothes that I had bought earlier in the day didn't seem as clean as they did before I bathed. They didn't exactly reek, but they didn't smell fresh either.

I had thought I might take a nap before dinner. The nap happened, but in a tub instead of on a bed. To save money I skipped lunch.

There was still one thing I had to do. I had put it off as long as I could. I was surprised to find a toilet indoors, in a small room near the stairs. Pre-industrial civilizations had outhouses, and chamber pots. The Beetle's Lair's lavoratory was a combination of the two. A wooden box with a circular opening straddled a nearly full metal bucket. Dried corn cobs and pieces of bark were beside the toilet. There was also a wash basin. The water looked unused, evaporation residue coating the top half of the basin. There were a couple of things that made the experience manageable. The room was reasonably ventilated, with many slots cut into the exterior wall to allow bad odors to escape and fresh air to enter. There was also an air-freshener. Nothing too obnoxious, just some herbs and spices simmering in water. I gained some respect for the innkeeper. He had his faults, but he preferred his toilet experiences to be as pleasant as possible.

It was only mid-afternoon. That was about the best I could approximate the time. My stomach was already growling. Maybe I wouldn't be able to skip too many lunches. Before I was arrested I could buy food any hour of the day, but here.... I walked downstairs.

# Chapter 7

# FOUR DIRECTIONS

The three men I pseudo-communicated with were still at their table. I couldn't find the innkeeper. I debated whether I should wait for him or return to my room. Before I could make up my mind I was drawn into the gentlemen's conversation. It wasn't that I was exactly eavesdropping. They were just talking so loudly and with so much emotion it was difficult not to be drawn in.

"I don't think the three of us is enough," said the man who defended me.

"Three normal men," countered the tall man. For emphasis he placed his gleaming, well-polished blade on the table. Maybe he was as talented in its use as he implied, but the weapon looked like it rarely left the scabbard. Even less likely, it ever got dirty.

"Although it sickens me to say it," added the rat-faced man, "I agree with Stick. He's so successful with his blade because he rarely has to use it. My bow may not be as pretty as his sword, but I'm as accurate at one-hundred meters as he is at one. I don't think we should screw things up by adding anyone to the group."

"If Gaea herself offered to help us you would turn Her down," said the older man.

"The more people we have the more diluted our cut."

"And not wanting to associate with more people doesn't have anything to do with it?"

"What has anyone done for me? My dad ran away before I was born. And my mother soon after that."

"Didn't you live with a foster family? They must have cared

39

for you?"

"Many foster families. They cared more for the money the government gave them to look after me." The rat-faced man began to scratch, first casually, then with gusto.

"Foster families don't earn that much money, probably not even enough to compensate for what they spent on your food and clothes. Quit scratching yourself. You're going to draw blood and leave a scar."

"I can't help it. Whenever I'm upset my skin itches."

"Then you must itch all the time," commented the tall man.

The rat-faced man ignored him. "My foster parents cared so much that they kept giving me back to the government."

"After you stole from them."

"BORE YOU!"

"You must admit, we haven't always been aware of our surroundings, to the extent we could have been," said the older man. "We've missed out on some salvage opportunities. Sometimes too few men can't watch every direction."

"Then the logical solution is to have enough people to watch every direction," suggested the tallest man. "There's north, south, east, and west. It looks like we need one more man. That may be enough. In time, Pebble may even be able to adapt. Hate for a person he hasn't even met can't be sustained."

"You'll be surprised," spoke the rat-faced man.

"Who can we find in Bluewood willing to risk their humanity for the potential of prosperity?" asked the oldest man. "Most people think we're foolish. That's not to say they didn't do the same when they were younger."

"If you're going to ignore my fervent and justifiable objections about adding someone to our group, I think I should be the one to choose that person, because I'll be the one most affected."

"By all means. If you want to do all the leg work and the lip-flapping, I won't stop you."

The rat-faced man waited as long as it took him to turn towards me. "How about you? You've obviously been listening to us. And even more obvious, you're an infant. Would you like a little adventure, and to pad your wallet? If you survive a couple of deaths, you'll have enough gold after a year to live off it for the remainder of your human existence."

"Good call," said the tall man. "An infant is perfect. Even a monkey can be trained as a lookout, and if he isn't talented enough to survive, we'll only have to split the spoils three ways."

It was like I wasn't there. Didn't I have some say in the matter? It wasn't that I hadn't considered offering to tag along with those men. I had to do something to earn some money, and I still didn't have a clue what that would be. I didn't have to do this forever. Maybe I could start a business with the money I'll make. Not this far out in the boondocks. In a real city, with more customers, and fewer monsters. But did I really want to do this? If some of the treasures they spoke of were real I could become a wealthy man. But some of those monsters were probably real too. Relative safety but poverty versus constant danger---including mutating into a monster---with the possibility of collecting a fortune. Even if I didn't make much money, I would at least be getting some experience. Raisin's enthusiasm for his job got me interested in joining the town watch. "I'LL DO IT!"

The men looked at one another. "Agreed."

I just realized something. "How do I know you'll not kill me some day, to take my share of the treasure?"

The oldest man replied, "Limbo generates enough dangers and rewards without us having to create any. There is an undeclared oath of solidarity among humans."

"There is a pact we can make to bind our brotherhood," said the tall man. "We three have already done it, but if you're to be part of our group, we must re-construct the pact."

I followed them outside. We walked to the back of the inn, stopping beside a large blue oak. They pulled down their pants.

41

What had I gotten myself in for?

"You, too," said the rat-faced man.

The oldest man pointed to the tree. "Now." The three of them urinated on the oak, all of them hitting it in the same spot, the streams combining a few sims in front of the tree, creating one large stream. I was almost too late. My stream combined with theirs just as their streams began to dissipate.

"That may happen to you if you stray," said the tall man. "Our flows will cease, and you'll be all alone."

"Remember," said the rat-faced man, "you are one of us now, a member of our company, our family. If you betray the pact, I will kill every re-creation of yours until you become an insect, then I'll torture you by pulling off your wings, your antennae or any other appendages you might have."

The oldest man slapped me on the back. "Pebble may torture you, but he'll also sacrifice himself, for any one of us. Now, even for you."

After we returned to the inn my three new companions introduced themselves. The oldest man began. "My name is Centaur Beetlewoods. I was sentenced for killing my wife's lover. I earned my name for attempting to ride an equine-human hybrid. If I wasn't as strong as a horse, I would have never survived the encounter. I worked as a freight-hauler until the lure of riches overwhelmed me. Salvaging has become more than a rich-quick scheme to me. The anticipation of what's in that cave or beneath that rotting corpse becomes addictive. I entered Limbo in the Beetlewoods." My blank response warranted a clarification. "The Beetlewoods are southwest of here, near the Frontier."

Pebble came to my rescue. "He's just an infant, Centaur? He's probably not even potty trained."

"Raisin also mentioned the Frontier," I remarked. "It's at the perimeter of the penal colony, where the most extreme mutants live?"

"Not just the mutes with the most extreme physical

mutations," said my tallest new companion, his name still unknown to me. "The most morally extreme also live out there."

"The most evil?"

"And the most good. What many of us aspire to become, but aren't worthy of attaining."

"Without Gaea's assistance," Centaur added.

"Being too good is boring," Pebble commented.

"Do people here really believe in the earth mother?" I asked.

"All of us to some degree," Centaur responded. "Many believe She determines who we mutate into."

"Some of the older inhabitants of Limbo have forgotten this planet is a prison," said the taller man. "They believe Gaea created it for them. Others believe Gaea is the planet."

"What's beyond the Frontier?"

"No one knows. There's an energy shield there to keep us in our prison, but no one has been able to penetrate it."

"My name is Stick Bluewood, by the way. As you can tell by my name, I arrived in this area. I've been on Limbo less than two years. I earned my name by defending myself from squirrels. Not the cute ones that play in trees. These SQUIRRELS were the size of dogs." I nodded in acknowledgment. "I skewered one of them, and later ate it over a campfire. The others fled. I have lived in and around the Bluewoods my entire life."

"Limboans consider life beginning the day of our arrival," Centaur clarified. "Pre-Limbo is viewed as a gestational stage."

"Since my near fatal arrival on Limbo I have practiced my swordsmanship every day," Stick continued. "No one in the Bluewoods---excuse me, the world---is my equal."

"Or has a greater ego," added the rat-faced man.

"If deeds confirm the boasting, it's sharing the truth. I may have only committed petty crimes before I was incarcerated, but I did so consistently. I didn't steal for the profit, but I enjoyed that too. I'm susceptible to the enticement of finer things. I enjoyed the challenge of pulling off capers. My downfall was surrounding myself with people not as proficient. I thought I would never be able to trust anyone again, because they could never live up to my standards. That was before I met Centaur and Pebble."

Taking his cue, the rat-faced man began. "My name is Pebble Rhinopolis. Blah, blah, blah. I arrived on Limbo in the same area as Centaur, but in the city. Gulag might be larger, but it can't compete with Rhinopolis's character and culture."

"Gulag is at the geographical center of Limbo," Centaur illuminated. "Limboans consider it the capital, although it doesn't have any jurisdiction over the rest of Limbo. Settlements here are primarily city-states, with the largest having some influence on the surrounding villages and towns."

"I began my life of crime stealing candy as a toddler. I worked my way to stealing transports as an adolescent. Being small my entire life, and being bullied because of it, caused me to pick on those even weaker than myself---as Centaur has hypothesized. I stole from children, and the elderly, the sick, anyone who was an easy target. I became a pick-pocket, a thief, a burglar. I even mugged, for the few dollars I would usually receive. I didn't care if I hurt my victims. I didn't try to hurt them, but if they did get hurt that was just part of doing business. I once killed someone when I hit him too hard with a brick. I was more upset from the manhunt and my eventual imprisonment than for my victim's life. I thrived in Rhinopolis, before the human pact changed my outlook. I couldn't hurt anyone anymore, and later wasn't even able to force myself to steal from them. I left Rhinopolis for the wilderness, first in the Beetlewoods, then in the Grasslands, where I met Centaur, two years ago. He was much more eager than I to form a partnership."

"But I persisted. Two was much safer in the wilderness than one. A rattlesnake had bitten him. If I hadn't suck out the venom he would have died."

"I didn't fear the pain of death, or the potential mutated re-creation. But someone stealing from my corpse.... One of the tenets of our partnership, the one that sealed the deal for me, was that the surviving member must safeguard the other's possessions until he returned."

"It was a substantial oath. It sometimes took weeks for a person to return to their corpse. It was rare under the Human Pact for a human to betray another. Those who did so, who wanted to retain some honor, made the excuse that their latest mutation had changed them enough to no longer be considered human, voiding the Human Pact."

"Feek concealed in flowers not only still stinks, it damages the reputation of the flowers. I never had a partner before, so it took awhile to adjust. To actually have to consider what someone else thought, was an insane concept, but some of those crazy ideas that Centaur came up with, and later Stick, saved my life, and added to my wallet."

"How did you earn your name?" I asked.

"A dozen rats attacked me seconds after arriving on Limbo, closer in size to capybaras than hamsters."

"Does everyone have such an encounter when they arrive?" I asked.

"Apparently," said Centaur. "A mute's heightened senses must be attuned to an infant's confusion."

"The one's that attacked me definitely were," Pebble continued. "It was like they knew I was clueless in defending myself. They picked the wrong infant. I looked for a stick or other make-shift weapon. All I found were small stones, but they were sufficient. Every stone hit its target. Those rats that didn't die fled when they grasped what they had gotten themselves in for."

"We met Stick a year later," said Centaur. "He looked up to Pebble."

"No one was more surprised than I," said Pebble. "No one had done that before. My disdain for him joining us diminished. Within a day I even tolerated him."

"It took weeks before he felt the same for me," said

Centaur.

"Pebble had exchanged his stones for a bow by the time I met him," said Stick. "I couldn't believe someone could shoot that far and be so accurate. He had become a celebrity in my eyes, but one I could become friends with."

"Do you still prop him up on a pedestal?" I asked.

"Until I became acquainted with his bathing habits."

"It's bad for my skin to bathe more than once a week."

"And effective in scaring away unwanted associations," Centaur added.

"That too. From Pebble I learned that perfection didn't have to be legend. It was possible to achieve something close to it."

"Close?" Centaur's mouth dropped.

"For Pebble."

I just thought of something. If the three of them had been salvaging so long, why hadn't they struck it rich already? Maybe I won't be able to retire before I mutated into a monster. I could always quit after a year or two if things weren't progressing. If Pebble didn't kill me for eternity. He was kidding about that, wasn't he? What had I gotten myself into?

"I smell something," said Stick.

"I took a bath as soon as we got back to town."

"Splinter began cooking earlier today," commented Centaur.

The innkeeper burst into the great room from the kitchen. "And you can actually eat early too if you promise to leave afterwards. Some of the things you three talk about sour my customers' stomachs. No one wants to hear about blood and guts while eating and drinking. You've suckered this infant into your schemes, haven't you?"

"He is a willing participant," Centaur replied, sounding injured.

"About as much as that woman was who I had intimate relations with. Why does the law have to butt into people's private business? If she didn't want it she should have said no. It's not my

46

fault she was unconscious at the time."

"You're disgusting," said Stick.

"But you'll still sleep in one of my beds and eat the food I cook for you. You get a choice of bison stew or boiled fowl today."

"How were you able to catch a fowl?"

"I didn't exactly catch it. I found it dead beside the road."

"I think we'll have the stew," said Centaur. "And don't forget to bring bread. If there aren't some vegetables in the stew, bring some. We salvagers need our vitamins."

"Salvagers, huh. Real salvagers can afford to stay at a better inn."

"That's true," said Pebble.

"And we'll like another round of beer," said Stick. "And bring a mug for, ah....."

"Hornet, but I don't want one."

"You'll have one." Pebble's expression alternated between a frown and a perpetual grin. When the latter was forced he looked like Satan incarnate.

The innkeeper returned with four mugs. "That will be 25 coppers."

Pebble spit out the beer that had already made it into his mouth. "TWENTY-FIVE?!"

"This is your fourth round. You are regulars, that's why I let you keep a tab, but I won't bring out food until we're clear."

"But two-and-half silvers?"

"I'm willing to reduce it by four coppers if we omit the bread."

"We'll pay." Centaur handed the innkeeper seven coins---two silver and five copper.

I pulled out my wallet. "How much of that is mine?"

"Nothing at the moment. I carry a community wallet. Periodically we contribute to it, usually after a big score. And that next big score better be soon. A couple of strong ants could drag this away." He tossed the leather pouch into the air. The ease of movement and muted jingle confirmed his claim.

Moss was the one to return with the stew and bread. He lingered before returning to the kitchen. I waited to see if any of the others were going to tip him. They declined. I followed their lead. Perceiving we weren't going to communicate with him, either positively or negatively, he rushed back into the kitchen.

A wooden spoon stuck out of each bowl. I didn't want to think about how long it had been since they had been cleaned. I wasn't too worried about the stew being safe to eat. It was hot enough to kill anything harmful in it. It was surprisingly good. The natural flavors of the bison meat, and the carrots, onions, and potatoes came through, with a hint of herbs and spices. They smelled similar to those simmering in the water by the toilet. The innkeeper must have made that stuff in bulk. What else might he use it for?

The beer was hardier than I was accustomed to drinking, yet I still had a feeling it was watered down.

After spending more time with my new partners, and downing my first beer, I became bolder. I didn't consider them my friends yet---more like associates. "So, what is this thing you need help with?"

"Need?" said Stick. "I'm confident we could do it with just the three of us. Having you along will just make it easier for us."

"Okay. So, what is this thing that someone tagging along will make it easier for you to acquire?"

"There's a guy in Three Rivers willing to pay 200 gold for an emerald pearl. That isn't enough to retire on, but a good start."

"You think it actually exists? Or is it just rumor? I never heard of a pearl being green."

"I don't really know. No one I have talked to has actually seen it, not first hand."

"You think it's still in the Copper Forest?" asked Stick.

"Last time I heard. It at least gives us a starting point. I for one am getting tired of heading into the wilderness and looking for random treasure---and trouble."

"You think the arbols still have it?"

"The last time I heard."

"Arbols?" I queried.

"Arboreal mutants living in the Western Frontier. They have a passing resemblance to monkeys."

"Human or animal?"

"Definitely human," Stick answered.

"Stick likes his women exotic."

"Not THAT exotic. Arbols look human...for the most part."

"From a distance. I admit, their lithe, athletic bodies are attractive, but I can't get past their hair---and tails."

"Arbols don't have tails."

"The ones I have seen do."

"Then they weren't arbols."

With so few women on Limbo one---apparently---can't be too choosy. "So a person doesn't have to become a freak after he is mutated?"

"There are two major categories of mutations," Stick elaborated. "A specific mutation is where human genetic material is mixed with another species, such as the arbols having some simian characteristics. Most of these mutants look more human than animal. A diverse mutation is when either non-specific genetic material is mixed with human DNA, or human genes are modified without cross-contamination."

"So, are we going after this pearl? Or do we need to break into sub-committees and discuss it for another two hours?" Pebble had rubbed his left arm raw, and was beginning to work on his right.

"Hornet?" asks Centaur.

"Whatever you guys decide. I'm new to this."

"It needs to be unanimous."

I nodded my affirmation.

"Then it's decided."

Shortly before dusk people began to trickle into the pub. The innkeeper looked at the four us. Following through on our word, we headed upstairs. "We'll make plans tomorrow morning," said Centaur as he followed Stick and Pebble into the room the three of them shared.

I usually didn't fall asleep easily if I had taken a nap during the day. Marvin Tinker couldn't. Apparently, Hornet Polygulch could. When I woke the next day I didn't remember any of my dreams. If I did would they have been of my old world or my new? Of teaching mathematics to high school students or stealing an emerald pearl from arbols?

# Chapter 8

## ELEM

Being the leader of our company, Centaur took the responsibility of us being properly provisioned and packed very seriously. When one carried his own gear it was crucial nothing was left behind, or fell off. I being new to such endeavors, Centaur spent the most time on my pack. He adjusted the straps on the newly purchased pack, too robustly.

"OWWW! Do they have to be pulled so tightly?"

"If they're too loose they will chafe."

"But do they have to cut off my circulation?"

Centaur loosened the straps, but just a bit. "We're going to have to be especially careful when we enter the Copper Forest. Arbols harness elem."

"Elem?"

"Short for elemental energy. Elem are the---unintended---precipitants of terra-forming. Think of them as complex molecules that have the potential to release inordinate amounts of energy. Without elem, re-creation wouldn't be possible. Elem seeps into the soil, the air, the water, rocks. It glows faintly, making it marginally detectable. Elem are constantly spewed from Gaea, like radiation from an isotope, but finding them is still an arduous task. It sometimes takes days, for even an experienced prospector, to find a single elem."

"But worth it," Pebble added.

"So you want to be an elem prospector now?" asked Stick.

"Too monotonous. A gold per elem makes it tempting though, doesn't it?"

"Wizards will only pay a gold for an elem if it's delivered." My confused expression warranted an elaboration. "Many years ago---closer to the creation of the penal colony than to today---a group of elem peddlers, calling themselves WIZARDS, began combining and packaging elem. Each combination of elem---called a penta---creates a unique effect. " Centaur looked at Stick, suggesting he take it from there.

"There are four varieties of elem. Elem aero is found in the atmosphere, but sometimes is captured in airflows between mountains. Elem aqus is found in water. Elem terra in the lush soil of forests. Elem fiero in dry, hot desolate areas. When five elem come into contact they bond, forming a penta. The creation of this bond causes energy to be released. The form of this release depends on the combination of elem, and to some extent the person directing it."

"You consume it?" I asked.

"There are other ways of releasing its energy, but it is directed the most accurately from within a human body. Being as much a part of Limbo as elem, especially after being re-created, we are linked to it, allowing us to tap into its power, becoming its conduit."

"It sounds like magic, doesn't it?  The penta peddlers even call themselves wizards."

"Magic is just a name we give to things we don't understand. To a primitive, CPR looks like we are breathing life back into a corpse."

"You haven't mentioned black elem," Pebble prodded.

With hesitation, Stick added, "Black elem is a myth.  But one that's likely valid, because it takes five elem to create a penta.  Elem essence, as it's also called, is supposedly the life force, what we call the soul.  It's hypothesized that combining someone's soul with four elem will cause a more powerful effect than that achieved from a standard penta.  It's an abomination.  Theoretically, once a soul becomes part of a penta it is consumed.  If someone's soul is consumed they can't be re-created."

Centaur added, "Another hypothesis suggests the soul will mutate when bonded with the elem, becoming part of what was created."  Neither outcome sounded very appealing.

"And these WIZARDS have a monopoly in penta packaging and distribution?" I asked.

"They also use elem for their own purposes, but a majority of the elem sold to them is resold, in a relatively safe, user-friendly form.  Most penta are sold as capsules, what we call stones.  Runes indicate composition.  Unless someone is extremely confident in the nature of the energy released, they shouldn't buy penta from a secondary source."

"Wizards also sell rods," said Stick.  "Bulk penta receptacles. The advantage of buying a rod is the discount a person receives by buying in bulk."

"The most expensive receptacles are rings," said Pebble. "Their cost is offset by them having---allegedly---unlimited charges. There's enough elem within to attract surrounding elem, like a magnet."

"Have you ever found penta?" I asked my companions.

Considering their resources, it was doubtful they would have been able to buy one.

"Only once," said Centaur. "Two stones. One, I was acquainted with---a healing stone. The other had three dot runes, representing air, and two asterisk runes, representing fire. Not wanting to risk setting myself on fire, or drowning, or electrocuting, I was only going to use it as a last resort. Or, if I was hungry enough, I might sell it. My desperate moment came three months before I met Pebble. I was in the Grasslands and stumbled upon what looked like an octopus. I was two hundred kays from the nearest sea. The absurdity of finding this thing where I did delayed my reaction. I didn't notice it until I was almost on top of it---it was hidden in a gully. From its reaction to my prescience I assumed it did so intentionally. I backed away from it, but not soon enough. I was ten meters away and that thing was still able to hit me with one of its tentacles. It felt like a whip had struck my leg, but a whip with a claw at its tip. My thigh had a ten sim gash, and I was rapidly losing feeling in it. A second tentacle hit me, this time in my side. It was a less substantial wound, but it was another location to lose blood. I was becoming dizzy, and the thing was moving towards me. I wasn't going to out run it with a limp leg. I swallowed the unknown stone. The air began to sizzle with electrical energy. I was concerned I was going to be struck by lightning, but instead the lightning came out of ME. It struck the octopus, instantly turning it into charcoal. If it wasn't for the healing stone I would have died. I was lucky that day. My guess what that stone would do was correct, but what if it caused rain? I would have been clean when I died."

"Are we going to leave now?" asked Pebble. His right arm was as red as his left was the day before. He must alternate, to prevent him from digging down to the bone. "Or should we empty our packs a fifth time, and pack them a sixth?"

"It's too late to reach Jacob by dusk," stated Centaur. "We'll leave first thing tomorrow morning."

"Why not camp halfway?  Or walk through the night?"

"Your Fa blood that rich today?" asked Stick.  "Does leaving half a day later really matter?"

"Did Centaur bleed on you?  You're usually so hyper you can't sit still.  You sure you don't want to stretch your legs, today, instead of waiting until tomorrow?"

"I don't have as much Min in me as Cor, but I have more than you if you think hiking at night is a good idea."

"But we'll be walking on a road."

"You think a thin strip of dirt will keep a wild animal or mute away?"

I didn't know what to think---not surprising for someone with an equal mix of Min, Fa, and Cor.  Some people mocked me for being so muddy.  Being so balanced in intellect, emotion, and physicality, I was stereotyped as not having a back bone, never being able to decide on a course of action.  Others believed a person in perfect balance would be able to experience the world in its true form, without genetic filters to mutate it.  THE BALANCED, as those rare individuals were called, were often spiritual leaders, albeit passive ones.  With the general populace having trouble understanding such subtleties, mass market religions had highly unbalanced individuals as their spokesman, usually those with ninety percent or more concentration in one of the genetic houses.  Those in politics were also highly unbalanced, with each member of THE THREE being one of the most extreme from their respective House.  Was it worse to be despised, or cherished?

"Tomorrow will be best."  There was no more discussion.  Every member of our group had his role, and Centaur's role was leader.  Decisions were made in consensus, but Centaur's words swayed.

"Tomorrow."

"Tomorrow."

What might my role be in the group be?  Someone to watch a fourth direction?  Specific, but not very substantial.

"How far do we have to go to reach the Copper Forest?" I asked.

"600 kays," said Centaur.

BY FOOT?! If I was going to walk that far I needed to go bed. How often would we be allowed such luxury once the traveling began? Would most nights be spent on the ground? How long will it be before I slept in a bed again? "I'll see everyone at dinner. By the way, once we get to the Copper Forest, what are we going to do? What's our plan?" No one answered. That wasn't a good sign. Whatever confidence my companions gained in my eyes was lost. For all their boasting they weren't much more equipped for what we were doing than I. After a minute of silence I returned to my room.

Once I shut my door, I released the straps on my pack. The 30 kilos hit the floor with a thud. My arms felt like they were floating. How heavy was that pack going to feel after hiking hundreds of kays? I fell onto my bed, relishing every second. Beds were welcomed when one was exhausted, but sometimes they just felt good---the softness, relinquishing the battle against gravity.

# Chapter 9

# FOWL

Leaving Bluewood City filled me with both jittery elation and perspiration drenching fear. An incredible adventure was beginning: unimaginable sights, but also unimaginable danger.

We were more cluster than military procession. The first

few kays consisted of taunts, seasoned with ambition. Weariness and reality eventually sunk-in. We needed something to initiate the adventure. Action superseded anticipation.

We travelled upon a road, wide enough to accommodate three abreast, through a moderately dense deciduous forest. Brief detours into hollows and upon ridges occurred often enough to relieve the potential boredom of a route lacking deviation. The shortest distance between two points might be a straight line, but it wasn't always the most scenic.

"Who lives over there?" I asked, pointing to a rundown house, barely visible through the leaves.

"Someone not wanting to live in town," said Stick, "but also not wanting to be too far away from it, in case of attack."

"You think someone still lives there?" asked Pebble.

"I don't know. I've never seen anyone around it, or smoke coming out of the chimney."

"What are you getting at?" asked Centaur.

"If no one is occupying the house any longer, maybe we can help ourselves to what was left behind."

"Is that ethical?" I asked.

"It's more ethical than squandering it to forest decay."

"If someone's living there, we'll withdraw," Centaur assured me. "We won't know until we investigate."

Confidence of finding our first treasure grew when we didn't see evidence of a path leading to the house. It must have been years since someone last traveled to the wood and stone building for the forest to grow up that much.

We paused at the door of the cottage. It was ajar, providing a narrow strip of illumination into the building's interior. Too narrow. Walking around the cottage didn't earn us a better view. The only windows were five-sim slits, two per wall that let in less light than the door.

"Can't we just walk-in?" I whispered. "It doesn't look like anyone's inside."

"We probably can," said Centaur. "But it doesn't waste too much time to be cautious. After a thorough visual inspection, we'll listen for sounds, and sniff out any unusual odors."

Pebble already had his ear to the door, and Stick's nostrils were flared as he peered into the slits in the walls. They rejoined Centaur and me, twenty meters from the cottage. Pebble was first to speak. "Something's in there. I heard rustling. No voices, no sounds of walking---just rustling."

"It smells rank in there," said Stick.

"Maybe the people who lived there died," I suggested. "They may have been old, and it was their time."

"People don't age on Limbo, Hornet," said Centaur. "Not in a traditional manner. If there are people dead in there it wasn't because they died of old age."

"It's not a human smell," added Stick.

I shuddered. "Ghouls?"

"Ghouls don't make that much racket," said Pebble.

"Like you have ever seen, or heard, a ghoul," said Centaur.

"I've heard tales."

"It smells like a chicken coop," said Stick.

"Those scattered tracks do look like they were made from birds," said Centaur. "I'll go in first. Stick will follow, and you two will keep watch."

"Don't be helping yourself to more than your share of the loot," said Pebble. "Maybe I should also go in, in case you need some help in opening something. I've been picking locks before I could walk."

"You need to help Hornet. He's new to this. If we need your expertise, we'll call."

Centaur kicked the door open. The rustling sound intensified. Centaur backed away. There was enough light in the cottage now that some of its contents were seen. Bats hung from the rafters.

"A torch would help to fumigate," suggested Centaur. He

wrapped moss around a stick and lit it by striking a flint. More smoke was given off than light. He thrust the flaming vegetation in front of him as he entered the cottage. The noise within intensified. Bats escaped through the doorway in a swarm.

What we thought were bats. A second glance transformed them into a combination of bat, bird, and bee. They had bat wings, but also feathers, a round, bee-like body, and a hummingbird proboscis.

Instead of flying to the safety of dense woods, the fowls attacked Pebble and me. Neither of us was prepared for the onslaught. Upon learning birds were our antagonists we eased up on our resolve. I was pricked in the side as I brought my sword up and around to defend. The thing remained attached to me, like a tick. I attempted to extract it with my sword, but the blade was too long to be effective. Pushing it away caused its four limbs, and the claws at their ends, to tear my flesh where they clutched. The only solace I had during that first wave of attack was my success in keeping the others away from me. The birds stayed clear of my mad dervish-like spinning and hysterical screams. I begin to get light-headed. I stopped spinning, which was a red flag for the fowls to re-attack.

Pebble killed one attacker and held off two more with a dagger. If he was in range he could have eradicated the entire flock with his bow. The problem wasn't that they were too far away, they were too close.

I not only continued to feel light-headed, but became more so. I felt like I might faint.

Stick and Centaur came to my rescue. Centaur pulled the bird attached to me away with one of his massive arms. He tossed it 10 meters. It hit with a THUNK against a tree. It popped, spraying more blood than it should have had in its body. Stick handled the remaining beasts. He truly was an artist with his sword. Every swing contacted. In the end, fourteen corpses surrounded him.

I looked down at my puncture wounds. "The bleeding is

slowing."

"That's because you don't have enough blood remaining to leak out," said Centaur.

That faint finally arrived.

I woke on a bed. "He's lucky," said Stick. "I've heard of men becoming completely drained by one of those blood-sucking fowls."

"I thought they were scared of people," Pebble commented.

"If we didn't stir them up like foolish infants they would have probably left on their own to get away from us," said Centaur.

"If we had a healing stone we could fix you in a couple of minutes," said Pebble. "You're going to need bed rest. Maybe another day here, then back to Bluewood City."

"But I have a healing stone."

Pebble looked like he was going to kill someone, me in particular. He stormed off instead. A moment later he yelled back at us, "I'LL SEE IF THERE'S ANYTHING OUTSIDE WE CAN SALVAGE!"

I was more scared now than when the fowl was attached to me. Recognizing my concern, Centaur said, "Pebble thought you might die. He was scared for you. He's not angry that you kept the healing stone a secret. He's angry because what you didn't make him aware of almost killed you. Ever since he began living a more moral life, he has become very concerned for his companions' well being. We are his family now, including you. He has never been part of a family. If he had, maybe he wouldn't be here."

I tossed my wallet to Centaur, who pulled out the healing stone, and the remaining gold coin. Centaur rotated the metal disc between his finger and thumb.

"I think we chose wisely, Centaur," said Stick. "An infant this resourceful will only become more so with a little experience."

"Did you find any treasure?" I asked.

"Whoever lived here took everything of value with them," said Centaur. "That bed is the only piece of furniture the fowls hadn't completely ruined. You'd be lying in guano if we didn't flip the mattress."

"Take the coins and tell Pebble you found them."

"They were yours before we met," said Stick. "They should stay yours."

"If you weren't here with me I would have died beneath a pile of feathers. Not a very noble way to die. I would have been ashamed to come back to life. Take the coins."

I swallowed the healing stone. I immediately felt better.

Pebble returned. "You look better. Maybe we'll be able to leave soon. I didn't find anything of value."

"We did," said Stick. Centaur threw the wallet to Pebble.

Pebble's eyes grew wide as he opened it. He poured the contents into his left hand and counted. "Almost two gold here. How could I have missed that?"

"Hornet found it beneath a loose floor board beside the bed," said Centaur.

"Not only does Hornet's injury delay us, so we spend more time looking for treasure. He's the one who finds it." Pebble looked at my completely healed side. "May you mutate out of humanity only after I do, Hornet Polygulch. And may we have many profitable adventures together before that happens."

We should have spent the remainder of the day, and evening, at the cottage. We were weary from our skirmish with the fowls, but more eager to continue our journey---and the building stank.

It was the middle of the day when we finally left. What I thought was the middle of the day. Conjectures were problematic when the sun didn't move.

# Chapter 10

## LOST

As the forest became progressively more dense, the noises it emitted became louder.  We heard birds, squirrels, monkeys, even a hair-standing-on-end howl of a large cat.  Although I was protected in the middle of our group---Stick and Pebble were in front of me, Centaur was behind---there was still enough unprotected space on my flanks to keep my nerves on edge.  It would help if I could connect those sounds to what made them.  One's imagination was one's worst enemy.

We stopped abruptly.  Two of the largest cats I had ever seen were in the middle of the road, about 50 meters in front of us.  The black and white felines weren't acting aggressive, but they didn't appear intimidated by us either.

"Should we go around them?" I suggested.

"They're just cats," countered Pebble.

"More tiger than tabby," added Centaur.

Stick drew his sword.  "Most things go the way you want them to after a bit of encouragement."  He darted towards the cats.  Instead of fleeing they turned around and lifted their tails.

"GET BACK HERE!" Centaur lunged towards Stick like he was a child that had just run towards a busy street.  He stopped about halfway, then began to back-peddle.  He could always have more children.

Something vile squirted out of the backside of the cats.  It smelled like someone vomited on a decaying animal.  Even from the distance I was from the stench it was so strong I felt like I was going to pass out.  Eventually my scent glands did overload.  I vomited, then darted, into the forest.

I got scraped up pretty badly, the underbrush being substantial, but it was better than remaining near that odor.  My pack kept getting caught.  Remarkably, I didn't lose any gear.  Seconds later I was forced to stop to vomit again, then a few steps after that to vomit a third time.  After a fourth hacking, nothing came up.  I felt completely drained, and not just the contents of my stomach.  I could still smell the rotten, acidic stench.  The odor had diminished but it hadn't completely dissipated.  If it was this bad for me what must it be like for Stick?  He had to have been hit directly with that discharge.

I looked in the direction I thought I came from, expecting to see my companions.  I couldn't see them or the trail.  Maybe if I sniffed the air.  The forest was so permeated with the stench I couldn't tell where the odor was the strongest.  I had to have left a trail through the brush, but every time I spotted a broken twig in one direction another would appear in the opposite direction.  For an instant I panicked. "CENTAUR!  STICK!  PEBBLE!"  No counter bellow.

Did I actually run THAT far?  I ran off to the left of the trail, which meant I headed east.  If I now headed west I should eventually meet up with the trail, but up trail or down trail?  Was I heading slightly to the south or north?  I had no clue which direction I should go. Would my friends wait for me?  Would they begin searching?  They would search, because I was an infant, someone who wasn't able to take care of himself.  If the sun never moved and it was slightly northeast of being directly overhead, it should be easy for me to find my way back to the trail.  I had to have shot forward slightly when I veered into the forest.  At the time I was facing south, so I should head northwest.

After five minutes of hiking I became concerned again.  I should have intersected the trail by now.  I was moving at a good clip away from the cats, and it was slow traveling without a trail---in addition to the brush, there were fallen logs to hop or climb over, depending on their girth---but I still should have reached the trail. WAIT! Did I turn around before I ran off into the brush? Maybe I headed northwest instead of southeast. No, I was reasonably confident I fled into the brush without delay.

Who would have expected cats to do that? Cats were so fastidious in their grooming. One would think they would be repulsed as much by that odor as humans were. But...they weren't really cats, were they? Their size had confused us. That white stripe on their backs should have given them away. I had been on Limbo for just a few days, but I had already been attacked by a giant hornet, blood-sucking chickens, and now enormous skunks. How many ENCOUNTERS will I have by the end of the week?

There was a ridge ahead of me. If I climbed to the top of it I might be able to see the trail or my companions. "You are almost here," spoke a voice in my head. Could I be going crazy already? Did the fowl attack count as my first death and re-creation? Was a doppelganger---past or present---speaking to me? "Pleasure awaits."

At the top of the ridge I didn't see anything I didn't see below, just more of it. "Closer." Maybe it wasn't me who was speaking. I felt too exposed on the ridge. I began to descend, but was only able to take two steps. My feet were cemented in mud up to my thighs. I was dismayed. How could it be that wet up here? I tried to lift each leg, first under their own power, then with assistance from an arm. It was like my legs were now part of the soil, like roots of a tree. "A little exercise before dinner creates a healthy appetite."

Frantically I retrieved the bow on my back and tried to line up the notch on the back of an arrow with the bow string. After many arduous seconds I was successful, but the arrow was accidentally launched when my jittery hands could no longer hold the shaft.

I attempted to load another arrow. Before I could, my bow

was pulled out of my hands by invisible arms. It rose twenty meters, then fell into brush beyond sight. "It needs to stay alive so it will remain juicy, but its claws might scratch."

A long, slinky shape appeared. Its eight legs slowly followed the rocky ridge towards me. It was feline, but the oddest cat I had ever seen. Two slightly upturned antennae jutted out from its forehead. Its mottled green coat terminated at a forked tail.

I was surprisingly calm. Yes, I had made peace with my inevitable demise, but that desperate escape from the skunks had also sapped what little resolve remained within me.

A dense fog suddenly blocked my view of the cat. It began to rain, but just in my immediate area. The mud I was stuck in softened. I was able to pull one leg free, then the other. I ran down the ridge, away from the rain and cat. The fog began to dissipate, but not completely. The sun remained blocked. Without using it for orientation, how was I going to find my way back to the trail?

I continued in the direction I had been heading. It was as good a direction as any. I had to keep moving. That cat might have escaped the fog already.

I came to a stream. It was shallow enough to cross safely if I didn't mind getting my feet wet. Like that mattered, considering I was already soaking wet and muddy. I washed the mud off, then began walking downstream. Creeks led somewhere, which was better than I could guarantee wandering aimlessly on my own.

The stream eventually fell over a cliff. I climbed down to the grotto below, pausing at the spectacle before moving on. The waterfall warped. A lizard's head appeared---a very large lizard's head. Its body followed and followed, and followed. Forty meters later the lizard's entire body was revealed, including two wings that were folded against its scaly flanks.

"You have caused considerable change to my routine," said the lizard in a sultry tuba voice.

The day just won't improve. As I attempted to remove myself, expeditiously, from the encounter, a stream of scalding vapor swooshed past me. How could I be so lucky that the lizard was such a poor a shot? Ah. A large, sleek shape just meters away shook and shrieked as blisters erupted upon its reddening hide. "That just won't do," boomed the lizard's voice. A gust of wind pushed the cat backwards. A few seconds later it was no longer in sight.

I had stopped moving once the lizard attacked. I turned to face the creature. If it had wanted to kill me it would have. The cat was a substantially more challenging adversary. "I hate doing that. The octocat would have lived another day if it had not come so close to the grotto. It played unfair. That is why I helped you. There was no sense of competition in the hunt. Octocats are bullies and I do not like bullies. I despise conflicts almost as much as I despise losing my solitude."

And I entering this grotto probably didn't endear me to the lizard any more than the octocat. "Thank you for the help, but I must be going. I need to return to my companions."

"The three humans you ran from are four kays away. They are not very proficient in tracking you."

"If you can point me in the right direction I'll return your solitude to you."

"Once peace is lost, it takes some time for it to return. But without chaos, order would not exist, would it? Our world is no longer balanced. Without evil, good could not exist, but there is too much evil now. What did the creators think would happen with a planet inhabited by criminals? Positive energy must catch up to the negative, or Limbo is doomed. I probably will not live to see it, it still being decades away---not in this form anyway." The lizard became pensive, pausing for what I considered to be an eternity. "You see, drak are the most powerful life forms Gaea has created, but they will ultimately mutate into other forms. My morals are balanced, which means I do not intentionally harm, or help. I have a tendency to ramble---as do all drak---because we live the longest. Excluding the gent, of course. Once a gent, always a gent. The maxim is not completely accurate. They too arrived human. I have been a drak for 71 years. Life is slower for us, so we do not have the urgency to get to the point as quickly as others do. No one really knows what a drak transforms into. Some of my associates suggest there is a limit to the number of mutations, and when a drak dies he really dies. I believe drak have become so accustomed to their unhurried lives that when they die they mutate into the non-living."

"Ghouls?"

"Gaea help us---or curse us---if that ever happens. The devastation would be too terrifying to comprehend. I speak of unconventional organisms."

"Plants?"

"A tree or a weed? That's the ultimate question, isn't it? In our next life do we watch the world from a lofty height, or do we randomly pop up in places we are not wanted? No, not plants. Limboans can mutate into vegetation much earlier in their evolution. I believe drak mutate into rocks, soil, water, even the air."

"I don't think I would like being a rock."

"What experiences do you have to support that opinion? Never having to move may be paradise."

My friends were probably another kay away by now. I hoped I was never this verbose if I became a drak. Being a drak would be kind of cool---to fly, to breath fire, or steam, to control the weather. "I could leave your area sooner if you flew me to my friends."

"Do I look like a taxi?" The drak unfolded its wings and extended them.

"You look strong enough."

"This is not some fairy tale." The drak re-folded its wings against its body. "Drak aren't animals. We can't be...tamed."

"Maybe you could zap me to my friends, then."

"Some mutes, including drak, possess certain abilities, but

with limitations.  In exchange for our ability to develop elem naturally, we do not interact very well with the external variety.  A healing stone will not heal me.  Balance.  I believe I am finished with you.  I am getting sleepy.  Drak live long lives, but they do not stay awake any longer than any other species.  Balance.  Head west.  Your friends are coming from that direction.  Once you walk a couple of kays you may start shouting for them."

"So nothing---else---becomes aware of me?"

"Everything within five kays is probably aware of you.  No, I just prefer you do not make so much noise while you are near me.  Good day, infant."  The drak waddled its massive bulk back through the waterfall.

# Chapter 11

# LYNN

"Infant, you look like you've wrestled a tempest," said Centaur upon seeing me.

"And you guys still smell like you've been rolling in fermented manure."

"We should do something about that."  Pebble wrestled me to the ground, rubbing some of his stench onto me.

Stick helped me up.  Considering what he had been through he didn't smell much worse than Pebble, or now, me.  He wasn't wearing his travel clothes.  They must have taken the brunt of the discharge.  "You bury them somewhere?"

"I left them on the road where I stripped them off.  The

skunks were fascinated by them. After sniffing them they both had insane grins on their faces, like it was intoxicating. You would think they would be familiar with the odor of something that came out of their own butts."

"You get any on you, Centaur?"

"Pebble unintentionally blocked the attack for me, but he later shared the offensive odor, in the manner he shared it with you." Pebble grinned in response.

"I'm looking forward to a bath in Jacob tonight," said Stick.

"With the pace we're going, make that tomorrow night."

"Stop scratching."

I became concerned. "We're not going to travel through the night are we?"

"You worried about getting lost again?" asked Centaur. "Stay on the road this time. It's wide enough that even after we lose our light we'll still be able to find our way."

"It's not that. Aren't wild animals more dangerous at night?"

"Not to a party of four."

"Even an octocat or a drak?"

"A drak hasn't been seen in these woods in more than a year," stated Stick.

"He's back."

"You sure it wasn't just a big lizard?"

"With wings?"

"We better get moving," Centaur decreed. "A drak on the move doesn't care who he cuts a path through."

"I don't think he's going anywhere for awhile," I said. "He's napping."

"And how do you know this?" Pebble asked.

"He told me."

"You waited until now to share this with us?"

"I guess I was just happy to see you guys. Considering all I've seen this week, I didn't think speaking to a drak was that unusual."

Centaur smiled. "Being ABLE to return to us was more remarkable than the conversation."

"He didn't seem that vicious. Annoyed, but not vicious. I don't think drak think too much of us."

"It's mutual," said Stick.

"Apathy, not antipathy."

"I guess if I was that powerful I wouldn't think much of us either."

"Power doesn't have to breed contempt...or apathy," said Centaur.

"Too often it does," added Pebble.

"A tree or a weed," I added.

Three confused looks.

"Just something I heard."

"Maybe it would be best if we set up camp," Centaur suggested. "Travelling in the dark is more dangerous than during the day. And we'd be less tired after a night's sleep. More aware of our surroundings. Better at reacting."

"I think we can hold our own," Stick responded. "Hornet's ADVENTURE with the drak is proof of that. A warm bath and bed beckons."

"Pebble?"

"Is getting to Jacob a day early important enough to risk potential---lethal---complications?"

Centaur looked at me. Great. So I had to be the one to make the life and death decisions, someone who had been on Limbo for less than a week. I didn't think it was going to go well either way, so it might as well happen sooner, to get it over. "Let's head to Jacob. No reason to delay that bath."

With the approaching darkness came night sounds. Most of them must have also been present during the day. The darkness amplified them. Our sense of sight was diminished, so we had to rely on our other senses, especially our hearing. There were some animals that were nocturnal, but overall there were probably fewer animals active at night than during the day. Be it perception or reality, the dangers of the forest seemed to multiply after dark.

We choose to not light torches. Not only would we not be able to see outside a 10 meter radius, everything within a couple kays would be drawn to the illumination. The dimmed sun---which had become a full moon---didn't emit enough light for us to distinguish details, but it was bright enough to permit cautious movement.

The adrenaline rush of new adventures and potential danger kept us alert for the first minutes, but our weariness resumed with a vengeance. We slowed considerably and began to imagine things. Tree limbs became arms. Rocks and fallen logs became entire deformed, monstrous torsos. "Maybe we should have camped for the night," commented Stick.

"Now you say it," said Centaur.

Stick led. He knew the area the best and was the most experienced outdoorsman. Pebble followed. He had an arrow cocked at all times, and twice prematurely released a shaft, sticking tree trunks that startled him. I was safely third. The strongest member of our company, Centaur, protected our rear, the most dangerous duty. Sometimes the position was called the caboose, but most often the proc.

Every position in a protective queue had a name. First was the scout, then the art---short for artillery. Middle positions were just third, fourth, etc. In front of the proc was proc's second.

Scout tumbled into art, who tumbled into me, who tumbled into proc. We were back on our feet within seconds, but it felt like minutes.

"Don't walk any further," spoke a voice. We all turned towards the voice, but in different directions. "I've come to warn you, not to fight you. I'm not the danger. Look closely in front of you, where the road continues. Look at the ground, but don't get too close."

"COVER ME!" Stick slowly shuffled down the road. The moon provided just enough light to reveal his astonishment. He snapped his hand up, palm out, halting us. We cautiously squeezed our heads past him to get a look. Vines overlapped, covering a pit that was as wide as the road. Its depth was cloaked in shadows.

"It drops six meters. A tunnel in one corner burrows much deeper. That's where you would have been taken, dead or alive."

"Then what?" I naively responded.

"You would have been consumed, dead or alive."

"I think we could have held our own," said Stick.

"Even if dozens attacked you? It's time for you to leave this area. They know you are here. They are beginning to surround you."

With our focus on the trap, we hadn't noticed the increasing pairs of pin point illuminations appearing 40 meters from us, in a rapidly expanding arc, exceeding a semi-circle before we were able to react.

"RETREAT!" Centaur squawked.

"You can't out run them," spoke the ethereal voice. "Climb the nearest tree."

"They can't climb?" Stick questioned.

"They can, but only on large, consistent surfaces. Their exoskeletons prevent them from being very limber. They won't be able to reach you once you escape to a branch or a narrow trunk. Climb. They have completely surrounded you and are now closing in."

We climbed, each of us up a different tree. My choice was a cedar. The dead branches near the bottom became rungs. Once up three times my height, I paused. The branches were healthy here, making it difficult to climb higher. There was no way a...gigantic insect?...was going to climb through that pincushion below me.

Something crawled beneath and past my tree. It looked like an ant, but was larger than a cat.

"Not as large as this cat," said the ethereal voice. HOW DID

71

IT KNOW WHAT I WAS THINKING?! Was it reading my mind? "And it's fortunate I only read select thoughts. You humans have the dirtiest minds, and I have just washed myself before you interrupted the serenity of the forest."

Did everything in the forest feel that way? If so, why was the forest always so loud? The drak had thought that, and now this thing. Maybe it was the drak.

"I'm much prettier. And the forest being so loud IS the reason I like peace and quiet. I need quiet to contemplate, and to take naps. I would be even more beautiful if I could sleep more."

"Who are you?"

"Look for yourself. I'm directly above you. Why do you think you stopped climbing when you did? It was my suggestion."

I looked up. A cat not quite as large as me was lying on the branch above me. It had tufted ears and cheeks. Instead of a long, dangling tail it was bobbed, like a rabbit's. Its color was dappled, a mixture of yellow, red, and black. It was looking down, but not directly at me. It appeared to be focusing on something in the distance, farther out than my mind might comprehend. It stretched one paw, extending its four claws. They were about twice as long as my fingernails.

"No, I won't harm you," said the cat. "I didn't help you escape the ants just to save the kill for myself. Then why did I help you? Curiosity, predictions of adventures with you. Yes, I can foretell the future to some degree, the accuracy depending on the number and reliability of the variables."

"Hornet, stay where you are," quivered the voice of Pebble. "Any sudden movement may cause it to attack."

"It's okay. It was the one who warned us about the pit."

"My name is Lynn, that's what you were about to ask. I mutated into this form many years ago. True lynxes aren't this large and don't have telepathy. I've never met another cat with human ancestry. I fear I may be the only one. I've been searching for a male companion for many years."

"So octocats weren't once human?"

"Gaea, no."

"The one that was stalking me appeared to be intelligent."

"Never confuse instinct with intelligence."

"So you're a mutant?"

"As one of your companions will become, soon. But not you. I can't predict your future at all. You're a complete mystery to me. By the way, positive or neutral mutants aren't usually called mutants. It's demeaning. Mute is acceptable. Changed is better."

"Who will mutate?"

"I must provide you the opportunity to remain curious. It will likely occur before you reach the arbols."

"I thought you couldn't read my mind?"

"I said I couldn't predict your future. Your present is wide open."

"I don't see any more ants," said Centaur.

"They may be trying to deceive us," said Stick. "We should wait until it gets light so we can see our surroundings better."

"The ants aren't that clever," said Lynn.

"They built that trap," said Pebble.

"That was from habit. They collectively think of something creative every decade or so. They have returned to their tunnels. I can see much better in the dark than you can. The last dozen are descending into the underworld." To emphasize her point, Lynn jumped from her branch to the ground, nearly a ten meter leap.

I was next to reach the ground, saving my leap for the last meter. My companions followed, in sequence. We clustered around Lynn.

"Thank you," said Pebble. "We never forget a friend."

"Your implication being you appreciate me saving you, but the longer you speak to me the more extended your delay."

Centaur jumped in, to provide damage control. "Pebble just thought you might also like to be on your way."

"Cats appreciate directness. Dogs, they are too cautious,

not wanting to harm the hand that feeds them. Cats feed themselves. I appreciate Pebble's sentiment, but it's inaccurate. I will be traveling with you. As I have mentioned, I seek male companionship. There is a rumor of a feline with human ancestry living in the Copper Forest."

"So you may not be the only one?" asked Stick.

"Gaea clusters mutants, but not exclusively."

"I thought we weren't supposed to use that word," I interrupted.

"YOU shouldn't. You'll continue to need my assistance, at least until the Copper Forest. You may no longer be infants, but you're still inexperienced. You do not yet have the skills or experience to survive on your own. In many ways you're in more peril now than when you were infants. You're more mobile, and more curious, and believe you are more powerful than you are. You're toddlers."

"We'll see about that," said Pebble as he re-cocked his bow.

"You are compelled to defend your friends, while wishing I would flee, so you won't have to fight. It's never a good idea to stay in the same spot in the forest too long, especially at night. Many things, and I do mean THINGS, are converging on us as we speak. Follow me. I'll lead you safely around the ants and back to the road. We'll clear the forest at dawn, and be crossing the Neutral River half-an-hour later."

We followed Lynn without further argument. Only once did she pause to respond to the night sounds. A piercing banshee-like wail erupted from her, banishing the cacophony for a full quarter. Slowly the silence dissipated, but it never got as loud as before.

# Chapter 12

# EXOSKELETONS

The river was half-a-kay wide. "We're not going to swim across?" I asked rhetorically. I hoped it was rhetorical.

After climbing a rise, the question was answered. A ferry was docked on the far side of the river, where the road continued. We waited patiently as the ferryman brought his craft back across. "We can afford this?" asked Pebble.

"It's just two coppers each," Centaur replied. "The ferryman doesn't dare charge more. There's a ford a couple of kays downstream---in the opposite direction we're travelling. A nuisance, but it does give travelers another option."

The ferryman was squeamish about Lynn, but allowed her aboard without argument. She probably sent him a subliminal message.

A fish the length of the raft swam by, bumping it. I lost my balance, but caught myself before falling. "Don't be concerned," said the ferryman. "The cable will hold." It was strung between the banks of the fast moving river. It slid through two metal hoops placed fore and aft of the raft. A pedal powered water wheel propelled the craft across the river in three minutes.

Another half-an-hour of walking brought us into a cultivated area. Compared to the computerized, homogenized, flawless farms of the collective, they looked like fields of weeds. I recognized corn and tomatoes, but they were irregular in size, and discolored. The other crops either grew so poorly that they looked unfamiliar to me, or they were mutations.

"Breakfast?" Stick eyed the crops with as much trepidation as I, but he was also hungry. Some people became extraordinarily brave when their stomachs spoke for them. I also had become hungry, but rapidly lost my appetite upon seeing the crops in more detail. I promised myself if I died of food poisoning I would be re-created as a farmer and improve the state of agriculture on Limbo. They couldn't have grown THAT poorly. If they had been damaged, by whom? Or what?

"I think we can wait another hour, until we reach Jacob," suggested Centaur. He considered the lack of a response, confirmation. We kept to the road.

"Beware the beetles," said Lynn. I looked at the ground beneath me. Nothing. I scanned the fields. No amorphous cluster. No approaching swarm to engulf us. All I could see were a few large shapes two fields away. Cows no doubt, or a mutated similarity.

As we approached, the animals transformed. Four legs became six. Hides became exoskeletons. Horns remained, but they elongated, to two-thirds the length of the animals, which grew to more than three meters.

Centaur halted us at the edge of the field. "I think we now know what damaged the crops."

"We should do something about it?" asked Stick. "The Knight-Errant's of Olde would have."

"We're not defenders of the faith," said Pebble. "We're salvagers seeking our fortune."

"We can be both. Jacob's farmers will pay plenty for us to rid them of this nuisance."

"This opportunity does look like it was handed to us on a silver platter," said Centaur.

More likely a bloody platter. I had my hands full with one hornet. How was I going to fight something twice my size?

"Everything has its weaknesses," said Lynn. "Crop beetles are big, but slow. They have poor sight and hearing."

"Then we ought to be able to sneak up on them," said

Centaur. "Pebble, you can probably stick them with arrows before they even know we're here. The rest of us will take care of the ones you don't have time to finish off." Pebble nodded.

Stick headed towards the beetles, who didn't even look up. Centaur followed him. I begrudgingly followed Centaur. Pebble began walking too, but at an angle. His destination was a low-lying bluff adjacent to the insects. Lynn lay down, with her large paws before her, in sphinx stance.

"Aren't you coming with us?" I twisted my neck around in the lynx's direction while continuing to move forward.

"Everything has its strengths. The beetles' natural armor is difficult to penetrate. They are unlikely to run away when threatened. They are too stupid to be fearful for their safety. You'll have to kill most of them. This is not my battle. I'll still be here if any of you survive."

"What's the likely outcome?"

"That is something I choose to not share with you. There are some things you must discover for yourselves. Good luck."

Well, that wasn't very encouraging. Didn't Lynn say one of my companions would die before we reached the arbols?

Stick stopped 25 meters short of the beetles. Centaur and I stopped beside him. A moment later Pebble stopped on top of the bluff. He placed eight arrows into the ground beside him and cocked a ninth. He looked at us. Centaur nodded.

Pebble released the cocked arrow. In rapid succession he reached for an arrow beside him, cocked, and released. Three arrows were in the air before the first one hit. The first made contact, but only briefly. It bounced off the beetle's carapace. Seven of the nine arrows hit their targets, but only three penetrated.

The previously docile beetles became anything but once they were attacked. Their oral pincers clicked. Their horns were lowered, bull style. Only one of the beetles had been killed by the ranged attack. The other two hit received minor injuries. Pebble's second barrage was as unsuccessful as his first, but it did bring down one more beetle.

This time the beetles attacked back. They charged, their double lances aimed carelessly before them. I easily dodged them as the miniature stampede slowly passed through our ranks. I struck a beetle with my sword, but the blow caromed off, causing no damage. Stick poked an insect from underneath. His strength was just enough to hold his ground as the creature's momentum forced the sliver of metal to rip through the tender flesh. It slumped to the ground, blocking the insect behind. It slammed into its companion, horns first, puncturing it. As it swung its head around, attempting to free itself, Centaur swung his battle axe over his head, allowing gravity to do most of the work as it fell with a crack as it tore a path through the creature's shell, nearly splitting it in two. All that practice chopping firewood had finally paid off.

Before the beetles could turn around and begin their second attack, Pebble released his third barrage of arrows. Another beetle was removed from battle, permanently. The odds were looking better, and none of us had been killed, not even injured. That all changed, or nearly so.

Somehow I tripped. I must have stepped into a hole. The shock from the sudden, acute pain made it impossible to think clearly. The beetles were charging, just meters away. At best, I was going to be trampled, and maybe even skewered.

Then something remarkable happened. That same hole that I had stepped into caught one of the beetle's legs. It veered like a tank losing traction on one side. Head first it struck the beetle beside it, puncturing it with its horn. Stick and Centaur made quick work of the beetle that stumbled. The remaining two beetles finally gave up, racing off towards the forest. What little intelligence they had finally kicked in.

My companions rushed to my side, then helped me up. As soon as I put pressure on the leg that stepped into the hole, I fell back down. Pebble showed concerned. "Is it broken?"

"I don't think so. I believe my ankle is just sprained."

"This would be a good time to have a healing stone," said Stick.

Not only did I feel stupid for stepping in a hole, I now felt guilty for delaying my companions, a second time. "I'll be able to walk, I think. It's not that bad." I put pressure on it again. I winced, but didn't fall back down. "Maybe if I had a walking stick." A blue oak, much larger than those in the forest, was on the perimeter of the field. With an abundance of sunlight and room to expand it was able to achieve its potential.

Lynn appeared in front me, blocking my route to the tree. "I thought you were going to wait for us from a safe distance?"

"So did I. My slumber was interrupted when two of the beetles attempted to massage me---with their hooves."

Pebble was shocked. "You napped while we fought for our lives?"

"It was very likely you would survive."

"But you didn't know about those two beetles," said Stick.

"The selectivity of my predictions is indeed unnerving."

I found a relatively straight branch about the right length beneath the oak. I walked back to my companions. Centaur had his dagger drawn, and was cutting a horn off a beetle. I looked at him, questioning. "Proof. If someone came up to you and declared a reward for doing something, wouldn't you want something more than their word?" Two more horns were cut out, verifying that we had killed at least two of the beetles.

# Chapter 13

# ALGAE

With pride, we carried the lances the remaining five kays to Jacob. My leg continued to improve. On the outskirts of the village I threw away my walking stick. I still walked with a limp, but when I concentrated I could mask it. First impressions were said to be everything. I didn't want strangers thinking I was crippled. Illogical, perhaps, but that was how I thought.

"Hold up." Centaur turned towards the river we've been following since we crossed it on the ferry.

"I understand that old men sometimes need to take breaks," said Stick, "but we're within sight of Jacob, unless your eyesight has become as weak as your stamina."

"We need to freshen up before we greet the village."

"If I don't primp myself before entertaining a woman I'm surely not going to before I meet a gaggle of farmers," said Pebble.

"That's why you never get a second date." Stick followed Centaur to the banks of the Neutral River, just a few meters away.

Pebble looked at me. I responded, "We do smell like a landfill."

"Aren't heroes suppose to smell like they've done a hard day's work? We're not perfume salesmen."

"COME ON, PEBBLE!" Stick had taken off his pack and was well on his way to removing his clothes, as was Centaur. "If I have to strip and take a plunge, so do you?"

"But you like showing off your body, every chance you get, even when there's no women around. It becomes unnerving at times."

Stick no longer was paying attention to Pebble. He had finished undressing, and without hesitation leaped into the river. The current was almost non-existent beside the bank, inhibiting him from drifting. "Hey, what are you doing?"

Centaur frisked Stick's pack. "There it is." He pulled a cloth away. He jumped into the water a few meters upstream of Stick. Once he popped up to the surface he began washing himself with the cloth.

"That's my sword cloth."

"You wiped worse with it."

Stick's expression relayed the contrary.

"You have two others in your pack."

Stick wasn't convinced.

"Once I rinse it out it, it will be as good as new."

Centaur was quite thorough in his washing. Stick now believed that burning the cloth might be its only salvation.

I followed my companions' lead, removing my clothes before dropping into the river. Modesty was often viewed as meekness. A prison wasn't the place to appear meek. "Wouldn't we become cleaner if we had some soap? Even better, tomato juice. Isn't that what people are supposed to do when they get sprayed with a skunk?"

"You got some?" asked Centaur. It was amazing what one took for granted. How little people have changed through the millennia, physically, intellectually, emotionally, spiritually, but they were able to pamper themselves better. What I would do for some modern conveniences about now. I wasn't asking for much. Deodorant soap. A shower with plenty of hot water, with a massaging head perhaps. And transportation of some sort, other than my feet. Modern men weren't conditioned to walk so much. I wasn't sure if my blisters were more pronounced or my calluses. Actually, it was an easy call. Calluses developed over time. It took just minutes for a blister to develop. If I was lucky the water would have enough grit in it to act as pumice. I jumped in. Yep, it was my lucky day. But did my mouth need such a cleansing? Without toothpaste on Limbo maybe it did.

Centaur tossed Stick the sword cloth. Apparently Stick had forgotten his disgust, because he was as thorough as Centaur was in his cleaning.

"You coming in?" Centaur asked Pebble.

The rat-faced man watched us from atop the bank, a sour look on his face.

"It can't be that bad. You're not afraid of the water are you?"

That last comment was the catalyst he needed. He reluctantly removed his leather boots and tunic, then jumped in.

From the looks Centaur and Stick gave him, they apparently had the same question I had. His reply: "It doesn't make sense to wash only ourselves does it?"

"I guess we better wash our clothes as well." Centaur begrudgingly climbed out of the water and up the bank. A woman suddenly emerging nude from the water might have been a wondrous sight, but seeing a man, not so much. It reminded me of those pictures of the progression of evolution---a fish climbing out of the water and transforming into a human. Centaur threw not only his clothes into the water, but also ours. With little or no current near the shore a haphazard approach was deemed the most efficient. He leaped back into the water. "I guess those rocks against the bank could be used as a washboard."

Stick tossed me the sword cloth, then helped Centaur scrub our dirty clothes. I examined the cloth before using it. It looked cleaner than the towel I dried off with in Bluewood City. That wasn't saying much. Now that the river was floating in clothing I could have used something else, but that just didn't seem right. I attempted to wash myself as I struggled to keep myself afloat, then I gave up and paddled close enough to shore to attach my feet to a rock. Better. When done, I tossed Pebble the cloth. Without

82

complaint the rat-faced man began washing himself under his clothes. "I'm surprised how modest you are," I commented to him.

"It's not the stripping that bothers me," he replied demurely. "It's the soaking. It makes my skin itch. It becomes red and scaly. It feels like I'm wrapped in sand paper."

"Lotion might help."

Stick brought his breeches up to his nose. "These clothes still don't smell too fresh."

I smelled the shirt I had been rubbing against a rock. "Mine do, but I didn't get the brunt of that discharge."

Centaur swam over to me. After inspecting the rock, he rubbed his socks against it, then examined them, both visually and olfactoryily. "I don't think they've smelled this good since I first put them on. And the stains are completely gone---the dirt and the blood."

"Let me try." Stick darted to the rock. A minute of vigorous rubbing provided the same results. He raised his underwear over his head like they were a trophy.

"Some plants are infused with elem," stated Centaur. "That algae on that rock must have cleansing properties. Elem aqua is associated with healing. Cleansing is a type of healing."

"So Mother was right," said Stick. "Eating your vegetables is good for you."

"It depends on the vegetables." With perturbed determination Pebble stripped off his underwear. He nearly drowned himself doing so. His clothes became as clean as ours, and he wasn't too happy about it. Somehow, having the algae assist in the cleaning was an insult to him. "Next thing I eat might cause a lightning bolt to burst out my ass."

The four of us crawled out of the water. We dripped dried as we wrung out our clothes.

Something was missing. "Where's Lynn?" I asked.

"She'll return," Centaur assured me. "Sleeping through that beetle skirmish couldn't have been enough adventure for her. And she still needs to reach the Copper Forest to meet that cat of her dreams."

"She's probably as put off with a city as I am." Between scratches Pebble put on his spare underwear. He lifted his head and scrunched his nose. "I should have washed these too." He wasn't exaggerating about his skin becoming irritated. It was red and blotchy, and his flaying wasn't helping.

"You could return to that rock," suggested Stick.

"I'm done with water---for another month."

"Quit scratching," said Centaur.

Pebble ignored the comment. "Cities wouldn't be too bad if they didn't have people in them. My friends preferred taking photos of people. I preferred landscapes and architecture."

"You had friends?" asked Stick. "How long are we going to wait for our clothes to dry?" Centaur and I had also put on a dry first layer, but the swordsman wasn't so hasty. He pranced around like a rooster.

"I guess our clothes don't have to be completely dry before we greet Jacob," said Centaur. "Once we rent a room we'll be able to lay them out again."

We chose to store our wet underwear. What kind of first impression would we make if we draped them over our packs?

# Chapter 14

# NEGATIVITY

It was atypical for travelers to enter the village dripping wet, but it was the beetle horns that caused the crowd to assemble. There were more than a hundred people enveloping us and gawking by the time we reached the village square.

Jacob was larger---in area---than Bluewood City, but less populous. Living on the fringes of a prairie, Jacobblers could see something coming from quite a distance. If that something threatened, they had time to cluster together to make a stand. Bluewood City was in the forest. Not only were the animals and mutes more dangerous, the limited visibility a vegetative mesh provided made it far more likely for something to leap out at you. Bluewoodians didn't have time to huddle, forcing them to sustain a defensive stance, the wooden palisade being the most visible evidence. Jacob being primarily a farming community, homesteads were farther apart than they were in Bluewood City, with hectares of crops in between. The Jacobblers were friendlier than Bluewoodians. They acted more laid back, making me feel more at ease. They did an honest day's work. Viewing others in their own image, there was more outreach than fear. When greeting visitors for the first time the village put its best face forward, the collective voice of the settlement acting as a single individual.

The mayor and village patrol met us at the square. Without exterior defenses---not even watch towers---it was the first time we were impeded since spotting the first resident of the village. The man in charge wore overalls, like most of the people in town. The sheriff and his deputy also looked like they had overalls on, but each was partially shrouded by a wire mesh vest. A ladder emblem was over their hearts. The mayor, who was nearly as wide as he was tall, was first to speak. "Welcome to Jacob." He glanced at the horns. Who couldn't when something two meters long was pointing at you. His smile diminished marginally as concern plowed through. "If you've come to sell trophies, you may have to wait until fellow travelers come into town. Jacobblers are wealthy of spirit, but poor of gold."

Pebble was bursting with statements that had to be expelled. He was barely able to hold them in until the mayor was finished speaking. "The horns are proof of a great service we have done for you. If gold is scarce, silver will suffice."

The three villagers looked at one another like they were mentally discussing which sanitarium Pebble should be put away in, for the remainder of his life.

Centaur was aware of the tenuous relationship Pebble had created. Something had to be done to rectify the situation, immediately, if we hoped to profit from the community. "What my good friend and business associate was attempting to inform you of is our good fortune of entering your northern fields as a herd of crop beetles were devastating them. Being the neighborly folk we were, we took it upon ourselves to rid you of this menace. We brought these horns to donate them to the village, to be used as a monument perhaps."

"You are kind," responded the mayor, returning to his pre-Pebble joviality. "Thank you so much, gentlemen." He gave us each a generous hug. "Our crops are guaranteed to prosper now."

It was time for Centaur to complete the sale. "Jacob, being a neighborly place, we thought you might be willing to share some food and supplies...and coin."

The mayor's smile dropped again, but this time it was replaced with seriousness. Responsibility and leadership bloomed upon withered cordiality. In the midst of playing happily with a child, the playmate became guardian. "All coin and gem is scarce here. Most Jacobblers never leave this area, except to Rhinopolis during harvest. There are few opportunities for exchange, of currency or commodity. Quality of life sustains us. If the quality of life was better before our incarceration would we have been sentenced?"

"Violence is the root of all negativity," added the sheriff. "Violence brought us here. Violence will eventually strip us of our humanity. Jacob has chosen, on many occasions, to circumvent violence, even to the short-term detriment of its citizens."

"Yes, we will be happy to feed and lodge you. And we'll even provision you when you leave. We can't pay you for something we chose not to do ourselves. Deputy Pike will escort you to your room. Enjoy your visit."

Not knowing how to respond, we followed the deputy, sans horns, to a two-story building adjacent to the village square. Instead of there being a pub on the first floor, customary for most inns, there was a produce market, interspersed with tables and chairs.

Two sets of bunks and a bench were the only furniture in the simple room we were escorted to upstairs. Pebble exhaled deeply and dropped onto one of the lower beds. "This is much more pleasant. Being around all those people was making me...annoyed."

Centaur's face tensed. He turned to Deputy Pike. "Pebble wasn't specifically referring to Jacob. He's a bit anti-social."

"No apologies. I feel that way myself sometimes. Even in a peaceful place like Jacob there are a few individuals who are less peaceful when they've had too much to drink."

"You sell alcohol here?" asked Stick.

"Fermented cider. It's provided without cost, as is all sustenance."

"Rotting apples?"

"Where do you think alcohol comes from?" Centaur

87

inquired.  "From Gaea's teats?"

Stick had this whimsical look on his face.

"And don't even think about having a relationship with one of those wholesome lady farmers.  We're here strictly for business, and being ridden out of town on a rail won't be very profitable."

Stick now looked embarrassed, and a little sad---a little boy caught being naughty, and his candy taken away from him as punishment.

"We don't have to go back out there today, do we?" asked Pebble.  "Lynn had the right idea about bypassing this place.  I've heard there aren't a lot of people in the Frontier.  Maybe it would be better just to mutate a couple of more times and win a free trip there."

"Again, Pebble is referring to cities in general, not to Jacob."

Deputy Pike either chose to ignore the comment, or found it to be too insubstantial to disturb him.  "I've often wondered what it would be like in the Frontier.  Those ordered areas of it have to be similar to Jacob, peaceful, but hopefully not as boring.  Trogs are supposed to be stodgy, but the few who have passed through here were more lively than most of our citizens.  Its unlikely trogs who travel are representative of their race.  Leaving home, for whatever reason, is chaotic.  Fun, but chaotic.  Or maybe that's what fun is about---chaos."

"Have you also seen arbols?" I asked.

"You know, one would think being chaotic the arbols would be running helter-skelter all over the world.  They are the reclusive ones, not the trogs.  I don't think it's because they fear the world.  Maybe they are so happy with their lifestyle and where they live they have no desire to leave."

"But even the most content person sometimes wishes for a change of scenery," said Stick.

"From what I heard," said Centaur, "the arbols act like children, playing all day, staying up late into the night, and sleeping 'til noon."

"Some of the things they do are quite adult," added Pebble.

"But even that is playful. There is a complete lack of shame in it."

Deputy Pike sighed. "What would it be like to live without shame?"

"They're supposed to be as many female arbols as male," said Stick. "The opposite is said to be true for trogs. Or maybe that's because one can't distinguish a trog man from a trog woman."

"So a man is more likely to be set in his ways and stodgy, and a woman more playful?" I commented.

"A sad state of affairs, indeed."

Deputy Pike continued to linger in our room. Didn't he have anyone to arrest? Considering the people who inhabited Jacob, probably not. Talking to people passing through was likely his only entertainment. "Well, I hope you enjoy your stay here. I can guarantee it will be peaceful. Dinner is served in the market at dusk. Being a farming community we adhere to farming hours."

"No lunch?" pleaded Stick.

"The farmers take a snack in the fields with them. You may forage in the market, but you'll have to wait two more hours to eat a formal meal. Good day." Deputy Pike closed the door behind him.

Packs were opened and our underwear draped over the head and footboards. Centaur stripped out of his wet outer clothes. He placed them beside the underwear. "I'm going to take advantage of this bed, and I'm not going to feel guilty about it. Old men like me can't stay up 10 hours a day."

"You've just begun your second decade," said Pebble. "I hope I'm not that worn out, decrepit, and senile in two years."

"Hey, I never said anything about being senile. I still have my wits about me. Sometimes I just don't remember where I put them."

"I can't wait until dinner," said Stick.

89

"I'll join you," said Pebble. "Maybe we can still profit from this settlement. Everyone can't be working in the fields." He dug out a deck of cards from his pack.

Centaur gave him a stern look. "Pebble?"

"If I happen to win, I won't bankrupt them. I remember what happened in Reed."

Stick sighed. "And Reed had the best ribs on Limbo."

"If?" Pebble didn't respond to Centaur's accusation. I had a feeling if luck wasn't on Pebble's side there were ways he could improve it.

"You coming, Hornet?" asked Stick.

I didn't know when it happened, but I now sat at the adult table. "I think I could use an hour of horizontal myself." With exaggerated grunts of offense Stick and Pebble stalked out of the room.

From the hallway I heard, "I thought you didn't want to be around people, Pebble?"

"I'll make the sacrifice. The few coppers I have are lonely and need some friends."

Centaur eyes were closed and he was breathing heavily. He lay on one of the lower beds. With my sore ankle making me feel all of MY 10 years, I chose the other lower bed after I stripped off my outer clothes. Let the youngsters climb.

Minutes later---what had felt like minutes---I was woken by a door opening abruptly and slamming.

Pebble paced the room, looking distraught. Stick leaned against the wall, looking gleeful. Deputy Pike was also there, no expression at all, with his arms crossed. Uh, oh.

Centaur twisted around to place himself into a sitting position. "Is there some way to rectify this situation, Deputy?"

"I hope not," he replied. "Pebble just lost three silvers to me." He tried to keep a neutral face, but a hint of a smile leaked through at the edges of his mouth. Stick cackled.

"Some of it was yours," Pebble dead-panned. That sobered

Stick, but not completely.

"These gentlemen attempted to rid some hard-working Jacobblers of their meager earnings. I had to teach them a lesson."

"So there are no charges against them? Being as ordered as this village is I worried that there might be some ordinance against gambling."

"There is, but the three silvers lost was sufficient to cover the fine. There might even be a way for you to recoup that."

"So, why are you so disturbed, Pebble?"

"I lost. I actually lost. I don't think I'll ever play cards again."

"Until the next village," said Stick. Pebble didn't respond. "Deputy Pike, you mentioned a way we can recover our fine." Stick sat next to Centaur. The deputy sat next to me. Pebble continued to pace.

"Not everyone feels as strongly about non-violence as the mayor and sheriff. Sometimes violence is the only cure for certain civic diseases. Those beetles aren't the only things that threaten Jacob. Being non-violent, Jacobblers are compelled to safeguard their village without committing violence. The previous mayor traveled to Gulag to exchange the village's accumulative profit---many years worth---for some protective penta from the Wizards. He returned with a RING OF SHIELDING. When activated the entire village is protected from attack by an energy hemisphere. Our salvation didn't last. The ring was stolen five years later, one year ago. We have been fortunate that no greater menace than the crop beetles has challenged us. Our luck will not hold forever. With Jacob unwilling to use violence in its own protection, it will one day be exterminated. A planet full of mutated criminals guarantees that."

"Didn't anyone pursue the people who stole the ring?" I asked.

"A posse was formed, and it even caught up with the man, but all it could do was ask for the ring back, pleading how important it was to the village. The man laughed and ran off again. The posse could have stuck the man with arrows as he ran, but of course it didn't. I was part of that posse.

"I've lived near Jacob all of my life. I entered Limbo in the middle of the Neutral River. A pike swallowed me whole before I could swim to shore. Being digested alive isn't a pleasant experience.

"I felt impotent not being able to help my village. But that helplessness is changing. My self-doubt and now, self-hatred, has simmered this past year. I think if the ring was stolen today I would be able to force myself to kill this man."

"No one knows where the man is, now?" asked Centaur.

"Not currently, but we know of two places he died. The ring wasn't enough for the man, although it was one of the strongest devices ever created. There's a cave at the bottom of the Neutral River, 11 kays upstream from here. It's laden with coins and rare gems---possibly even penta. The difficulty comes in retrieving the ring. The treasure is the remains of the people who attempted it. In addition to this cave being 10 meters below water, it is inhabited by poisonous eels. The scoundrel was re-created, but was too frightened to return to the cave to reclaim the ring. He died again days later, while attempting to rob a caravan of freight-haulers. His next re-creation had to be in the Frontier, because he wasn't seen again. If anyone had a short road to becoming a demon, it was he."

"Let's do it," said Pebble.

I had only listened to that point, my inexperience reinforcing my non-assertiveness. I couldn't hold back any longer. "YOU'RE CRAZY! What makes you think we could survive the attempt? In a year not only hasn't anyone been able to retrieve the ring, they haven't made it out alive. Just because we killed some beetles doesn't make us super heroes. I can't even hold my breath long enough to reach the bottom of a swimming pool."

"Jacob has a few penta," the deputy volunteered, "including a water breathing rod. I'm confident the mayor would donate it."

"It may be the opportunity we need to finance the

remainder of our journey to the Copper Forest," said Centaur.

"It's time we had a real challenge," said Stick.

"Jacob needs that ring, Hornet," said Pebble. "And we could use the money. Treasure worth hundreds of gold might be in that cave. If you needed something drastically, wouldn't you want someone to help you?" I didn't know if Pebble was being sincere about wanting to help Jacob, or just using the village's misfortune as a platform to nourish his greed.

"But it needs to be unanimous," said Centaur. "If we don't all agree, we go elsewhere."

If all infants had this much pressure put on them, they would return to the womb. I might die doing this thing, but if I didn't have any friends I would have died already. "Let's do it," I finally said, but without enthusiasm.

# Chapter 15

## CLOUDING THE WATER

Dinner wasn't particularly hardy. Retaining the theme of non-violence, Jacobblers were vegetarian---technically, vegan. "We still have that dried meat in our room," Centaur suggested.

"You've mentioned that already---three times." Stick stabbed his salad violently. The two kidney beans, previously tangled in vegetation, fell from his fork before it reached his mouth.

"What got into you inviting Deputy Pike into your poker game?"

"All money spends," Pebble replied. "At first I got frustrated playing with the Jacobblers. They didn't play right. They never bluffed. When one of them went all in I thought he was bluffing. Considering the cards that were displayed, and how he bet earlier in the hand, it seemed logical. He actually had an unbeatable hand. If I didn't have more money than he did I would have busted. Playing faithfully to the odds I easily won, but it began to get boring. When I was younger I preferred the easy score, but I've grown since then. When Deputy Pike walked by, instead of hiding the game or walking off, I invited him in, being very ambiguous what we were doing. He accepted. If I wasn't so put out with the way the Jacobbler's played I would have had more common sense. He played well and I was still in honest Jacobbler mode. I don't think I'll ever be able to play cards again."

The next day the horns were missing. The Jacobblers never intended to create a monument with them. They didn't want to be reminded of violence, particularly for it to be put on display. How much had we been humored the day before?

The Jacobblers lined the street as they saw us off, most of them believing we wouldn't return. It was a curiosity for them to see people choosing to confront violence. The mayor, sheriff, and deputy stood in the center of the village square. All three smiled, but for different reasons. "Here's what I promised you plus something extra." Deputy Pike handed Centaur the breathing rod--- and a penta stone.

"Thank you." Centaur placed the rod in his pack and the stone in his wallet.

"Good luck." Deputy Pike shook his head. "No, not that. It implies that you'll likely fail, and you need luck not to. I have confidence in you. Remember, you're not only doing this for yourself, but for Jacob. Our actions may have caused our imprisonment, but we can choose to change that behavior. If we don't on our own, Gaea will do it for us." I didn't know what to think. Deputy Pike's speech did inspire me, but it may have also put too much pressure on me. I was stressed before being burdened with responsibility.

The road south of the village hugged the Neutral River, staying within a few meters of the cottonwoods that huddled even closer.

It was a beautiful day. The morning coolness was beginning to give way to a gentle warmth. There was enough of a breeze to flicker the leaves, making the river sound more violent than it was. The aroma of warming grass was only superseded by the occasional waft of sage.

We talked very little, in contrast to the morning we left Bluewood City. How were we going to overcome a school of poisonous eels? "I think swords would be best," Stick suggested. "Being narrow, elastic, and agile, slicing would be better than pulverizing."

"Daggers would be better," Pebble argued. "Being smaller, they'll move through water easier. FEEK! Which means I won't be able to use my bow. Do you think Jacob has any harpoon guns?"

"We're already halfway there. Too late to turn back." Centaur hated delays. Sometimes adults were as bad as children when trying to keep them on task.

We passed a fork. To the right was Rhinopolis.

"We're going that way after we find the ring," Stick informed me.

"How far is it to the Copper Forest?" I asked.

"Too far to worry about right now," Pebble sniped.

"About two more kays---to the cave," Centaur estimated. "Deputy Pike mentioned four trees that formed a **W**. The cave should be directly across from them, a third of the way across."

Ten minutes later Stick announced, "There they are."

At the base of the **W** Centaur dropped his pack. He opened it and removed a rod. He examined it, as the rest of us huddled around him. I was completely engrossed. The rod was about the size of one of those over-sized pencils elementary students use. It was metallic: silver and glossy. Five runes spanned its length: three dots alternating with two waves. There was a small knob five sims from one of the ends. The rod was open on the other end. Centaur set it down carefully on a rock. "We better take our clothes off first. If we are changed physically, they may tear or strangle us." We did as he suggested.

Pebble looked down at himself. "It feels like I'm waving bait. I'm going to put my underwear back on." Centaur and I followed his lead.

"What else might we need down there other than weapons?" asked Centaur.

"Rope."

"A net."

"How about food and water?" I asked.

"We're not going to be down there that long," Centaur declared. "I'm not anyway."

"I don't think I want my food to get that soggy or mixed with fish water," said Stick, "but I wouldn't mind grabbing a couple of fish on the way back to shore. If I spend another day grazing I'm going to grow hooves."

"We need something to put the treasure in," said Pebble. We attached sacks, rope, and a net to the belts we wrapped around us. Not the best fashion statement, but functional.

"We better hide our gear in the bushes," said Centaur. "Not much traffic heading to Nine Palms, but why risk it."

I began to brainstorm. It seemed crazy what we were going to do and I wanted to be as prepared as possibly. What else might we need? "What are we going to do about illumination? Even if the water isn't that murky there's probably no light in that cave."

Centaur paraded the penta he received from Deputy Pike between his fingers. "This might help."

Stick studied it. Recognition was expressed almost instantaneously, followed by perturbation. "At least one of us will be able to see, and he can direct the rest of us, I guess. Maybe the eels will take it easy on the blind."

"The one who consumes the stone will be able to choose what he wishes to illuminate: a sword, a branch, a rock, even himself. The wielder is the tap, not the reservoir."

"How long will the effect last?" I asked.

"It depends on the penta, but usually a day. Some pentic energy dissipates once an action is taken, or can be temporarily suspended, then resumed. Each penta is unique. Some varieties, like water breathing or healing, go into effect without direction. Be thankful we don't have to use more complicated penta. Many novices---and even some masters---destroy themselves unexpectedly.

"Here we go." Centaur pointed the rod at Pebble first. The stress that had been building in me released. I still had a few more minutes before I would be transformed. Already my anxiety level was rising again. My puss-filled wound was mental. No matter how many times it was drained it continued to fill. A spectral wave of light struck the rat-faced man, dissipating within seconds. Stick was next. A second release of stress drained. As the colors faded from the tall man Pebble began to transform. His neck began to bubble, then crack open. GILLS! Pebble grew GILLS! Now it was my turn. The stress vanished. Dread nourished anxiety. The present brought relief. Being struck by the projectile felt like being shocked by static electricity, more startling than painful. I began to feel unsettled. Something was happening to my body, something that hadn't happened before. It was like going through puberty, compressed into a minute. I felt a breeze. I brought a hand up to my neck. I gently brushed my fingers against the ridges and flaps. They felt like that area on the roof of my mouth, but more defined.

Centaur finally injected himself. Once his transformation was complete he ingested the illumination stone. A moment later, he touched his axe. It began to glow, but not as brightly as I expected. I became concerned, before realizing it was a bright day. In darkness that axe will become a beacon.

97

"I thought we were just going to take daggers."  Stick sounded annoyed.

"I've never been very good with daggers.  In my big hands they become pairing knives.  I might be able to slice an apple with one of them, but not an eel."

"Then I'm going to use my sword."

"I think I'll stay with this."  I thrust my hornet dagger into the air.  "I'm equally inept with all weapons.  Considering how poor a swimmer I am maybe the dagger will be light enough to prevent me from swimming in circles."

"I'm also sticking with daggers," said Pebble.  "Two of them. I may be small, but I have claws."  He thrashed his weapons madly. We stepped back a step, Centaur two.  Pebble smiled wickedly.

"Shall we?"  Centaur was first to jump into the river.

"That was a short month," Pebble commented wryly as he jumped in.

Stick and I leaped in immediately behind him---we didn't want to lose our only light source.  After the initial shock of the cool water---it felt cooler than it did the day before, unexpected considering we were just 12 kays upstream from where we washed---we adjusted to the temperature.  It approached 20 degrees, warm enough for us to survive in for an hour, but compared to the air temperature, and our bodies, it felt chilly.  What had Jacob done to the water to make it so much warmer?  We had bathed in it, and not just externally.  Those mouthfuls weren't intentional.  Neither was that grit ending up in places grit just didn't need to go.

The current took us downstream at first, but after we descended three meters, it no longer effected us.  As with most large rivers, it was murky with sediment.  If it wasn't for Centaur's glowing axe, we would have become separated.

I was concerned I wouldn't know what to do once I was submerged in the water.  I was afraid I would start choking, but the water breathing kicked-in automatically.  I no longer breathed through my mouth and nose.  Water passed through my gills, extracting oxygen and releasing carbon dioxide.

I expected---hoped---fins would also develop, to make me a better swimmer.  No luck there.  I made do with what Gaea provided---or in my case, what Gaea hadn't yet provided.  I reaching out with my arms and kicked with my legs.  Once into a rhythm, I was able to move briskly, passing fish and debris with ease.  Nothing challenged me, most of the fauna frantically dodging the chaotic churning.

Centaur slowed, then stopped.  Rocks jutted up from the riverbed ahead of us.  He dropped seven meters, landing in silt.  A plume of it billowed around him.  He signaled for us to not come any closer.  He swam back up.  Slowly the water cleared, too slowly for people wanting to get a dangerous job over with and return to shore.  He repeated the signal to stay put, then swam off.  With our only light source leaving with him, it immediately began to darken.  We could barely distinguish one another, but Centaur was clearly seen peeking around one rock, then another.

Three minutes later he returned.  He signaled for us to follow.  On the far side of the rocks was a 150 sim aperture.  There was no need to question if it was the one we sought.  A persistent stream of meter long eels entered and exited through the opening.  I expected more from them.  They didn't glow like electric eels, and they were smaller than I imagined them to be.  They looked like flat, black garden snakes.  This will be easy:  robbing a bank without guards with the safe already open.

With our weapons outstretched, Centaur's blazing in the lead, we headed towards the cave.  As we neared, the eels darted inside.

Centaur entered, the rest of us nearly bumping into him, we being that tightly bunched together.  The orb of light invading the cavern became a burst, completely filling the cavity.  The eels darted into three tunnels, spokes of the seven meter diameter spherical entry hub.

Coins glittered on the floor among an assortment of rusting

weapons and one nearly disintegrated boot. We scurried towards the copper, silver---and even gold---coins. We filled the pouches tied to our waists. No ring, yet.

The eels slowly evacuated the tunnels, looping back to them after darting towards the center of the cavern. We instinctively formed a four corners defense. I was surprised how efficiently my reflexes responded. Being the weakest link, I faced the exit. Centaur backed up to me. Pebble and Stick flanked me.

One particularly brave eel darted from the tunnel left of me. It swam completely around us before darting back. Others began coming closer to us, but none were careless enough to be struck. More came out of the tunnels, nearly two-dozen now. They swirled around us, causing a small whirlpool. I was beginning to get dizzy. Any moment I felt like I might tumble over.

Centaur detached the net. He pointed to the right tunnel. He counted down with his fingers: five, four, three, two, one. We lunged toward the tunnel. The eels attacked. We defended by knocking them away and slicing them in two. Centaur was having difficulty. Holding the net in his left hand while striking with his right, kept him off balance. I was last in line. Pebble pushed me past him with a hand holding the hilt of a dagger. We both rushed into the tunnel, seconds before Centaur and Stick stretched the net over the opening. The eels slammed into the two-sim mesh, jarring it backward, but not enough to allow an eel through. Pebble and I tied the ends of the net firmly with the rope we brought. The eels continued to bang their heads, pushing the net inward, but not at its vulnerable perimeter.

Centaur made a fish mouth, then tapped his finger against his body in several locations. Stick gave him a thumb's up. Finally comprehending, Pebble and I also raised our thumbs. No one was bitten by the poisonous eels. Now we just had to escape unharmed.

We began to search the tunnel for treasure. The ring had to be there somewhere. Smaller tunnels, about 50 sims in diameter branched out from the central tunnel. There were a dozen of them, six on each side, each about three meters deep. It was going to be a tight squeeze if someone wished to crawl to the end of one of them. With stretching, I was able to extend an additional meter. Nothing in the first one I searched.

During my egress I heard a loud gurgle. Stick flaunted a capsule. He added it to his pouch.

With renewed enthusiasm I searched another tunnel. Again I came away empty-handed. Stick found another stone. Pebble found his first. It was like an Easter egg hunt, but with every plastic egg I opened being empty. One more tunnel each before we were forced to move into another wing. And how the hell were we to manage that? We had to find the ring in the first wing.

Pebble gurgled as he jumped up and down. He had found the ring, or at least a ring. We weren't told what runes were on it. Rings were so rare, though, that the RING OF SHIELDING was probably the only ring here.

I searched my last tunnel, and was rudely met---by an eel that hadn't fled with its companions. It darted out to escape, biting me on my shoulder as it swam past. Stick sliced it in two before it slammed into the net.

Centaur rushed to my side as I become nauseous. As he examined my shoulder and shook his head sadly, I vomited, clouding the water. Of all the places to die. I felt better after throwing up, but in seconds the nausea returned. I vomited two more times. Half of the tunnel was now cloudy with the contents of my stomach.

Centaur pointed upward. The remainder of the day was a blur. After the net was ripped down, most of the eels attempted to enter the tunnel. Stick and Pebble made short work of them. The ingress became a food processor. The remaining eels backed away until we were almost out of the cave, then they attacked in mass. Centaur carried me away in front, followed by Pebble, who protected me, and Stick who fought off the rest of them. Pebble wasn't even paying attention to the eels that attacked him.  He was completely focused on my well being.  Pebble got bit, maybe more than once.  I wasn't sure.  I was unconscious most of that time.

When I woke it was dark.  I found myself beneath a tree, above the banks of the river.  A fire blazed 150 sims away.  Centaur and Stick looked out into the prairie in the direction a coyote howled.

They must have heard me rustling, because they both turned around seconds after I woke.  "Pebble?" was the first word out of my mouth.

"He didn't make it," Centaur replied softly.

# Chapter 16

## RE-CREATION

"Pebble didn't allow an eel within three meters of you," said Stick.  "I may be better with a sword then he, but I'll never be that tenacious."

I looked around.  "Where is he---his body?"

"We couldn't bring him back with us," said Centaur.  "I could only carry one of you, and Stick had to protect the three of us. Most of the remaining eels returned to the cave, but there were a couple that just wouldn't give up until Stick finally skewered them. By then we were nearly to shore."

"Pebble will be re-created, Hornet.  Hopefully he'll retain his humanity a bit longer.  He probably will.  He hasn't been on Limbo that long.  I think he's only been re-created twice before."

"Will he be re-created where he died?  Only to drown and be re-eaten?"

"Re-creation, like everything else on Limbo, is unpredictable," said Centaur.  "Sometimes, if a body isn't too badly damaged, a person is re-created in his old body as it self-heals.  Pebble will not have that option.  After he was struck for the third or fourth time and no longer able to move, he was carried away, probably to be consumed by what remained of the eel colony.  Annihilation is best for rapid re-creation.  The soul is immediately released, allowing it to inhabit matter more quickly."

"So Pebble could be re-created already and is wandering aimlessly nearby looking for us?"

"Not so soon.  There is a minimum delay for re-creation: about 10 hours.  Best case scenario, Pebble will be re-created in five hours.  But he won't necessarily reappear nearby.  If the morality of the mute he is becoming is pulling strongly, he could be re-created anywhere, including the Frontier.  Sometimes a person is re-created in a random location for no particular reason."

"So we may never find him?"

"We'll look for him tomorrow after we return the Ring of Shielding to Jacob," said Stick.  "I wouldn't mind holding on to it, but Pebble would want to donate it to the village."

"And if we simply take it, it would be trading Pebble's life for treasure, and I would never do that," said Centaur.  "Pebble had to have died for a more noble cause."

Jacob was ecstatic to have their protection returned.  A feast was held in our honor.  Fresh cucumbers and tomatoes were added to their staple:  a blend of recently harvested lettuces, supplemented with legumes and nuts.  Dessert was walnut halves glazed with corn syrup, and clusters of grapes.  The mood turned sour when someone inadvertently swallowed a bug on a lettuce leaf.  The shame the person felt for killing a creature forced him to leave the festivities early.  With the instigator of the deed no longer present to remind, the revelry returned.

"I wish I was leaving with you." Deputy Pike shared in the celebration, but not with enthusiasm. He was going through the motions to refrain from dimming the village's collective mood. He would much rather be patrolling the village's outskirts---or staring at a wall.

"Why don't you, then." To retain his bulk Centaur had to eat a lot of food. There weren't many calories in vegetation. He had constantly grazed since food was first set on the tables. He worried about the eventual release at the end of his digestive cycle. A human body wasn't built to consume that much roughage.

"If the ring is stolen again...."

"You can't live your life to please others." Stick had finished eating long ago, a token consumption, at best. He didn't like putting anything into his mouth that didn't first speak to him. "Bitterness and resentment will be your reward. You need to start thinking about yourself."

"That's the problem. I am thinking about myself. I couldn't live with myself if something happened to Jacob because I wasn't here to defend it. I apologize again for Pebble having to die for a cause the people it affected the most didn't have the backbone to do themselves."

At dawn we returned to the camp Centaur and Stick had established to wait out my recovery. We searched for Pebble the remainder of the day, and the next. It was becoming frustrating. "If I knew he was eventually going to appear I would be willing to wait indefinitely," said Centaur, "but he could be hundreds of kays from here and no longer human."

"Maybe he isn't re-created yet," said Stick.

"One more day."

"Why rush off? Does arriving a few days earlier make that much of a difference?"

"It's not just the day we arrive, but the days leading up to that arrival. We replenished our bank from the coins we collected from the cave, but not substantially. We can't live off it forever."

"Let's just give it a few more days. I agree we can't stay here until our money runs out, but I can't abandon Pebble if there's a possibility of him returning."

I contemplated adding my thoughts, but I really didn't have any, none that mattered. I had known Pebble for just a few days. How could my opinion compare to those who knew him for years? Everyone could add insight, but the decision we had to make was more emotional than rational. I didn't know Pebble long enough to be vested.

There was one thought I was confident I could share. "Where is Lynn? She's been gone for three---and a half---days. Has she also abandoned us?"

"Who can predict what a cat might do," said a voice in my head. Centaur, Stick, and I stood up simultaneously.

Ten minutes later Lynn appeared, but she wasn't alone. Pebble was walking behind her. He smiled at us broadly, but with effort. He looked exhausted, but still human.

"You need to lie down." Centaur directed him to a spot beside the fire. Pebble promptly fell asleep.

I suddenly felt as tired as Pebble looked. Having him back put me in such a state of peace I had trouble keeping my eyes open. The burst of adrenaline I got from first seeing him had run its course, making the drop in energy feel even more severe than it was. I had many questions to ask, but they could wait until the morning. Centaur and Stick must have been of like mind. After confirming Pebble's health, and that he was sleeping soundly, they also drifted off.

Pebble was still sleeping when we woke. By unspoken consensus we allowed him to continue.

"Why don't we give him a healing stone?" I broke my fast with a handful of dried fruit the mayor provided in gratitude for us returning the ring of shielding. He also gave each of us a healing stone. He felt guilty about Pebble dying. To ease his conscience he emptied the village's coffers.

"It won't help." Centaur also nibbled on dried fruit, alternating it with hazelnuts. "A healing stone heals. It doesn't replenish strength. It takes awhile to recover from re-creation. Pebble's body needs to normalize naturally. Sometimes it takes a week or more. If he had traveled a ways to get here he probably used the remainder of the reserves he didn't have. He doesn't have to be completely recovered before we leave, but closer to it than the state he's in."

"There ARE supplemental means to return his strength." Stick chewed on a piece of dried meat we had provisioned ourselves with in Bluewood City. It was dwindling, rapidly. At the rate we were consuming it, it would be gone before we reached the next settlement.

"True, but not from a healing stone. What Stick is referring to is an energy stone. It does what it sounds like it does. It returns energy to a person. Sometimes people become so weak they actually die from the state. With aging so sluggish on Limbo it doesn't happen very often. The main use for an energy stone is the lessening of down time. A week can be reduced to an hour."

"That's not the only reason some people use the stone." Stick frowned, looking more disappointed than sad. "Sometimes athletes use energy stones to enhance their endurance. I can understand why someone might want to replenish his energy after a battle, especially if it's likely he'll have another before he recovers. But to consume an energy stone to better someone in a competition? How is that proving your athletic superiority? If you are the best at something, it needs to be the product of YOUR merit, not a Wizard's."

Centaur looked at me. "Athletic events were popular on Limbo many years ago. Science might be limited in a medieval society, but people can still run, jump, and throw. Another activity that doesn't require modern technology or techniques is gambling. As stakes became higher, athletes and their sponsors implemented artificial means for success.  As sporting events became more sullied interest in them dwindled.  It was difficult to root for a favorite when you didn't know which substances he had in his bloodstream, or what hidden mutations he might have.  Before the influx of energy stones and other enhancers the best athletes were rumored to have hidden mutations.  Mutes were forbidden to compete, but it was difficult to recognize one if they didn't show any exterior physical characteristics."

I became impassioned.  "If we had these healing stones when the eels attacked us, Pebble may have survived, and I wouldn't have gotten sick.  He didn't die because of low energy, so he might have been saved."

"The healing stone would have mended the damage to his flesh," said Centaur, "but it wouldn't have been able to counter the poison.  Countering harmful foreign substances, like diseases and poisons, requires a curing stone."

"What if he consumed a healing stone prior to the attack? Wouldn't the extra energy have enhanced his immune system?"

"We can't store excess energy.  And again, health, energy, and immunity aren't synonymous."

Pebble continued to sleep.  We took the opportunity to inventory what we collected in the eel cave.  Combined with what we had before entering the cave, we now had five gold coins, 18 silver, and 37 copper.  Three charges remained in the water breathing rod.  In addition to the three healing stones there were four others of unknown function.  Unknown to me.

"I recognize three of them: reveal, soften, and fire." Centaur studied the fourth.  Still looking puzzled after a couple of minutes, he handed it to Stick.

Stick brought the stone up to an eye.  "Three dots bookend by two trees."

"Trees represent soil, flesh, and solids.  Dots, air, gases, and illusion."

"An almost infinite number of outcomes."  Stick handed the

stone back to Centaur, who placed all four, along with the three healing stones, in the communal wallet.

# Chapter 17

## ILLUSIONS

Pebble woke intermittently the remainder of the day. We couldn't wait for him to revive to hear his tale, so we coaxed what we could from Lynn. Once she began it was impossible to shut her up. "While you were celebrating your victory over the herbivores, I was sprinting towards Pebble's re-creation."

I interrupted. "Pebble hadn't died yet."

"But it was likely he was going to die, and I wanted to be where he would be re-created. The odds of us reaching the Copper Forest are greater if we keep our group intact."

"So you were thinking about yourself?" said Stick.

"Exactly. As we all do. When we help someone, we do so because we feel good about ourselves when we do it. Good deeds sometimes transpire, as side-effects of selfishness, but they are never the primary goal."

"Sometimes you speak of making predictions," I commented. "Other times it's almost like you can see the future."

"Given enough variables, and their reliability, predictions can sometimes mimic premonitions."

"So you didn't know for certain Pebble would die, or that he would be where you found him?"

"Nothing is for certain. Gravity keeps us planted on the

ground, but there is the possibility---extremely slight---that an electromagnetic pulse could counter it, flinging you and me into space. Due to the likelihood of danger and Pebble's reckless nature when it comes to protecting others, it was likely he would die. Due to his current morality relative to the location of his last re-creation I was able to pinpoint where his essence should re-inhabit a body."

"You left us before we chose to enter that cave."

Lynn smiled, which for a cat, looked like they were up to something. She continued her tale. "I knew where to go. The problem was getting there. I had to travel 50 kays...."

"Which direction?" asked Centaur.

"Northwest."

"The Grasslands?"

"At times in grass taller than me."

"That's some beautiful country. Green, lush, and rolling."

"It may be pretty, but it slows travel. It took me an entire day to reach the place Pebble should appear, that was with me walking day and night. I napped while I waited. Pebble appeared midday. As was customary with re-creations, he awoke immediately, but with barely enough strength to stand. He felt better once he stretched his new muscles. After coming to a consensus he was reasonably fit for travel---he stubbornly, me after balancing his health with my anxiety for the event to be over---we began walking back to Jacob. It was going to take us three days, so I wanted to put a few miles behind us before we slept for the evening. We should have been able to cover that distance in two. I contemplated what would force us to need that extra day."

"How could you make a prediction if you didn't know the parameters of the variables?" I was becoming annoyed. I never liked listening to people who were full of it. I wasn't sure about Lynn. Either she was a great storyteller or she had special abilities she hadn't yet shared with us.

"Clusters of variables are often more predictive than individual variables. It was possible, but not likely, a hare would cross the road in front of us.  For any species to do so it was almost guaranteed.  Advanced predictive science often requires a holistic approach.

"I discovered what was going to delay us the following day.  I began seeing things."

"Wild animals?" asked Stick.

"Nothing that mundane."

"Monsters?" I asked.

"Or dangerous.  I saw orange balls and violet string. Something wanted to play with the cat, and the cat wasn't amused. Pebble had an odd look on his face, implying he also saw the balls and string, or something just as odd.  He didn't say anything, he probably thinking the visions were caused by re-creation fever.

"Other illusions appeared---flying fried chicken, fluffy pillows---all very colorful, and in directions we had no intention of going.  If we hadn't been so goal oriented it was likely we would have examined the diversions more closely.

"Pebble was first to see the burrow.  Something glittered inside it.  It was too tempting to pass up.  And it was directly in front of us.  Pebble went inside while I guarded the entrance.  The aperture was less than a meter high, forcing Pebble to crawl.  He didn't mind.  In his weakened state any reduction in his fight against gravity was welcomed.  Two meters in, the tunnel must have enlarged, because Pebble was able to stand up.  He departed with a grass-weaved bag full of gold coins---very full.  There must have been hundreds of coins in that bag.

"I THINK WE CAN CONTINUE OUR JOURNEY NOW, Pebble announced, looking whimsical, standing proudly in his re-creation suit, carrying a sack full of gold.  He was so anxious to depart, he pushed past me in order to lead.  I had to re-direct him numerous times, but he didn't mind, as long as we maintained our pace.

"We were intercepted.  Diminutive men and women with long legs bent backwards appeared in the glade in front of us.  They were shorter than the vegetation.  To match Pebble's height, they stood on a companion's shoulders.  They moved by leaping.  Their shortest bounds were many times their height.  They wore colorful clothing, the men in cotton shirts and shorts, the women in dresses that looked to be full-length, when they were standing, but were knee-high when they were airborne.  RETURN OUR GOLD, said one of the men who wore a large wide-brimmed green hat.  His mustache looked like some of the grass in the glade was glued to his face.

"Pebble walked off, oblivious to the encounter.  RETURN OUR GOLD, repeated the man.  Pebble proceeded, without deviating his stride.

"A woman hopped next to him, her dress rustling in the breeze her movement created.  Her elbow length hair was the color and texture of the man's mustache.  THREE WISHES TO MOLD FOR HE WHO RETURNS THE GOLD.  Pebble stopped in his tracks.  Three things was more than one measly sack of gold.

"YOU PROMISE TO FULFILL MY THREE WISHES IF I GIVE YOU THE GOLD?' asked Pebble.

"WE WILL GIVE ALL YOU ASK IF YOU WISH THREE, said a second woman.  She had hopped next to him seconds after the first.  Her hair was longer than the first woman's, but it wasn't as lush or vibrant.  Not only was its color washed out, it looked brittle, like it might break if it was bent.

"Pebble looked at me. YOU HAVE THE GOLD, I told him. YOU MUST DECIDE ITS FATE.

"Pebble handed over the sack of gold coins.  Without delay, he stated his first wish."

"Pebble always knew what he wanted," said Stick.  "It may be constantly changing, but only because there was something better to replace it."

"FIRST I WANT TO BE HEALTHLY---PHYSICALLY AND MENTALLY.  Pebble waited for his wish to be granted, but nothing happened.

"IF YOU REMEMBER, I told him.  YOU MUST DECLARE ALL

YOUR WISHES BEFORE ANY ARE GRANTED.

"MY SECOND WISH IS TO ACQUIRE THE EMERALD PEARL---
TODAY.  MY FINAL WISH IS TO HAVE ALL THE SILVER WITHIN 100
KAYS.  HAH, YOU THOUGHT YOU ALMOST HAD ME.  IF I WOULD
HAVE ASKED FOR ALL THE GOLD I WOULD HAVE WENT BACK ON MY
WORD, AND THAT WISH, AND PROBABLY THE FIRST TWO, WOULD
HAVE BEEN VOIDED."

"Why didn't Pebble ask for gems?" I asked.

"People don't think well under pressure," said Centaur.  "I
think choosing silver instead of something more valuable was the
least of Pebble's worries."

"The hoppers all smiled when the third wish was declared.
YOU HAVE CHOSEN WISELY, said a second male.  MUCH MORE
WISELY THAN MOST.  WOULD YOU LIKE A FOURTH WISH?  IF YOU
CHOOSE A FOURTH, STATE IT NOW.  WE CAN'T GRANT A SINGLE
WISH UNTIL ALL WISHES ARE DECLARED.

"I WISH I WAS BACK WITH MY FRIENDS, NOW, SO I WON'T
HAVE TO WALK THE REST OF THE WAY.  The hoppers laughed
hysterically, those on shoulders falling into the spongy grass unhurt,
those already on the ground hopping madly.  WELL?  The hoppers
stood back up---those who weren't already---and smacked their
hands together---one giant clap.

"We were now beside a river, and it wasn't the Neutral,
unless we were much farther upstream.  The sun being in
approximately the same location made that impossible.  The grass
was dry as it is here.  We had to be due west of Jacob, beside the
West Fork.  We were farther away than when we began the day.
WHAT WENT WRONG? Pebble asked me sincerely.  I knew
immediately the trap the hoppers had set, but was obligated to
allow fate to play out.  This encounter was why our journey
required an extra day."

Comprehension flashed in Stick's eyes.  "The hoppers agreed
to give three wishes, not four.  When Pebble stated his fourth wish,
all four were negated."

"Correct.  A final prank was to send us away blindly.  It would have been too kind to send us in the direction we wished to go."

"So the gold was just a gimmick?"  I asked.

"Not necessarily," said Centaur.  "I've heard of hoppers being great gamblers.  The higher the stakes the greater the pleasure if successful."

"It sounds like these hoppers worship chaos," stated Stick.

"Chaos isn't a deity," I said.  "You can't base a religion on it."

"Why not?  Parishioners of Min worship intellect.  Fa, emotion.  And Cor, physicality."

"Good versus evil isn't the only moral dichotomy," stated Lynn.  "You'll find as many highly chaotic---or ordered---mutes in the Frontier as those excessively negative or positive."

When Pebble woke he re-told the tale, emphasizing the betrayal at the end.  "Only cowards win on technicalities.  If I ever see one of those grass-haired midgets again...."

"We were certainly fortunate," said Lynn.  "Legend states that only once in our life are we permitted to see hoppers."

"You didn't sound too fortunate when you were complaining about blisters on your paws."

The reason people didn't see hoppers a second time was probably more mundane.  With their ruse coming to light, it was unlikely they would be able to play additional (successful) practical jokes (on the same person).  That or they just didn't want their butts kicked.

# Chapter 18

# CURED

Pebble hadn't fully recovered---physically. That didn't prevent us from breaking camp. They say attitude is everything, and Pebble had more than enough to compensate for lingering limitations. "So you think we can make it to Rhinopolis in three days. That means walking 40 kays a day. I'm an invalid not a marathoner."

Stick walked beside the rat-faced man on the dusty road that was wide enough for twice as many abreast. With the horizon being empty neither had a weapon drawn, which lasted five minutes for Stick. He felt naked without clutching a sword. Some people had to have a coffee cup in their hand, Stick needed sharpened steel. His right arm was noticeably larger than his left. All those repetitions lifting that elongated piece of metal created quite a work out. It was rare not to see a sword in his hand during daylight hours. Sometimes he even had a hilt clutched as he fell asleep. Men were said to never grow up, they just bought more expensive toys. Stick's sword was his security blanket and teddy bear all wrapped into one. "Don't be such a wimp. Your re-creation sickness has to be over by now."

"Don't forget that walking I did before I recovered."

"That's called conditioning. With all that extra work you should be able to run laps around us."

"After we sell the pearl maybe we can buy an ox or something to ride."

"An ox? You can walk faster than an ox."

"But it would be doing all the walking, not me. And why stop at an ox? I'm also going to buy a wagon, for it to pull. I could lie in the back on pillows to cushion the ride."

"Why not hire a rickshaw." That last comment came from Centaur. He was directly behind Pebble, beside me.

Lynn was everywhere. Whenever a hare leapt, or a prairie dog poked its head out of a hole, she darted off. She never caught anything, not permanently, but that wasn't her intention. Catch and release was less messy than ripping into a carcass with her incisors, bloodying her fur. When she was hungry she would eat, but she wasn't yet hungry enough to clean up after herself, something that wasn't optional for her. If a human had such a drive for fastidiousness they would have been diagnosed as having a disorder. For a cat, constantly cleaning itself it meant it was well adjusted. Sometimes Lynn would dart when nothing was around her. Did she sense something a human wasn't able to, like a dog hearing sounds outside the human range? It was one of those things cats never discussed. They all did it, they just didn't talk about it.

"Maybe I will," Pebble replied. "Even better, I could be the one providing the transportation. Not just in cities, but between them. With exhausted runners being replaced every few kays with fresh ones. The Rickshaw Express I could call it. There would be substantial start-up costs, but profits would be enormous. It would be the noble thing to do, to reduce travel time between cities, and provide jobs."

The lack of transportation on Limbo was unfathomable. The prison world had been populated for more than a century yet it still didn't have any combustion engines. It didn't even have horses, not real ones. The creatures Centaur was named after were part equine. "Why don't centaurs rent themselves out?" I suggested. "If God had any role in their creation, it's apparent He intended them to be taxis."

Centaur shivered. It wasn't that long ago that he

experimented with that idea. What had he been thinking? "The only god on Limbo is Gaea, and I don't think She puts much thought into anything she does. Now, the engineers who built our prison, they knew what they were doing. Denying us horses meant slow growth. Our lack of technology can attest to that. We have substantial resources here, but without adequate transportation there are few things we can do with them. It's like having hundreds of batteries, but only one flashlight. Most of the world will remain dark."

"If horses weren't included in the genome how did centaurs develop?"

"That's where Gaea comes in. Genetic transmutation. Lead into gold. A deer into a horse. On the sub-atomic level everything looks pretty much the same."

Something was different about Pebble---not substantially. He didn't grow an extra head or lose a finger. His mannerisms had changed. He didn't bring his hands to his body as much. His perpetually dry, scaly skin compelled him to relieve himself of the irritation, temporarily. A five minute period wouldn't go by where Pebble wasn't scratching some part of his body. Now he had suddenly stopped. "Pebble, does your skin no longer itch?"

So abrupt was the realization, the rat-faced man stopped moving. He pulled up a sleeve, then a trouser leg. His skin wasn't red and it didn't have any scaly patches. "I'M CURED! Maybe being re-created isn't that bad. I wonder what my next re-creation might do for me. Make me taller?" Pebble no longer dragged his feet. Whatever fatigue he might have had from being re-created, real or imagined, had vanished.

The remainder of the first day's journey---from Jacob---was without incident. The only potential danger was when a buffalo herd intersected the road. My companions had shown on numerous occasions they could handle one animal or a small group of them, but a stampede? We made the necessary detour, to not to startle them.

The evening was also uneventful. Nothing disturbed us during our 150 minute watches. The night sounds were less than they were in the forest or beside the river, diminishing the concern for the unknown. I had the most restful night of my incarceration. The calm before the storm? Possibly, but I'll take what I can get.

# Chapter 19

# A HOLE

The following day was nearly as unremarkable as the previous, until we discovered irregularities in the sparse grassland. Depressions, one to three meters deep appeared. Soil was turned over in other spots. In areas still intact, the sod was wrinkly and slightly raised.

"Over there." Stick pointed with his sword. "A hole." But it wasn't any rabbit or gopher hole. It was fully two meters across.

We walked over to investigate. As usual, Centaur was proc. If any other member of our company had been, he would have been dead. The earth rose up beneath him. A black, bulbous head as large as Centaur poked out of the ground. Mandible pincers crunched down on one of his legs. Centaur shrieked. The beast---monster---thing---loosened its grip for an instant to move up his leg. Taking advantage of the interruption, Centaur clutched the jaws, attempting to halt their progress up his body.

We rushed to our friend's aid. Pebble and I struck the creature as Stick prepared to pull Centaur free. Lynn sat on her haunches patiently waiting for us. Our weapons did negligible damage to the beast's natural armor. Most of the blows were deflected. Our opportunity came when the creature rose. Pebble pierced its belly, which uncorked a yellowish goo, as Stick pulled Centaur free.

Lynn ran past us. "Into the hole." Not having a viable alternative, we scurried towards the aperture, dragging Centaur with us.

It spit at us, hitting me in the side as I helped Stick drag Centaur the last couple of meters into the hole. My body felt like it was on fire. My clothes, on the side of me that was hit, melted, including the mesh armor. The flesh underneath looked like plastic that came too close to a fire.

Pebble rushed to my aid. He scraped away the liquid that remained on me with one of his daggers, aggravating my anguish. Pulling a cloth from his belt, he wiped his weapon clean, then threw the rag to the side. "I NEED A HEALING STONE!" After retrieving one for himself from Centaur's municipal wallet, Stick tossed the pouch to Pebble, who flipped it over, emptying it. In a single motion he snagged a capsule from the ground and placed it in my mouth. The healing energy rushed through my body. My side tingled as my wound closed over and healed. I thought I might faint, but within seconds became clearheaded again.

Centaur was similarly tended to. His wound was more severe. The healing stone Stick gave him closed his wound and dissolved the digestive acid, but his femur didn't fully heal. Stick returned all but the final healing stone to the wallet. "No," pleaded Centaur. "We might need it later. I'll be all right." To demonstrate, he stood up, but when he put pressure on his leg, he fell back down. Not to be defeated, he picked up his battle axe and placed the business end of it on the ground. He held onto the handle, using the weapon as a crutch.

"IT'S HEADING TOWARDS THE OPENING!" Pebble announced. Its full length was now seen---nearly ten meters.

"This time I'm proc," said Stick.

With the shuffling of roles Pebble became scout. He led us down the moderate descent. After 10 meters the tunnel curved, as it did in an additional 10 meters. We could barely see our hands in front of our faces. "We better light a torch," said Centaur.

"Won't that make it easier for it to find us?" I asked.

"There is only one way to follow us," said Stick, "unless you want to dig us a new tunnel?"

Centaur struck a flint, creating a spark that landed on an oiled rope wound around an arm's length piece of wood. The torch erupted. We were blinded for a moment before we became accustomed to the intense light. Gray, dry earth surrounded us. As a child I feared caves. How could such brittle dirt support so much weight above it? I'll survive, I told myself. I had to. We couldn't go back the way we came.

A fork. "Our goal is to find an alternate route to the surface," stated Centaur.

"Preferably away from that thing that attacked us," added Pebble.

"Which route would that be?" asked Stick. "Only one might lead to our escape."

We looked at Lynn. "I don't know everything." That may have been a momentous occasion if their situation wasn't so dire.

Centaur lifted his axe and pointed left. Someone had to make a decision. Centaur took his leadership role seriously. He may not always be right, but half the battle was being determined enough to make a---any---commitment. As we moved into the tunnel he shared with us the rationale for his decision. "When people are given a choice, a majority choose right. So, to get somewhere quicker, to bypass the crowd, it's wiser to go left."

"Then let's hope that thing is part of the majority," said Pebble blandly.

The tunnel did appear to be rising. Rounding a curve we met another borrower, or maybe it was the same one. There go the odds. We back-peddled around the curve. It looked different than the first one. "I think it's dead," said Stick.

"Are you willing to test your theory?" asked Centaur.

Stick was already back around the curve before Centaur finished his sentence. A moment later Stick's voice echoed, "It's dead."

When we re-rounded the curve, Stick was practicing his fencing on the stationary target. It was amazing how good a person became when his opponent was dead.

"Do we cut our way through?" I asked. The beast occupied most of the tunnel.

"I think we can climb over it," Pebble suggested.

"IT'S MOVING!" I shrieked after seeing the thing shudder.

"Maybe it was just an involuntary reflex," suggested Centaur.

It shook again, followed by a popping sound. A small version of the thing broke through the exoskeleton. Then two more. They looked at us, contemplating their odds.

We didn't take as long to decide our action. "Let's try the other tunnel," said Centaur.

"If it isn't too late," added Pebble.

The three youngsters rushed us. Stick fought them off as the rest of us scrambled down the tunnel, guiding left at the fork. One of the youngsters was struck down before I lost sight of the melee.

Stick caught up to us, with a frown. "You're not harmed?" asked Pebble, concerned, but also a bit disappointed.

"After I skewered the first one, the other two stopped fighting and ate their brother."

"You'll fight again soon," said Lynn.

"Immediately?" I asked.

"Before we return to the surface."

"At least that means we'll make it back to the surface," said Pebble.

The new tunnel persisted in its descent. "Maybe it's safe

now to go up the way we came," I suggested.

"Something's coming," said Pebble. "Sounds like thousands of footsteps. I still don't see anything."

"I do, now," I said. "Black worms. More than a dozen."

"Centipedes, I think," said Centaur. "Worms don't have feet." They were 30 sims long, and maybe a thumb's width in diameter. A few meters closer to us, details began to develop, in particular, a hundred legs propelling them.

Centaur dropped his pack and took something out---his stash of food. "Stay close to the right wall. Try not to move until the centipedes are past us. Their bite is said to paralyze." When the centipedes were about a meter from Pebble, who remained scout, Centaur threw his food behind Stick, who was still proc. The centipedes ignored us and bee-lined it to the food.

We waited until the centipedes were safely past us, and to the food, before we dashed off. We ran, Centaur not very gracefully, until the tunnel terminated at a limestone cave. "The food should sate them," said Centaur. "If not, let's hope that carcass was their destination. There are only so many battles we can fight before we become overburdened."

"What made you think to throw out food?" I asked. "Isn't fresh food more tempting?"

"You can defeat anything if you know, or can figure out, what it wants and use is to your advantage. Most creatures aren't evil, just needy. If I can satisfy their needs without killing them, or they killing me, all the better. I'm familiar with some species of centipedes. They will eat about anything. Food already prepared and placed directly in front of them almost guarantees it."

The cavern was five meters high. It was slightly deeper than that. To the right it terminated after three meters. In the other direction there was only darkness beyond the range of our torch.

"Exactly how far down are we going before we begin heading back up?" I asked. "To the center of Limbo?"

"That is something to consider," Stick commented.

"That's assuming there are tunnels beyond Warden's Shield," said Centaur.

"I don't think I want to be down here long enough to find out," said Pebble.

My confused look warranted an explanation. "Warden's Shield is the name given to the energy barrier that prevents us from leaving the penal colony," said Centaur. "It's beyond the Frontier, supposedly. I've never met anyone who has actually been to Warden's Shield, but I have talked to someone who has talked to someone. Every time the tale is passed along it becomes more altered."

It didn't make sense to me for only part of the planet to be used as a penal colony. What was the function of the rest of the planet?

"Lynn said we'll make it out of here," said Centaur, "so I'm confident we will. The detour might just take a little longer than we planned."

Lynn smiled. Was it in acknowledgment of her abilities, or did she know something about what was down here she wasn't sharing?

We continued our round about journey back to the surface. We walked cautiously into the darkened portion of the cavern, Centaur hobbling along the best he could.

"You sure you don't want to use that last healing stone?" Every few minutes Pebble would ask him that question. Centaur persistently declined.

When we traveled through the dirt tunnels the light from the torch persistently illuminated our surroundings, the space being significantly confined. Now, in a more open space, it felt eerie not being able to see more than 10 meters in front of me, and even less behind---the torch was up front. Something could be lurking out there, just beyond our vision.

"You can see in the dark, can't you, Lynn?" asked Centaur. "How far can YOU see?"

"Twice as far as the light if it wasn't blinding my night vision. As long as the torch blazes, I'm as blind as you."

"I need a break," Pebble announced. "We haven't stopped since entering this hole." Centaur may have seen through Pebble's ruse. If he did, he didn't comment on it. Centaur wasn't going to request a delay to rest, even with a bum leg. Pebble certainly didn't need it. He may occasionally complain---about doing physical activity---but when circumstances demanded it, he tapped into his inexhaustible reserve of energy, becoming part whirling dervish, part Tasmanian devil. Many of my most troubling students had an excess of energy. Sometimes fidgeting wasn't enough for them. The walk to the principal's office released some of that energy, but it was, at best, a temporary fix. The cure would be combining gym with mathematics.

# Chapter 20

# MUSHROOMS

The cavern narrowed, becoming a gallery. The ceiling varied from two meters in height to higher than the torch light could reveal. In those dark-ceiling areas stalactites would occasionally hang down into view. I thought of them as floating heads---brains without the brawn. Creepy, yes, but what hadn't been since we ran into that hole?

Whenever we paused, our feet no longer slapping against the stone floor, the sounds of the underworld became more pronounced. Water was dripping somewhere. And there was this high-pitched sound, likely coming from bats.

"In such a confined space, sound probably travels for kays," Centaur hypothesized. "Let's keep moving."

We spotted something translucent stretched across the passage in front of us. Getting closer we saw individual gossamer strands. They crisscrossed one another, forming a mesh. From wall to wall, ceiling to floor, it blocked the passage. While examining the substance, my hand got stuck. In the attempt to free myself, the same happened to my other hand. Pebble came to my rescue, resulting in him getting stuck. "This will cut through anything," said Stick seconds before his sword became attached to the adhesive mesh.

We saw its shadow first: eight legs supporting a bulbous body. Then a second shadow. Then more. By the time we saw what had created the shadows, they had surrounded us, on both sides of the mesh, 15 arachnoids, two-thirds of a meter in diameter. Pebble thrust the torch in his free hand towards them. They were intimidated by the fire, but more importantly, the mesh closest to the torch melted. Pebble burned his hand free, then mine.

Stick and Centaur pulverized the spiders behind us. Those in front of us fled. "Anyone hurt?" asked Centaur. We shook our heads. "That was a pleasant break in our routine." Seeing Centaur smile for the first time since he was crushed and dissolved was the spark needed to renew our enthusiasm for escape.

I should have known that wasn't going to be our final obstacle. After passing through an additional hundred meters of gallery, the passage widened into another of those areas without a visible ceiling. The remaining spiders, or maybe another group, fell on us. With the scarcity of game down here, they had to be persistent to survive.

Stick was unstoppable, slicing left and dicing right. Centaur was the least successful. No longer being able to protect his weak leg in an enclosed area, a spider broke through his defenses and bit him---on that leg. He slumped to the ground, the spider still attached, like a tick. Pebble set the torch down, leaning it against a boulder. He replaced it with a second dagger. He stabbed the spider attached to Centaur, then pealed it away, its legs flaying momentarily before flamboyantly ceasing.

We didn't allow the spiders to escape this time. The last one climbed a wall and was almost to the darkness when Pebble struck it with a dagger he hurled. It fell, cracking, then exploding as it landed on its back.

Centaur vomited. Stick handed him the healing stone. "It would be wasted," he choked out. "It can't heal toxins."

"Then how about that leg?" pleaded Pebble. "It's not only hobbled, it's bleeding again."

"Bind it," he said after a second vomit. "Not much can hurt it now. Don't worry about me. If the poison was strong I would be dead already. The nausea is a good sign. I should start feeling better in a few minutes. From the amount I expelled there can't be much of the poison still in my system."

We waited for Centaur's health to improve---hopefully improve---but not in an area with three fronts to defend. We returned to the narrow part of the gallery, with Stick watching behind us and Pebble leading. Lynn and I watched Centaur. His coloring seemed to be improving. He was able to stand in fifteen minutes. "If it wasn't for eating flies I wouldn't mind mutating into a spider. Climbing walls and making webs would be kind of fun."

We resumed our journey. A high-pitched wail was heard again, louder than before. After a minute it stopped. "I don't know what I like less, the screaming, or the screaming stopping," said Pebble. "Is it worse to meet the thing that made that sound, or the thing that silenced it?"

I was becoming concerned. We were no longer taking a brief excursion down a hole. The journey was becoming a whole day affair, and then some. What if we never saw sunlight again? The only thing that kept us moving was faith, and most of that relied on the predictions of a lynx.

The terrain was beginning to change. No longer was there one route to follow. Small alcoves began to pop up on both sides of the wide central gallery. Some of them were connected to narrow tunnels. Most of them were so narrow they could only be traversed on your belly.

"MUSHROOMS!" From the sounds Stick's stomach had been making it wasn't surprising what his senses focused on. The eight meter wide alcove on our right was ripe with fungi. They were a meter high. Hanging beneath their umbrella heads were gelatinous spheres.

"They look like fruit," I commented.

"Eating them won't harm you," said Lynn.

Stick reached out to harvest a sphere. Before he made contact with it, its host mushroom shook, detaching three of the fish egg-like globs. One hit his arm, spattering like a water balloon. Before he could wipe it away, its consistency changed, to firm rubber. "It tingles." He attempted to pry it off---unsuccessfully. The glob had oozed completely around his arm, connecting to itself, forming a cast.

Pebble looked at Lynn with malice. "I thought you said it was safe?"

"I said eating them won't harm you. I'm sure they're delicious."

"Are you losing your circulation?" asked Centaur.

"It's not numb. It tickles, like ants doing calisthenics."

"Lynn. It's time we got out of here. I think we're going to need a specialist in Rhinopolis, or a curing stone, which we can buy there."

"A majority of our spelunking is over."

"Then let's get a move on."

Something looking like a wart began to grow from Stick's fungus cast. We increased our pace, Centaur with a pinched look on his face, and sweat on his brow. He had to been expelling twice as much energy as us, hobbling on his bad leg.

The flickering torch light revealed more mushrooms ahead. The fungi were taller and their caps smaller then the one's we already had the displeasure of experiencing. The loud piercing wail we heard twice before erupted in our skulls. A small flap opened in the center of each stalk. They vibrated in sync with the cacophony.

We clutched our ears and ran past. At our closest point to them we veered, expecting to be attacked. They were content to strike at us vocally.

Greeting us on the other side of the mushrooms were the parents of the centipedes we encountered earlier. They were a meter wide, four times that in length. Eight tentacles whipped furiously outward from their heads. One of them stood its ground, but the other climbed the cavern wall with its small pick-like feet.

We attacked the creature on the ground, while keeping an eye on the one working its way towards the ceiling. It was difficult to concentrate with the fungal siren blaring. Stick led the attack with more gusto then the rest of us combined. With his damaged arm he felt he had nothing more to lose. The wart on his arm had grown into a mushroom. A daring thrust by the swordsman impaled the beast, but by doing so Stick exposed his parasitic arm. A tentacle struck it, numbing it. The numbness crept to his shoulder, then down his side. The mushroom on his arm wilted, dried out, then fell off. The fungal cast lightened, then became porous. Sim long chunks broke away, shortening his arm with each departure. A moment later only a powdery residue remained, scars on his cauterized shoulder being the only evidence that Stick had a fourth limb.

With the calmness of picking up a dropped pencil, Stick snatched his sword from the ground with his offhand. He was ready when the second centipede attack arrived, this time from above. It was awkward tilting our heads back to fight, which was apparently the creature's intent. But it didn't know how much we had already put up with. In unison we jabbed upwards, skewering it in four places. It became motionless a moment later. Its pick-tipped feet did their job so well it didn't fall upon its demise.

We didn't rejoice in our accomplishment. If we didn't escape that din soon we felt we might go insane. Slowly the piercing wail diminished as we put distance between the mushrooms and ourselves. Eventually the sound could no longer be heard at all. It took longer for the ringing in our ears to do so.

Our moment of peace was brief. The pitter-patter of many feet, and an army of squeals, approached. "It's time to make our last stand." Centaur dropped his pack, then removed the remaining penta, prepping them for consumption. Following Centaur's lead, we also dropped our packs, providing more maneuverability. We stood in a semi-circle, posed for the onslaught.

"THAT DAMN SIREN IS BRINGING EVERYTHING TO US!" Pebble shouted.

"Which was probably the mushrooms' intent," said Centaur. "All organisms have defense mechanisms. Humans have their intellect. Those mushrooms apparently call others to do their fighting for them."

Rats the size of house cats scuttled into the torch light. "Now it's beginning to get interesting." Lynn began to salivate as she made clicking sounds.

Centaur placed one of the penta in his mouth. In the moment it took the rats to travel those last eight meters, Centaur raised a hand. A stream of fire burst from it. He moved his hand back and forth until all the rats were consumed by the flames.

"That wouldn't be one of those effects that last ten hours, would it?" I wistfully conjectured.

"Sorry. Offensive penta is powerful, but doesn't last. One good blast of heat, or cold, or water, or electricity is all we can expect."

"Why did you have to burn them," Lynn moaned. "In time I would have done the job, and provided dinner."

"I'm losing my patience with these delays," said Centaur. "Almost there, you say. Good. If not, maybe one of us will be left behind. We'll be able to return to the surface as quickly without you."

"No you won't." Lynn looked at the charred rat remains and shook her head.

We walked through the charcoal, walking around what we could. It was an impossible task. There were too many carcasses. Crunch, crunch. It sounded like we were walking on egg shells. "I'm worried this sound might attract something," I said.

My companions began to laugh, initially a chortle, which progressed into a guffaw. I joined them after becoming cognizant of my unintentional sarcasm. The stress relief was just what we needed.

# Chapter 21

## STUPID

"Hold up," said Lynn. "Examine the floor in front of you." We found half a dozen trip wires about ankle high, spaced 50 sims apart.

"Someone....," Pebble began.

"...or thing...." I added.

"...doesn't want us to continue."

"At least not without causing bruises and broken bones." Centaur swung his axe at the first line, rupturing it. He examined it. "Cat gut."

"Indeed. Only the best."

"Cat's don't live underground, do they?" I asked.

"No cat with dignity. They would be constantly washing themselves."

"That means whoever---or whatever---concocted this trap makes trips to the surface," said Centaur.

"So there must be a route up nearby," Pebble concluded.

"Let's celebrate." Even with losing an arm Stick was still hungry. He took off his backpack. His jaw dropped, then his expression soured. All that remained of the pack was the pack. He displayed the incision in the bottom of it to us. His anger dissipated. What was done was done. Remaining upset would only diminish his reflexes. "I remember feeling the awkward weight when we were circumventing the rats, so it must have just happened."

"Hey, my pack is also empty," said Centaur

"And mine," Pebble and I burst out simultaneously.

We jumped into a four corners defense. In addition to the galleries and caverns on both sides of the main gallery, there were boulders and outcroppings. It, or they, could be hiding anywhere. "I didn't hear or see anything," Pebble confessed. "The thing that cut my pack must have held a hand or paw or tentacle beneath it so the stuff in it wouldn't fall to the ground."

"Who could be that sly?" asked Stick.

"Not just sly, but intelligent, to be able to construct that trap," said Centaur

"However, it was fairly obvious," stated Pebble.

"We almost fell for it."

"The ingenious levels of the two don't match," said Lynn.

"So the pick-pocketing and the constructing of the trap were by different creatures?" I hypothesized. It suddenly made sense. The two WERE connected. "The trip wires were a distraction. We were meant to stop to examine them. When we did, we were pick-pock...pick-packeted."

"We need to recover our supplies," said Centaur. For emphasis the torch began to flicker.

In single-file we rushed off, our attention focused on evidence of something recently passing by.  Pebble had his bow cocked and ready.  His eyes were pinpoints of determination.  A thief didn't like being stolen from.

"They went this way."  Stick bounded down a shallow tunnel on the right into a five meter deep cavern.  We sprinted after him.  Scattered throughout were some of the contents of our packs.

"That's just stupid," said Pebble.  He was referring to the coins, rod, and stones we found.  "They took everything but the treasure."

"What's of value to one, may not be of value to another," Centaur commented.

"Just plain stupid."

"Did they continue this way?" I asked.  "Or did they just sneak in here to examine their loot?"

"There are a couple more coins down this tunnel," said Stick.  The tunnel he referred to was 75 sims high, half that wide.

"What are they, rats?"

"This should be easy," said Centaur.  "Instead of following bread crumbs, we'll follow coins."

"How stupid," Pebble reiterated.  "I'll lead.  If this torch goes out, I'll be able to smell my way to them."

"You can't really smell money?" I questioned.

"Actually I can.  It has a distinct odor.  But I'll have to be much closer to it than we are now to be able to track it."

The diminutive tunnel made walking awkward.  Dozens of meters slightly bent and sideways was taking its toll.

"Maybe we should be satisfied with what we've recovered so far and head back a different route," I suggested.

"This way will lead us to the surface," said Lynn.

"There you have it," said Pebble.  "If you bend over for hours, damaging your back, rewards will follow."

"It wouldn't be a problem if you walked on four legs."

"Shut up."

Something dropped on us from holes in the ceiling. Mushrooms must be the weeds of the underworld. Spores burst from the fungi as they made contact with us. It was time to take a nap.

I woke beside my companions in a room barely tall enough for me to stand. It was narrow enough that I could touch my hands and feet to opposite walls if I stretched. The only other person awake was Lynn. She was staring at me with that far away look, kays or days distant. She was lying on top of both Centaur and Stick. The four of us, with our legs all facing the some way, looked like a raft, with Lynn the pilot. The room was constructed of stone, as was the meter tall door with a three sim slit chiseled into it, horizontally, two-thirds of the way up. The contents of the room became discernible after focused concentration. The only illumination was from a dim red light that shined through the slit. It faded in and out, like transport headlights passing by at night. Our torch wasn't in the room with us, or our weapons, except for the daggers we had strapped to our sides. I still had my wallet. "Maybe they are stupid."

"Just careless and self-absorbed," said Lynn.

Pebble woke up. "Get off me, cat."

"I'm not on you."

"Then get off Centaur and Stick."

Lynn looked around. So tight were our accommodations our bodies completely covered the floor.

"All right," Pebbled whined. He stood up, allowing a terminus for Lynn's leap.

The disturbance woke Stick and Centaur, who immediately reached for their non-existent weapons.

"Be prepared for anything." Centaur removed a stone from his wallet and brought it to his mouth. We detached our daggers, Pebble two of them. Centaur swallowed the stone. A moment later he sheened with pental clarity. He raised his hand. Expecting a burst of flame or a bolt of lightning, I was disappointed when nothing happened. Were some of the stones duds? But the elemental energy hadn't been ineffective, it had just been invisible. The wall in the direction Centaur stood began to melt. Stone became mud.

What was on the other side took our breaths away. It became understandable now, why a few coins weren't worth the trouble of holding onto. A stone pedestal was in the middle of a room similar in size to our cell. On top of the pedestal was a stone basin. Within the basin were dozens of diamonds. No one moved. It couldn't be real. Was it an illusion? A trap? One diamond was more valuable than our combined net worth.

"How stupid." Pebble paused a moment, a brief moment, before he rushed up to the basin and filled his wallet.

"They probably considered that wall to be impenetrable," said Stick as he helped himself to his share.

"Some mutes aren't familiar with penta." Centaur was also filling his wallet. "When a person is transformed, his mind changes as severely as his body. Some things are forgotten."

I was not left out. I collected 20 diamonds, not as many as my companions, but still a small fortune.

Lynn washed herself.

The vault had a door similar to our cell's. "Now what do we do?" I asked. "I'm guessing the penta you used is the kind that quickly expires."

"We go out the door," suggested Lynn.

"The vault has to be the most secure room down here," said Stick.

"To get in," said Pebble. "Why would they waste their resources trying to keep someone from getting out?"

One big shove was all it took. It got considerably lighter, but it was still dim compared to natural light, or even to torch light. Twenty-sim long beetles with glowing red carapaces passed to and fro down the tunnel we entered. The ceiling was as short as the tunnel we fell asleep in, but with the walls farther apart.  Which way?

The sounds of rats came from the right, answering that question.  We went left.  The squeaks and squeals intensified.  The rats were getting closer.  We turned to intercept their charge.  They appeared a moment later, and they weren't alone.  On the back of each giant rat was a miniature man dressed in prehistoric attire.  Each carried two spears the size of darts.  One at a time they flung them at us, most connecting.  One prick might be insignificant, but we were beginning to look like pincushions, and were bleeding from every wound.  The only one of us able to dodge every dart was Lynn.  When the last projectile was thrown I believed the attack to be over.  It was just beginning.  From within their grimy rags they removed gray cylinders.  Scraping them against a stone wall set them ablaze.  The flare-up was brief but brilliant, like a match being ignited.  Instead of throwing them staggered like they threw the darts, these projectiles were launched in unison.  Stick got the brunt of the attack, his clothes catching on fire.  Pebble tackled him to the ground, smothering him.  "Now's the time to use that last healing stone."  Centaur threw it to Pebble.

As Pebble attended to Stick, Centaur swallowed one of the two remaining penta.  This wasn't the time to be looking for hidden doors, so it must have been the unidentified stone.  Centaur hesitated before releasing the penta's energy.  Anything could happen, but the situation was dire.  He stretched his arms outward, toward our attackers and their mounts.  The ground began to shake.  There was a rumble.  The stone ceiling between us and our adversaries crumbled.  We backpedaled, a plume of dust following us.  When the murkiness dissipated, the passageway was completely blocked.  A lone glow bug was our only source of light.  It scuttled away before we could capture it, leaving us in darkness.

"Ah, Lynn," said Stick, who was still feeling the rush of the healing stone.  "If it isn't too much trouble, would you please lead us out of this hell hole."

"Someone hold onto my tail.  Someone else hold onto him...."

"Pulling your tail isn't like pulling on my finger?" asked Pebble.

"It's the freshest air you'll breathe if I leave you behind."

The tunnel we were in was a direct route to the surface. One of the most wondrous sights I had ever seen was the natural light on the wall a couple of crooks from the surface.  It took awhile for our eyes to become re-acquainted with the sun.  Moments later the sun dimmed.  Lynn got us out before dark, but just barely.

We emerged in an oasis.  Deciduous trees pocketed a lake. The hole we emerged from was within a blackberry briar.  A path was cut through it, but only a meter high.  We had to make our own trail, eating as we went.  The germs still had our food and we had no intention of going back to get it.  We also didn't have our weapons, sans daggers, which was a more problematic, in the long run.

"At least we're closer to Rhinopolis," said Pebble. "Vegetation like this grows near the Beetlewoods."

"Let's hope we're CLOSE ENOUGH to civilization for most of the wild animals and mutes to have been scared off," stated Centaur.

Stick looked different.  "YOUR ARM GREW BACK!" I squealed.  His burns were also healed, but that was insignificant compared to the regeneration of a limb.

"I was a bit concerned about that," he replied, "but we were busy, so I didn't have the time to fret.  The strangest part was not feeling any pain after the arm crumbled.  After awhile I got used to having one arm.  Maybe it really wouldn't be that bad to be mutated.  In time I think I could get used to about anything."

Centaur crashed to the ground.  "If you don't mind, I think we should camp here."  He had to be exhausted dragging that damaged leg for kays.

With silent consent the rest of us lay down on the lush grass beside the lake, our heads resting on our empty packs.  Hour watches were kept, with Centaur being omitted from the rotation.  Please, nothing bother us tonight.  Tomorrow we'll be able to re-provision, with the diamonds we extracted from the germs---the name we attached to the diminutive men.

# Chapter 22

## RHINOPOLIS

Our luck held.  No further delays until we reached the gates of Rhinopolis, mid-afternoon the next day.

"I need to leave for awhile," stated Lynn.

"Thank you for informing us this time before abandoning us," Pebble squawked.

"I'll meet you in two days...on the Briarwood Highway."

"We may stay longer," Centaur informed her.

"I'll meet you in two days."  Lynn ran off, her back legs crossing in front of her briefly before her front legs leapt ahead again.  She disappeared into the scattered trees a moment later.  Prairie had gradually transitioned into forest since noon. The transformation was nearly complete, leaving just the spaces between copses to be filled in.

"So where is this great convergence of waters?" I asked.  I was referring to the West Fork and Emerald rivers meeting.  Being from Rhinopolis, Pebble was an aficionado of Limbo's second most populous city.  Since waking he was relentless in sharing its attributes.

"It's the most cosmopolitan city, even more diverse than Gulag, because of its proximity to the Frontier. Arbols come all the way from the Copper Forest to trade goods here, as do mer from the Western Sea, trogs from the Platinum Mountains, amazons from the Honey Mountains...."

"Amazons?" Being on Limbo reminded me of some of the vacations I took. I was so immersed in the setting I no longer thought it strange to see the ocean or a palm tree, or snow.

"Some call them titans," Centaur clarified, "because of their size. Being all female, AMAZON is more often used. On a planet with five times as many men as women, gender is more of a novelty than size."

"Never confuse them with gents," Stick emphasized.

"Male giants?" I hypothesized.

"There are a few females mixed in," Centaur answered. "Amazons are not only female in appearance, but also in demeanor. Gents are more masculine, the women and the men. Brutish some might say. Being the largest mutes who have retained most of their humanity, they believe they are aristocracy. Most of them call themselves LORD THIS or LORD THAT. Many live in keeps, with dozens of followers doing their bidding."

"So they are something to aspire too?"

"Most people have a fearful respect for them," Stick replied. "For those wishing to become powerful, mutating into a gent would be welcomed."

"And you aren't one of them?"

"I view greatness on an individual level. I believe maximizing your potential makes you a more powerful person than someone who controls others. That's not to say we shouldn't concern ourselves with others. The greatest swordsmen defended fair maidens. They protected the meek and the righteous."

"The rivers meet on the other side of the city, Hornet." Pebble pounced when a break in the conversation developed. Even if one hadn't developed he was prepared to speak. He was not the

137

type of person who shied away from barging in. "The Isle of Gar is near the convergence. It's the only district of Rhinopolis's 11 that's outside the city's walls. It's renowned for its art community. If you want to buy a statue or see a play, that's the place to go. I wonder if THE MANY LIVES OF CHAMELEON is still playing. Its ribald, but the characters are well developed. It's amazing what a few mutations can do for sexual experimentation."

"I would be happy just to sleep in a bed again, and scrub off some of this grime."

"Most of the inns and restaurants are in Comida. There's a place there that has the best...you'll just have to see for yourself." Who could refute such enthusiasm?

The stone wall that surrounded Rhinopolis was eight meters tall. But was that high enough to prevent a gent from entering the city? The Jacob Gate was open. A dozen groups waited for the pair of heavily armored guards to give them permission to pass through. A third guard was seen on one of the towers adjacent to the gate.

The line was moving quickly. In a couple of minutes we should be up to the front.

"I forgot the gate medallion," explained the man at the front of the line.

"Then you need to go back to get it," one of the gate guards replied.

"Nine Palms is 200 kays away."

"You could buy another."

"If I did that I'll be lucky to break even."

"While you contemplate your options would you please step aside? You're holding up the line."

The freight-hauler did what he was told. He was too distraught for a rejoinder.

Pebble and Stick stepped forward a couple of steps, which Centaur and I automatically mimicked. The rat-faced man said, "Maybe we could help him out."

Centaur was so shocked it took him a moment to respond.

"You want to let go of your hard-looted coin? You're as stingy with your money as my wife was with her affections, towards me anyway."

"You're thinking of yourself. I was always free with spending my money as long as I had plenty of it."

"That's true. It does seem out of character, though, that you want it to benefit someone else." I also thought so, but I wasn't the most qualified to judge the character of someone I have known for...a week? I have only known Pebble, and Stick and Centaur for 10 days? Maybe his re-creation had changed him. Mental mutations didn't necessarily reflect physical changes.

"I thought you hated PEOPLE," Centaur continued. "And if you hate people so much why do you like this city? 70,000 is a lot of people to hate."

"In a large city a person can become anonymous. It's possible to not see the same people on consecutive days. The loneliest people live in cities. I like being lonely."

"Don't you get tired of having us around? We're people too you know."

"But you're family. That's different."

"We were rewarded for returning that ring of protection to Jacob," said Stick. "We have the funds available to help our fellow man. Sometimes a tossed stone causes a ripple."

"Okay." Centaur begrudgingly handed two silver coins to the freight-hauler who hadn't moved, not even a swinging of an arm or a twisting of a head, since he had involuntarily extricated himself from the flow of traffic. The man was so unresponsive Centaur had to press the coins into his hand. Like feeding a jukebox, once the money had been recognized and accepted, the man activated. He returned to the line that had grown by a couple of groups since he had shut down.

"Next." The guard who spoke did so without looking at Pebble and Stick. They were just the next ears of corn or bolts of cloth along the conveyor belt. "Gate medallions, please."

"We'll need to purchase four." Pebble signaled Centaur.

"Am I your personal assistant?" Centaur searched through the communal wallet. He snagged five coins, then dove back in. He was only able to find one more. "Damn. If we hadn't given those other two away...." He returned the six pieces of silver and replaced them with a gold coin. Hornet remembered that many Limboan businesses conveniently short-changed their customers, forcing bills to be rounded up the next available unit.

"I can handle the money if you wish."

"I think I'll retain the burden a little longer." Centaur handed over the gold coin. He held his breath. The guard handed the coin to his partner. He recorded the transaction in a ledger, then dropped the coin in a slot cresting a metal box. From the shallow dinging it made the box had to be nearly full. From a leather pouch, much larger than the typical wallet, he pulled out two silver coins and four copper medallions. He handed them to the first guard.

"These will be good through the end of next month." He dropped the pieces of metal into Pebble's hand.

Centaur grunted.

"Okay." Pebble passed them back to Centaur.

"Next."

We shuffled through the gate into the city, half jogging. We were eager to be beyond the stress of entry, and to the precipice of exotic splendor.

A wonderful odor permeated the Green District. Vendors sprawled on both sides of the wide avenue. Fruits of various stages of ripeness competed with freshly cut flowers. For every waft of raw seafood, salty and pungent, was a billow of smoke laced with singed beef or fowl.

"I think it's time for lunch," stated Stick.

"We just ate," pleaded Centaur.

"An hour ago."

"I know just the place," said Pebble.

"After we re-provision. Wouldn't you like a new blade, Stick?"

"That means the Bronze District," said Pebble. "Follow me. And stay close. It's easy to become lost here, even if you can block out the distractions." Pebble definitely knew the city he was born in---the location he entered Limbo. He rushed from one narrow lane to another, through fruits and vegetables, grains and livestock. I was hard pressed to keep up. I had to keep my wits about me. One refrain from concentration, one examination of a tropical fruit, one ogling of a woman who used more than the quality of her wares to make a sale, might mean the abandonment of my guide. I feared that once I lost my friends I might never find them again. I enjoyed their companionship, sure, but they were also my safety net. It was just a week ago that I was walking naked through endless prairie, fighting a hornet the size of a dog. Dogs killed that woman. I was losing focus. Back to following Pebble.

We passed beneath an archway with the words BRONZE DISTRICT chiseled in it. Flanking it were thick wooden doors pressed tightly against a stone wall slightly lower than the one on the perimeter of the city. And two towers, unmanned, rising a story above the wall, bookends of the pseudo-permanent breach. I turned to the right, then to the left. Both sections of wall appeared to be without end. "Does the wall protect one part of the city from another? I thought with the Human Pact humans didn't wage war with one another."

Pebble paused in front of the archway to confirm he hadn't lost anyone before entering the new district. "As Rhinopolis grew it ran out of room within its walls, forcing people to settle outside them. Additional walls were built, to protect these people, and the plethora that followed. The interior walls still exist in case the outer wall is ever breached---and for aesthetics. Quaint districts are more appealing than a sprawling metropolis."

"Like Gulag," added Centaur. "That city continues to grow without boundaries, and planning. It was the first settlement on

Limbo.  People didn't know what they were doing."

"It sounds like they still don't," I commented.

"Habit."

"I kind of like the idea of a random, amorphous entity," said Stick. "It becomes the sum of its citizens, not the creation of the consensus."

"But there's no beauty in chaos, not when it's jumbled like that.  When brilliant colors are mixed gray is created."

"How often is Rhinopolis attacked?" I asked.

"I don't think it ever has," Pebble responded.

I was confused.  "Why waste so much time and money on its defenses?"

"Maybe it's never been attacked because of its defenses."

"That's like saying wearing garlic prevents werewolves because you never see one."

"Lycan flee from garlic because of the stigma attached it," Stick clarified.  "Being canine-derived their oral hygiene is scrutinized."

"Another way to look at it," said Centaur.  "With Rhinopudians feeling secure, their minds not befuddled with fear and uncertainty, they are able to pursue more intellectual endeavors.  That art community Pebble mentioned being an example."

"I'm surprised, even with its defenses, Rhinopolis isn't occasionally attacked, it being so close to the Frontier."

"The mutes in this part of the Frontier are primarily positive. Positive in the sense that they do things they believe benefit the common good.  Some of those things are too exotic for my taste."

"That's what I like about them," said Stick.  "They aren't afraid to abandon the norm."

# Chapter 23

# PROVISIONS

The Bronze District was more orderly than the Green. Instead of having two major perpendicular avenues, and many narrow alleys, it was organized in blocks. Travel was less demanding. Not only was the street system more organized, without street vendors one didn't have to detour around as many people, or worry about someone darting out from a hidden alcove. With his back turned towards the street, Centaur emptied the municipal wallet into his left hand and examined its contents. "Before we buy anything here, we better exchange our diamonds for coins if we don't want every vendor rounding prices up to the nearest diamond. You remember where the bank is, Pebble?"

"The Bronze Locket is a block over. Feek. That reminds me. I put over a gold in the Bank of Comida four years ago."

"You've probably earned quite a bit of interest then," I said.

"You don't understand. Banks in Limbo don't pay interest. They charge rent. They are high security storage facilities."

Centaur elaborated. "Criminals have a tendency to not trust one another. It's too easy for someone to skip out or become lost in the wilderness or the Frontier."

"What happens if you don't pay your rent, Pebble?"

"Oh, rent is paid. It's probably no longer worth my time to make a withdrawal. I'd be too embarrassed to collect the coppers that remain."

Pebble beckoned Centaur to lead them into the Bronze Locket. He thought strongly about staying outside. At the last minute he shuffled behind us. The bank's interior was a mixture of wood paneling and steel. Three burly guards scrutinized us. Above the three cavities in the far wall was the Rhinopolis Bank Association's motto: NO UNAUTHORIZED WITHDRAWAL WITHOUT A FIGHT.

Centaur walked up to the right window. He placed the diamonds on the shelf that jutted into the room. Two eyes looked back at him. An entire face had to be there, but without sufficient illumination or a larger aperture I couldn't be certain. "I would like to exchange these for coins, at least ten percent being silver or copper." Two disembodied hands carried them into the shadows. I was concerned that the bank might try to rob us. What could we really do if the bank didn't provide coins in return for the diamonds? A moment later the eyes, and hands, returned. A wooden basin was full of gold, silver, and copper. "Thank you."

I mentally counted the money. It didn't add up. There weren't 400 gold there, the value of the 40 diamonds, but I couldn't be certain unless I physically counted the money. Centaur picked up the basin and was on the verge of pouring its contents into the municipal wallet, when he abruptly set the basin back down and transferred the coins by hand into the purse.

"Shouldn't we count the coins first to make sure they're the right amount?" I asked.

"Bank Accountants have a reputation for being precise in their counting," Centaur whispered.

"It doesn't look right to me. It doesn't look like 400 gold."

"Because it isn't. Banks charge a five percent fee to exchange money." Oh. Centaur finished emptying the basin. One gold coin missed the bag and clattered on the floor. He bent over to pick it up, being quite obvious in what he was doing. He even held the coin out in front of him, showing the guards and those in the cavities what he held. Nervously he added it to the wallet and rushed out the exit, being careful he didn't walk too fast.

"Banks always make me nervous," said Stick. "People are

always watching, expecting the worse out of you, I guess. The only way we could get our hands on someone else's money was if we brought explosives with us."

"Don't ever say that," said Centaur. "Especially in public. The Rhinopolis Bank Association has a larger army than the city."

"Aren't you the mouse today," said Pebble. "You'll run into a mob of demons, but flee from a...." He looked back at the Bronze Locket. "Hmmm. What would it take to get back some of that money I lost on interest?"

"Shhh." Centaur walked away from the bank, taking Pebble by the elbow.

"Can't a man even consider?"

Centaur finally stopped walking, but not until he entered the HAMMER AND MAIL. Dozens of weapons and armor covered the shelves and tables. We spread out, each of us focusing on a different style of fighting and protection. Centaur liked axes, the bigger the better. He preferred the one-headed variety. They weren't as efficient against multiple opponents, but one-on-one they caused a lot of damage. One or two strikes was all it took to incapacitate. He picked up one particularly beautiful piece of weaponry. Its arced head was 75 sims long. "Is it terran crafted?"

"I only sell the best in my shop," the proprietor answered, equal parts pride and refutation. "Terrans haven't been making as many bladed weapons. Some of them have come to believe drawing blood is more negative than pummeling. Dead is dead in my book."

"It looks like the prices have gone up, or is Rhinopolis just more expensive?"

"Supply and demand. The blunted weapons have dropped in price. You get a better value in Rhinopolis than you do in most villages and towns. There's too much competition here."

I was drawn to the bladeless weapons. I didn't have the same moral philosophy as the terrans, whoever they were. I didn't mind blood, I just didn't want to see my own when I cut myself after mishandling a weapon. I had my eye on a club about a meter long. Pieces of metal stuck out of it. They weren't sharp, but they were irregular enough that they would rend flesh when they made contact. "Did the terrans also make this club?"

"Yes. This mace is one of the finest they make. No matter how many times it makes contact, even on bone, the studs won't become embedded or fall out."

"I thought mace was something you sprayed at someone?"

"It's also the name of clubs used as weapons. Some people still call the most basic maces CLUBS, but those that are well-crafted, most of them augmented with studs, are called MACES."

"Do trogs and arbols also make weapons?" It seemed logical that each race might specialize in a particular style of weaponry.

"The trogs are too busy fighting their holy wars to make weapons, and the arbols are...uh...too busy playing. When the trogs do have some free time they mine a bit. The metal for weapons has to come from somewhere. Trog is a derivative of troglodyte, a cave dweller."

Stick looked at swords. Most were more ornate than functional. He settled for both a two-hand and a one-hand. Centaur was shocked when he saw the prices, more so than when he saw the price of the axe he ended up buying. "Perhaps you ought to settle on just one weapon."

"Does a man settle on just one arm? Who does most of the fighting? Don't governments spend a majority of their money on defense? I'd rather go hungry and naked than be without adequate weaponry."

"When you start asking about dinner I'll remind you of that. Okay. I guess we can afford both. Just don't lose them this time."

"You also lost yours."

"But they were half the price."

Pebble split his time between daggers and bows. Although much smaller than an axe or sword, a dagger was nearly as expensive. Centaur finally got around to looking at the rat-faced

146

man's potential purchases. "Don't you already have two of them?" He was referring to the knives sticking out of Pebble's belt. For some reason Pebble never stored them in a scabbard. Maybe they could be accessed more rapidly that way, but I thought it more likely Pebble just liked the way they looked. The sharpened ends couldn't gleam if they were hidden.

"Maybe I should return this bow to save money."

"We need to be able to hit a target before it hits us."

"Wouldn't it be better if we had more than one of us hitting these targets early?"

"You're probably right. It's just that you're so much better at it than either Stick or I." Or me. I didn't really want to learn a new way to kill something, but I didn't want to be dismissed about doing it either.

"Then why don't you buy something more accurate. Maybe a crossbow. They take longer to load, but a shot or two is usually all a person can get off before the target is too close."

Centaur headed towards the crossbows. "I haven't forgotten about the daggers. I still think you only need two or three, not a half-dozen."

With that said Pebble still bought what he intended to buy. Centaur found his crossbow, the least expensive he could buy that was functional. He also had to buy bolts for it, and Pebble, arrows for his bow. Combined, the weapons cost us 30 gold.

Armor was also bought. There were more choices than there had been with the weapons, with every type in every size available. Consequently, the variety of each sub-class was poor. "How long would it take to customize chest and legs?" asked Centaur. He wasn't as excited about weaponry as Stick or Pebble, but armor, that could make or break a mission. Centaur was more a meat and potatoes fighter, a person who pounded away at someone or something instead of performing flashy maneuvers that were named after the masters who created them.

"Normally a week, but for a bit more coin I could have the

chest plate and leg guards ready in three days."

"Still too long.  I think we'll have to settle for what you have in stock."

I didn't know what to look at, so I did the best I could, looking like I did.  It reminded me of it being every man's duty to look under the hood of a stalled transport.  I found a set of armor about half the size of the others.  "Children buy armor?  I didn't think there were any on Limbo?"

Pebble nearly fell over laughing.  The proprietor came to my rescue.  "That was made for a partial, a partial man:  halflings, thirdlings, quarterlings.  Most mutes provision their armor in their homelands, but occasionally one loses theirs, or wants an upgrade."

Centaur settled on buying each of us a scale coat and breeches.  The overlapping pieces of metal didn't provide as much protection as plate, but it was lighter and more maneuverable---a good compromise.  He also bought us helmets, under Pebble's protest.  "How am I supposed to see with this contraption on my head?"

"It doesn't cover your eyes."

"But I feel it pressing down on me, stifling what little intellectual prowess I possess.  And I can barely turn my head."

"What if someone smacks your head?  You might have a hard head, but bone won't prevent an axe from splitting your skull."

"I'm willing to take the risk."

"Do what you like then, but if you die of a preventable head trauma don't expect me to save your stuff until you're re-created and return.  I'll sell it the first chance I get."

"Fine."

"Does that mean I don't have to buy a helmet either?" I asked.  Centaur gave me a look a parent reserved for a child.  "I guess not."

The armor, including the three helmets, came to another 80 gold.  The seemingly bottomless pile of coins Centaur received in exchange for the diamonds was a third gone already.

# Chapter 24

# DESSERT

Comida was an interior district: a district not bordering an exterior wall. The other two were the Citadel and Australia. Australia, America, Africa, Europe, and Asia were residential districts, to honor the Garden Planet's continents. Many theologians believed God created the first man and woman there. Not having much to do, they did a lot of procreating. I was taught in school that people related to one another by blood shouldn't have children together, to prevent mutations. Flawed genes, instead of being weeded out, would multiply. How were the decedents of the first man and woman able to reproduce without a majority of their children having eleven toes or two heads? That's assuming humans always had ten toes. Maybe they once had eight, or six. Could it be that the lack of common sense today is due to us losing a head a few generations back, losing half our intellect?

That may be why no one remembers the location of the Garden Planet. Knowledge of it was in that lost head. Some theologians suggest the planet is still as lush as it was when the first man and woman lived on it. After they began to sin they were expelled from it, which started the Great Galactic Expansion. Other theologians believe the first humans were expelled from a small region of the planet. The Great Galactic Expansion occurred millennia later, to escape the 40 Years of Turmoil, an unparalleled period of natural and self-inflicted disaster. A third group of theologians believe the Garden Planet can't be found because it no longer exists---in the state depicted by legend. Humans left the planet, after it lost the ability to sustain life.

As we entered Comida I was bombarded by odors. The Green District smelled like a garden. Comida was more pungent. Sautéing, grilling, roasting, frying, and boiling, overlapped and conflicted. It was wonderful, at times, but overwhelming: a complicated symphony too complex to enjoy. Sifting, analyzing, and re-organizing was challenging, not always entertaining.

Comida was renowned for its restaurants, but it was also Rhinopolis' garment district and provided lodging to a majority of its visitors. The streets were well designed. Similar to the Bronze District, but with enough breaks in the grid pattern, and trees and fountains and pools, that it felt more intimate.

Pebble stopped at a sidewalk café called the Taco Hen. A chicken surfing on a tortilla was painted in bold colors on a bamboo backdrop. Scantily-clad women served flamboyantly dressed men at small two- and four-person tables within a small, but efficient shade-producing copse. I still hadn't become accustomed to the scarcity of woman on Limbo. Why couldn't more of them commit crimes? It was common in poverty stricken areas for women to outnumber men. Desperate men had a propensity to commit crimes. With so many of them either in prison or dead, women were left behind to look after themselves and raise children.

Seeing the serving women dressed like that renewed thoughts that had lain dormant since my arrival. I had been more concerned about staying alive than romance. If I lived in a place as safe as Rhinopolis would I be able to find female companionship? How odd would that be, after not being able to make a lasting connection on a world with as many women as men, billions of them?

Pebble was last to sit. He was running the show. He couldn't relax until his guests were comfortable. "I wanted to share my favorite meal, at my favorite restaurant. We don't know how much longer we'll be together."

We looked at one another. It wasn't like Pebble to be this

150

sentimental. Enthusiastic? Emotional? Yes. But superficially. He never expressed his feelings this sincerely.

Centaur was first to respond. "If you're concerned about dying again, and us not being able to find you, maybe we can choose a place to meet. A backup plan if...."

"No, it's more than that. I've begun to mutate. I can feel myself changing. Not physically---except for my skin. Some of the things I used to feel enthusiastic about...I no longer do."

A waitress dropped bowls of chips and salsa on the table. Her cleavage was so extreme that when she bent over more than food almost hit the tablecloth. I attempted to avert my eyes--- unsuccessfully. Pebble was more goal-oriented. "Daiquiris all around, and fajitas after that, with all the fixings." The waitress smiled at the rat-faced man, then at the rest of us, making sure to make eye-contact with each of us. I felt a special bond between us. She walked away in a manner a man wasn't capable of. We breathed in deeply and released.

"Now what were we talking about?" spoke Centaur.

"We weren't," said Stick.

"You sure?"

"Pebble was talking. We were listening."

The rat-faced man continued. "I feel like I'm being pulled...westward."

"Towards the Frontier?" Centaur questioned.

"I've heard of that happening to people after they're re-created," said Stick. "Gaea's way of separating the most extreme from Neutrality."

"Are you feeling more...negative, Pebble? Do you feel like hurting someone?"

Pebble shook his head.

"Do you feel like going out of your way to help someone?"

"There was that freight-hauler at the gate. But I don't feel that way about everyone. My compulsions haven't increased. They've dwindled. I'm less...enthusiastic."

"You feel depressed?"

"I feel content...for the first time in my life. How about we hire a ship to take us to the Copper Forest? We have the money. It will save us a couple of days. And preserve our feet."

"You haven't changed that much. You still want to spend every copper you...we have. You're never satisfied until it's all gone."

"Oh, I think about spending money after that too. I just can't do anything about it."

"I have two problems with your suggestion, in addition to not having enough money to be looking for ways to spend it. One, Rhinopolis isn't a port city."

"Don't rivers eventually drain into oceans?" I asked.

"Let me be more specific. Rhinopolis isn't a sea port."

A different waitress brought out the frozen drinks, on a wooden tray carried on the palm of her hand. Her upper torso wasn't as well-developed as the first waitress, but her backside more than made up for it. It was ample, but well-defined. She smiled as warmly as the first waitress, making sure each of her patrons was personally greeted. When she walked away our mouth's dropped.

Centaur was last to begin sipping the frozen beverage. "Now what were we talking about?"

Stick began his attack with a bamboo straw. The lack of efficiency forced him to change tactics. He drank directly out of the glass, not caring if he stained his mouth. "You were rationalizing your penny-pinching."

Centaur looked like he had swallowed an overly ripe strawberry. His expression brightened. "Uh, now I remember. The West Fork empties into the sea, but not the Western. After it merges with the Neutral at Three Rivers it flows another 400 kays to the Crosshairs. If we wish to cross the Western Sea we need to hoof it to Sunset City. Even if it did save us a day or two, I don't like the idea of traveling a day in the wrong direction. We'll have to pass through Briarwood either way, so we don't have to decide now. I think that was my second point. Yep, it was."

A few minutes later four waitresses burst out of the kitchen with four skillets sizzling with peppers, green and red, onions, and chicken cut into strips---what I hoped was chicken. The waitresses also carried four plates with shredded lettuce, shredded cheese, sour cream, minced chives, and a stack of flour tortillas beneath a damp cloth.

The food looked so good I actually looked at it instead of the women, one of them being the waitress who had taken our order, another the one who had delivered our drinks. Okay, maybe I wasn't just looking at the food. The other two women were just as---uniquely---beautiful. The first two had both been blondes. The newcomers were a brunette and a redhead. The dark-haired one had eyes that sparkled and lips that were made for saying things you wanted to hear. The other had legs that were somehow both soft and toned. They started at her ankles and went up to her…. You can use your imagination. The newcomers gave their non-verbal greetings, then the four of them began to focus on a particular man, but for just an instant. They smiled one last time, before they walked off.

"Now what were we talking about?"

"You had just finished. Let's dig in."

The chicken was delicately seasoned, providing a subtle burst of exotic zest, underwhelming to not overpower the natural flavor of the meat. Each of us ate in our own manner. Stick filled his tortillas until they burst. By the time he consumed his last, his fixings were also gone. Centaur ate his fixings as courses, finishing one before going to the next, between bites of tortilla. He saved the chicken for last. Pebble ignored most of the toppings. To all his tortillas he added chicken. To half, shredded cheese. I put a bit of everything on my tortillas, but in small enough quantities that they didn't overflow. By the time my tortillas were gone half of my fixings were still on the plate, but just one strip of chicken.

Pebble was first to finish eating. He didn't consider food physical and emotional fuel, like Stick, or as an art form, like Centaur. Eating was just something that had to be done, like urinating or bathing---preferably every other week. "We better buy some penta. Arbols harness elem. We'll need to counter that."

"We'll never become their equals," said Centaur. "They use elem innately. It would take a hundred stones to imitate their abilities. And even then, we still wouldn't be able to activate them as quickly as they release their elemental energies---which they do as effortlessly as breathing. No, to claim the emerald pearl for ourselves we'll have to use something other than penta."

"Like...?"

"Agility, creativity, desire."

"Luck," added Stick.

"Plenty of that."

"I still think we should buy SOME penta. We can't have too many healing stones. And if we didn't have a couple of others we wouldn't have had this fine meal, and be discussing additional purchases."

"Agreed. But let's take a minimalistic approach. We still have hundreds of kays to travel. We'll stop by the emporium on the way out of town tomorrow."

"Just like Lynn predicted."

"Or could what she told us have influenced our departure?" I questioned. "Her words may have set our actions in motion." Maybe Lynn's predictive powers weren't so supernatural. She may have been a psychologist before she was sentenced. "I thought we had to go to Gulag to buy penta."

"It's less expensive if we buy it at the Wizard's Keep," said Centaur, "but it isn't the only place. Wizard sanctioned retailers are called emporiums."

"Penta is sold in franchises, like fast-food restaurants?"

"Not exactly. Emporiums are company owned. Wizards are too protective of their monopoly to share it with entrepreneurs."

"That's not to say there isn't a black market for penta," said Pebble. "It's lucrative, but hazardous. Who would you rather make your enemy, constables who must follow procedures, or elemental energy wielders who don't care about their public persona? No faction on Limbo is more powerful."

"How about Osquip?" Stick questioned.

"Shhhh." Pebble leaned into the table. He whispered, "Osquip has eyes and ears everywhere. If we're re-created we won't be able to leave Rhinopolis tomorrow. Damn. And I had been so looking forward to returning to the city. Why did you have to mention that name? Now I want to leave as badly as you."

Stick attempted to speak as quietly as Pebble, but didn't quite pull it off. "Pebble used to work for Osquip. He is the most powerful shadow boss in Rhinopolis. His extreme nature was the catalyst for Pebble modifying his behavior."

Pebble leaned in farther and spoke even more softly. "He killed people because it was easier than walking around them. Actually, he hires others to do most of his dirty work, including myself. My hands weren't as stained as some of the other people working for him, but they weren't clean either."

"I'm guessing this Osquip wasn't too happy about you leaving his employment?" I conjectured.

"Remember when you first joined us, I told you I would kill you if you ever left us?" I winced. I thought, half-thought, Pebble was kidding. "Children model their parents, and at the time Osquip was the father I never wanted. What I promised you was mild in comparison to what he sometimes did to those who wanted a divorce. After torturing them to the brink of death, he would heal them and start over again. Sometimes if he was particularly upset with someone it might take days or even weeks for them to be re-created."

I never imagined that having to resort to mentioning the Wizards would actually lighten the mood. "It seems to me the Wizards would want to sell penta to as many people as possible.

Wouldn't that mean more profit?"

"They enjoy their monopoly," Centaur responded. "If penta becomes too diffused their power diminishes. Becoming wealthy is just one way to become powerful. And power is relative. If I take from you, or prevent you from improving yourself, I become relatively more powerful than you even if I marginally improve my standing in the world. The Wizards are extremely conservative, both financially and politically. They are very set in their ways, even if it's to their detriment, which it isn't if they prevent others from progressing."

"You sure you can't make-up with Osquip, Pebble?" asked Stick. "A man in his position must have accumulated a few choice items. I've always wanted an enchanted sword. A greedy man might wish to give up something hard to come by if the price was right."

Pebble became stone-faced again, and his forehead began to bead. "You wouldn't want to handle the currency he deals in. I don't think you would be able to speak to him if he knew you were consorting with me. A man without a tongue can't communicate very well. He wouldn't intentionally have your tongue removed, but if the body parts it is connected to are sliced away it has a tendency to come off on its own."

"An enchanted sword?"

"Sometimes weapons, and armor, are infused with penta," said Centaur. "THOSE items the Wizards never sell to the public."

"So how would this Osquip be able to get his hands on some of them?"

"Sometimes Wizards misplace things," said Pebble.

"Are there really people foolish enough to steal from a Wizard? Why would anyone take that risk? But from what you said, it appears some do take the risk, and are even successful at it. In the manner you speak of the Wizards, they sound infallible."

"A stray calf can be killed, but not an entire herd. But you are correct, it does take a death wish for someone to be so bold. A parent losing a child becomes extraordinarily vicious. Most of the displaced artifacts have been returned."

"Some mutes are also said to be able to enchant things," said Stick.

"Mutes with innate elemental energy. The most powerful of them are rumored to be able to secrete elem directly into an object. Their weapons and armor also gets misplaced."

"It seems to me if Osquip is as cruel as you make him out to be he should be living in the Frontier," I commented. "Don't those with extremes moralities end up there?"

"After they are re-created," said Pebble. "Osquip has been quite adept at keeping himself alive." I couldn't imagine what it would be like for a person that evil to be simmering in his own foul juices for an eternity. Mortal men eventually die, but on Limbo re-creation is the only release valve.

The four waitresses eventually returned to clear the table of dirty dishes. "May I have a refill, please?" Pebble handed his glass to the woman with the long legs.

"No you won't." Centaur was quite firm in his rebuttal. "Coin flowed like water while living the lifestyle of your prior profession. You---we---can't afford such luxury today. Pebble will have some water, miss. Thank you." The waitress pouted, which made her seem even more attractive. She and the other waitresses left with the dirty dishes, swaying in a manner that made a boat envious. "Now what was I saying?"

The women returned with the bill. Centaur must have had some idea how much it would be, but his mouth still dropped. I never saw the amount, but I did notice Centaur pulling a gold coin from the communal wallet. The restaurant had a nice atmosphere, very aesthetically pleasing, especially the servers, but fajitas couldn't have cost that much. It had to be the daiquiris. It couldn't be easy creating crushed ice on a medieval world. Was it brought in from the mountains? It couldn't possibly be made, could it? It made sense now, why Centaur wouldn't allow Pebble to order another drink.

  The four waitresses returned a final time, to collect the money. After one of them scooped up the coins the four of them went into overdrive. Attractive, cute, beautiful, sexy, there weren't enough adjectives to describe them. As before, they gave each of us some of their attention, then fine-tuned their interest on one particular man. "Would you like dessert?" they asked in unison.

  "I'm stuffed," I responded.

  Stick whispered, "It's not food they're offering."

  "We must be going," said Pebble curtly.

  "It would be impolite to refuse a beautiful woman." Centaur held back as Pebble attempted to drag him away. Was Pebble just getting back at Centaur for not allowing him to have a second daiquiri, or was that more of the changes he was going through manifesting? Pebble didn't seem like the man who would turn down a woman, even if he was paying for the privilege. With regret Centaur finally gave in and allowed Pebble to lead him away. Did Centaur need female companionship more than the rest of us? He had killed his wife when he found her cheating on him. Was that the last woman he had been with? Did he still love her even after her betrayal? Maybe he had been loyal to her after all these years, even after her death. Would it really be that bad to have dessert? Children couldn't be conceived on Limbo. And it wasn't like the women were falling over a particular man when men outnumbered them five to one.  If we had the money for those daiquiris we certainly had enough money for some physical contact. It apparently wasn't illegal on Limbo, not in Rhinopolis anyway. It would help the local economy. The women probably received most of their income from dessert. Waitress wages were notoriously low. I wasn't sure if I could ever do something like that, even if the money was good and I was in complete control of the situation, in a place I felt safe. But I couldn't judge these women either, not if I considered doing business with them. With so few women on Limbo the sex trade must have been a lucrative business. It wasn't surprising that a venue like this had supplemental income---similar to planets with legalized gambling having slot machines in every supermarket and bar. I was tempted to have one more look at the beautiful women. Embarrassment prevented me. I felt bad denying their invitation, even if it was just a business opportunity to them.

Safely away from the restaurant Centaur vented. "The last time we visited an establishment like this you practically choked on the food to get to the dessert."

"It's one of those things I no longer have enthusiasm for," Pebble responded. "It's not that I can no longer appreciate women like that. The interaction feels immature. I'm too grownup to do that now. Playing with stuffed animals no longer excites me."

With Centaur still being out of sorts, he being worked up then denied, Pebble was able to push through us staying at a hotel Centaur would not normally agree to. BECHLER BAY was a theme resort. Waterfalls fell over a horseshoe shaped cliff. Underneath each waterfall was a stack of rooms. The hotel office was a straw hut.

The suite had in-room plumbing. Each of us enjoyed a long soak. After donning bathrobes the resort provided, we gave our dirty clothes---every article of clothing we had---to a porter to be cleaned.

We turned in early, each of us in our own bed. Before Centaur lay down he confirmed the door was locked and secure. "I need to borrow a couple of your daggers, Pebble." He barricaded the door with a dresser. Atop it he stacked the daggers, precariously. Any slight movement would bring them crashing loudly to the floor.

# Chapter 25

## EXHIBITIONIST

Something woke me. I crept over to the door. The daggers were still on the dresser. I spun around. The wall in front of me dissolved. "WAKE UP!"

My companions, being accustomed to danger, reached for their weapons before opening their eyes. Skeletons walked out of the wall---where the wall had been. The weapon vendor couldn't have created a better exercise to test our purchases. Swords and daggers were least effective on the animated bones. Their edges slid off the smooth surfaces. My mace was the most effective. It pulverized bones, crushing skulls and scattering limbs. With barely a scratch or bruise we were able to dismantle the skeletons. Bones lay everywhere. On the floor. On top of beds. Beneath beds. Even embedded in walls. What must the people next door think of the commotion?

"It looks like Osquip may have learned you're back in town," Stick commented.

"Do you know how Osquip got his name?" asked Pebble. He was taking the situation surprisingly well. Sometimes not knowing and fretting was worse than the experience. The attack now over, Pebble was able to cope. "He was named after a species of rat whose teeth are so strong they can bite through stone?"

"And it looks like he just bit through that wall," I stated. "It almost seems...cliché...sending skeletons."

"True, Osquip could have used more accessible objects," said Centaur. "I imagine he believed human bones attacking us would be more frightening then...that dresser against the door."

"But not as effective.  Something as sturdy as that dresser has the potential of doing considerable damage."

"For Osquip, the drama is as important as the outcome.  Remember what Pebble said about how he tortures people?  What concerns me most is the resources he put into this venture.  It takes a penta to animate something."

"Osquip is a wealthy man," said Pebble.  "Most venues in Rhinopolis make donations as compensation for the protection he guarantees them."

"He could have killed us more efficiently spending a lot less money," said Stick.

"That's if he wanted to kill us.  Remember what I said about him keeping his enemies alive."

"HOW DARE HE!"  Stick was more amused than offended when it was primarily Pebble's affair, but now....  "Even criminals have ethics.  This ought to lead us to Osquip."  Stick leapt through the wall---where the wall used to be.  With less fanfare, Pebble followed him, his obligation of supporting his friend superseding his trepidation.

"Here we go again."  Centaur shook his head, but smiled.  "We better go now or risk being left behind."

And that would have been such a bad idea?  "I thought we were trying to stay out of trouble for a while, at least while we were in Rhinopolis."

"Sometimes trouble is an exhibitionist."  Centaur leapt through the aperture.  Not wanting to be left alone, I followed.

We had no idea what might greet us on the other side.  It was opaque where the wall had been, like a lens out of focus.  There could be 50 armed guards, or a raging fire, water, or acid.  Nothing so exotic.  There was a room, much larger than the one we walked out of.  A stone statue, twice our height, was centered in it.  There were no windows or doors, just the opaque curtain, now behind us.

"I don't like this," said Pebble. "How can a piece of stone appear so menacing?"

In response the statue began to move, its hands stretched out like a mummy. We froze---in shock, not petrified. Bones were one thing. How were we going to destroy stone? Pebble, apparently immune to futility, charged, his daggers held high. Somehow he was able to chisel away part of the statue's head. The slight injury didn't faze the thing. With surprising agility it wrapped its arms around Pebble and squeezed. Pebble lost his grip on his daggers. They tumbled to the ground with a loud thud. Cognizant of our futility, we still rushed to our friend's assistance. We had to at least make the attempt to save him. Loud dings of steel on stone echoed in the hollow room. Except for a single shard I was able to detach from the statue with a lucky strike, the only evidence of our attack were a handful of scratches. Blood dripped from Pebble's ears, nose, and mouth, then finally his eyes. His head fell forward. There was a crunch as the stone vice continued to squeeze inward.

Centaur grabbed Stick and me by our shoulders and pushed us through the opaque curtain. He followed directly behind us. We fell together into our hotel suite, landing in a pile.

Stick untangled himself and looked back. "We abandoned him."

"What we left behind was no longer Pebble." Centaur had also picked himself off the floor, but instead of whining about what couldn't be fixed he was stuffing both his and Pebble's possessions in their backpacks.

I followed Centaur's lead. I was almost packed before Stick began.

"Come on, Stick. We need to get out of here before Osquip sends something else at us."

Stick finally broke out of it. He attempted to make up the time he wasted, but Centaur and I ended up having to wait half-a-minute for him to finish. "You really think it was Osquip?"

"Who else would it be?"

Centaur removed the dresser from the door and rushed us through the waterfall in front of our suite, not taking time to use one of the pathways around the falls. The jungle and lake beyond were deserted, as was the avenue in front of the hotel.

The moon was beginning to brighten---good timing, but not entirely. We would be able to see as we maneuvered through the city, but so would anyone following us.

"Feek." Centaur halted in the middle of the avenue, but for just an instant. "We still have to replenish our supplies. We should have bought them yesterday. What were the odds of something like this happening?"

"Considering our history, I would say they were almost guaranteed." Stick surveyed our surroundings. Still no sign of a pursuit.

"Lynn was able to predict something like this would happen," I commented. I was having trouble breathing. My heart was racing. We were just standing there, in the middle of the street. Any second now more skeletons, or statues, or...who knows what else, might leap out of thin air and begin attacking us again. If I was back in Bluewood City I wouldn't be wearing expensive armor or carrying this cool-looking club, but I would be safe. Hungry perhaps, but safe. I was having a panic attack, not full-fledged, but it was inevitable, unless we got out of here---now. I needed to get out of here, with or without my friends.

"Food and supplies first, then we flee," Centaur reiterated. He started moving again, beginning as a fast walk, then turning into a half-jog.

"Don't forget the penta."

"We may have to bypass the penta. We'll see after we buy the food."

"We'll pass the emporium on the way out."

"We'll see."

# Chapter 26

# PENTA

We returned to the Green District.  The markets were already open, but not yet busy.  It would have been better if their business was more robust.  We felt exposed not being able to blend into a crowd.  Bread, cheese, dried fruit and meat were bought, and even some fresh food for immediate consumption.

"Amphi would have to be on the other side of the city," said Centaur.  "We'll be less conspicuous passing through the residential districts."

"You sure about that?" questioned Stick.  "Travelers don't usually go into that part of the city."

"Which is why Osquip won't think to look for us there."

We passed through the Africa and Asia districts without incident.  Some of the people in the streets gave us inquisitive glances, but they didn't communicate with us.  Novelties were better gawked at than associated with.  I became concerned.  "Even if none of Osquip's men are here, word will eventually circulate---of our presence."

"With Gaea's grace, after we leave the city," said Centaur.

Most of the residences were low-lying, granting us views of the Citadel's spires.  I hadn't been in the city-state long enough to study its government.  As with most regimes, it was probably run by big business.  Without children to produce bloodlines it was unlikely to be an oligarchy.  There was no sign of totalitarianism.  It couldn't be a dictatorship, military or other.  With Limbo being populated with criminals it was surprising its societies weren't more chaotic and/or violent. Perhaps there was divine intervention here.

"Maybe Osquip just wanted Pebble," said Stick. "It's crazy to be hiding in alleys and behind corners if we're not really being chased." Which is what we had done since leaving Comida, before becoming progressively bolder. Out of sight was becoming out of mind. We still hadn't spotted anyone pursuing us.

"Do you really want to take that risk?" asked Centaur. "You do remember what Pebble said Osquip did to people he was displeased with. I don't want my fingernails to be pulled off or my skin burned until it bubbles."

"Pebble didn't look like he suffered much," I said. "He didn't look like he particularly enjoyed the situation, but he didn't look like he was in excruciating pain. He looked almost...content. I'm not saying it was good that Pebble died, but it's better to have a smile on your face than to go out screaming."

"Maybe we ought to wait for Pebble to be re-created, before we leave Rhinopolis," suggested Stick. "We could hide out for a few days."

"It may have been random," said Centaur, "but I think Pebble was found where he was after his last re-creation because he was being drawn to the Frontier. He mentioned something like that happening to him."

"Lynn spoke of someone mutating in our party before we reached the Copper Forest," I reminded them.

"We'll be there soon enough," said Stick.

"So we might see Pebble again?"

"We might," said Centaur, "but we may not recognize him.

"So we're still going to the Copper Forest?"

"We must. It's even more important we do so now. Our journey is no longer just a quest. It has become a memorial."

Amphi was finally reached. It was the most exotic place I had been to so far. Mutes resided there, temporarily and permanently. The fishing center of the city was also there, as were the outfitting stores.

Centaur walked into the PACK AND TACKLE. Knowing what he wanted he was ready to check out within minutes. We transferred the contents of our old patched-up packs into our new, plus sleeping pads, lanterns, climbing spikes, and other things too numerous and insignificant to mention.

"How about a pack for Pebble?" Stick suggested. Centaur responded with a blank look. "We might find him again."

"I don't think we should become too encumbered. Maneuverability is more important than accounting for everything."

"We still might find him."

We gave away our old packs to beggars, who became upset after rummaging through them and finding them to be empty. "BORE YOU!" shouted one of them.

Stick withdrew his sword. Centaur held him back. "We don't need any undue attention right now." The vagabond had already forgotten the incident and was happily transferring the trinkets beside him into one of the packs. Limbo was a harsh world to panhandle. Denials weren't limited to disregarding. "Let's head to the emporium." Stick's ire lessened, but not entirely. There was a reason he had been sentenced to a penal colony.

The emporium was on top of a small hill surrounded by a moat. It looked very much like a castle with its draw bridge, portcullis, and four corner towers. The closer we got to it the less formidable it became, becoming more playhouse than fortress, more middle-class residence than mansion. Its towers were as small as closets. On top of each was a statue.

Centaur paused in front of the moat to enlighten me. "Replicas of mutants from each of the dual-axis moralities. That one resembling a monkey is an arbol. Arbols are agreeable, but chaotic. The bald, stout fellow is a trog. Trogs also exist to improve the world around them, but much more rigidly. The primitive looking, hairy brute is a goblin. Goblins are persistently disagreeable. And finally, the sleek, long-limbed, big-nosed one with claws is a troll. Trolls are intentionally troublesome. The havoc they create is unpredictable---burning down a village one week, slaughtering a herd of cattle the next.  All four moralities are represented because Wizards consider themselves to be true neutrals, neither helping nor hindering, not too playful or too anal."

Centaur resumed his movement.  While walking across the moat via the drawbridge, a small electric charge passed through my body.  I was concerned at first I might get electrocuted.  Wizards had the means and apathy to carelessly take an anonymous life.

"Place your stone and rod on the shelf within the gateway," spoke a disembodied voice.  Did we really have a choice?  The portcullis was down, and even if it wasn't, a Wizard had more painful means to halt intruders than electrocuting them.

"I don't think I like doing business with people who can see what's in my wallet," stated Stick.  "What else might they be able to see?  Some of the most powerful people are perverts."

"Shhh," I pleaded.  "They can probably hear you."

"Let's hope they can't also read my thoughts.  Probably not, or I'll already be dead."

Centaur ignored Stick's rant.  "I prefer them showing a bit of their abilities.  A penta monger that can't manipulate elemental energy isn't worth our time.  Would you go to a doctor who knows less about medicine than you?"

Upon placing the stone and rod on the shelf, the portcullis lifted without anyone visible at the controls.  Expecting to see a courtyard on the other side of the gate, I become disoriented finding only a seven meter by fifteen meter room, with a small, elderly, balding, but very fit man behind a desk in the room's center.  So people did age here.  How many years did it take living on Limbo, without being re-created, to look like that?

The desk nearly wrapped around him, permitting just enough space behind for him to be able to free himself.  Three large tomes were opened on the top of the desk.  The walls were covered with shelves, and the shelves covered with penta.  There were thousands of stones, hundreds of rods, and dozens of rings.  There was a fortune there, worth thousands of gold---tens of thousands.

With an utter lack of emotion the man glanced up at us.

"We would like to buy some penta," said Centaur. That was stating the obvious.

The penta peddler handed us a slate with a stick of chalk tied to it. "Place your order here. One item or several. One slate per day."

Centaur took the slate. Stick was first to speak. "Should we just buy stones? Or also a couple of rods?"

"The advantage of buying a rod is the lower cost per charge," said Centaur. "The penalty is not being able to use all those charges before it gets displaced, accidentally, or forcibly. Losing one stone is painful, but not a tragedy."

"How about a ring?" I asked. "If rings can be used indefinitely, wouldn't it be even more economical to buy one of those?"

"Maybe if we had the money. Buying one ring would wipe us out. I was hoping to keep a reserve. Let's think about what we really need."

"Definitely healing stones. You would have had a much more enjoyable experience underground if we had an ample supply."

"And curing stones," added Stick. "Two of us almost died from poisoning."

Centaur became silently pensive, then said, "We could also use some shielding. Our improved armor will protect us better, but not unconditionally."

"Maybe something to help our offense too," said Stick. "There is nothing I can't defeat one on one, but some demons don't play fair. Elemental defenses make it---nearly---impossible to strike them, luck being more the determining factor than skill."

"And maybe another fire stone, and one that will turn rock to mud," I added. "We wouldn't have been able to escape the germs if that wall hadn't melted."

Our wish list became unmanageable, i.e., unaffordable. We settled on two rods: one for healing, one for countering diseases and poisons. Both had their full accompaniment of charges: 10. We also bought six healing stones, as a precaution if we became separated, or lost the rod. Other purchases: two fire stones, one cold, two lightning, two soften, one invisibility, two sleep, one grow, and one communicate.

"Many mutes no longer speak Esperanto," Centaur explained. "Some of them have mutated so extremely they can no longer make sounds we can recognize. Others no longer have the mental capacity to form thoughts into words."

We also retained the water breathing rod---with three charges---and the discovery stone.

Our bill came to 432 gold, 20% more than we would have paid if we bought them in Gulag.

"You sure it isn't worth a two week detour to save 72 gold?" I questioned.

"That's assuming we make it there safely," said Centaur. "With Osquip possibly pursuing us I don't think we can wait to purchase the penta."

Stick became fervent. "I'm not scared of any man."

"How about skeletons and elementals?"

"Skeletons are men without padding. Elementals, they piss me off more than scare me. It's going to take an hour to get those nicks out of my sword."

"This penta we bought better be worth it," said Centaur. "For what we just spent we could have lived comfortably for two years."

"It's been said that it takes money to make money," said Stick.

"Let's just hope we didn't sell the cow for a handful of beans."

"But wasn't there treasure at the end of that beanstalk that grew from the beans?"

169

"And a giant. It's more likely we'll see the giant than the treasure."

Centaur returned the slate to the penta peddler. He continued to read for a moment, then he snatched the slate, glanced at it, and in a whirlwind of energy, filled the order by removing a stone from this shelf, and taking a rod from that shelf. In slightly more than a minute he had placed all eighteen items in a leather bag with an engraving of the DENIZENS OF MORALITY, a circular arrangement of the mutant statues on top of the four towers. It was also known as the WIZARD'S MARK.

The emporium's proprietor sat back down to return to his reading. Centaur placed the money on the desk in front of him. Stick and I followed him out of the faux-castle. The penta peddler didn't even look up. Wasn't he going to count the coins? On second thought, who would be so stupid to short-change a Wizard?

We retrieved the stones and rod beside the portcullis. The gate dropped behind us as we crossed the drawbridge. We were passed by a large, muscular man who sneered at us. As the portcullis opened for him his boldness evaporated. His shoulders slumped. Concern rippled across his forehead.

"We better split up the penta, in case we become separated," suggested Centaur.

"Sharing the wealth, huh," commented Stick, raising an eyebrow inquisitively.

"Splitting it two ways should be sufficient." Centaur handed me the rods.

"Hey. You think I would gorge myself on penta like candy on Halloween?"

"Something like that. Let me have that healing rod back for a second, Hornet." Centaur injected himself with it, then handed it back to me. Within minutes Centaur's leg straightened out. Sullen since his injury, he suddenly became giddy. He flexed his healed leg and hopped about madly. Stick and I had to back away from him as he swung his battle axe. "It's time to send some demons home."

Stick smirked. "After we leave the city. I remember someone wanting to keep a low profile. And by the way, the next time something bursts from the earth and attacks you you're on your own." Stick's comment wasn't taken seriously. The first hint of distress and he would be in the thick of things again. Sure, a part of him did so because he wanted to help his friends---and the occasional stranger---but it was mainly instinct he reacted to. His body might constantly crave food, but his spirit subsisted on exhilaration. If Stick was an accountant a perfect ledger might have stimulated him. On Limbo he charged head on, towards danger. Situational and environmental stimuli, desired or not, directed his actions.

# Chapter 27

# BLAH

Two long lines of humans, intermingled with a few mutes, convened at the river gate, one of them entering the city, the other departing. A stone walkway connected the gate to the river. Two ferries passed one another, one heading to the mainland, one to the Isle of Gar.

The ferry we boarded became packed. It didn't leave until every sim of space was taken. The fare was just a copper, enough to cover expenses, but not too much to drive people away. The boat not only provided the only means of transportation to the island---excluding private charters that few could afford---but also, indirectly, Sunset City, the Western Sea, and the Frontier.

Being so close to people on the ferry, I had an excellent opportunity to study some mutes. The only ones I had conversations with so far were Lynn and that drak that had saved me when I became lost in the Bluewoods. Neither was humanoid. Why was I more comfortable around those least like me? Was it because I didn't see part of myself in them? Did they not remind me of what I would one day become?

Cognizant of my curiosity, Centaur said in a hushed tone, "A trog, an arbol, and a mer."

Two meters away was the trog. He was shorter than a majority of the ferry passengers: exceeding 140 sims, but barely. He was wider of torso and more muscularly built than the average human. What made him stand out most was his bald head. It was out of proportion to his body, making him look almost infantile. His facial features were stretched, distorting them. It was like looking at someone in a carnival mirror. His eyes, nose, ears, and mouth were twice as large as mine. His expression was blank, matching the sense of exacting calm he radiated. I imagined his countenance would retain its lack of emotion to eternity, even if the ferry was sinking. He was heavily armored. An axe, nearly as long as he was tall, was strapped to his back.

The arbol, a couple of meters further away, was taller than me, by 20 sims. His lanky limbs were much longer than a human's, making him appear even taller than he was. Fleece covered his rail-thin body. His head was of normal proportion, as was his facial features. A mischievous grin plastered his face, as stark as the trog's stoicism. He looked like he was up to something, not serious, like murder, more humorous, like placing water above a doorway, or tripping someone as they walked by. He wore a green leather vest and shorts. His head and feet were bare, of cloth. The bushiness of each made it unnecessary, even impractical.

The mer appeared to be embarrassed of his mutations. From a distance he looked like a normal human, but up close his peculiarities became apparent. His white button-down cotton shirt beneath his leather vest had a high collar that covered most of his neck. Whenever he moved, more of his neck became exposed. Gills grew on both sides of it, similar to the ones Centaur, Stick, and I grew after being injected with the water breathing rod. His skin was pale blue, like someone who had been standing in the cold too long.

"Mer feet are supposedly webbed," said Stick. "But I've never seen one without boots, to confirm the rumor." On his head he wore a short-brimmed hat. "They're as bald as a trog---even the women."

The ferry finally reached the Isle of Gar. I followed Centaur and Stick, who followed the horde up the slight slope to the broad avenue that crossed the two-kay wide island.

"Let's try not to get too distracted." Centaur waited for the crowd to disperse before he pushed through to the other side of the island. "Under no circumstances are we to leave the Boulevard. We've come this far without Osquip seizing us. Let's not get complacent now."

It didn't take me long to discover what Centaur meant by DISTRACTIONS. Every block or so I was tempted to examine this or ponder that. Sometimes I simply let the entertainment overwhelm me, becoming immersed for the minute my senses were within range of it. The Isle of Gar was not only Rhinopolis's most eclectic district, it might have been the most creatively diverse enclave in the known universe. Being isolated on an island, the art community was able to feed upon itself without diluting. If it had simply been a region within a civic sprawl, contamination from normalcy would have smoothed the rough edges of the innovative flux.

The Isle of Gar was an incestuous mix of painters and sculptors, performers and musicians, dancers and authors. Most of the artists worked with their mediums in silent ambiguity, but a handful every couple of blocks were more boisterous, performing to exhibit and market. Anything was considered art. One couple was in the process of arousing one another while any who wished to could watch for two coppers. What sacrifices people made for art. The artists were concealed behind an opaque curtain, but a hint was sometimes more erotic than an exhibition. It was also a good marketing tool. Who wouldn't want to peak behind the curtain for just two coppers? Apparently, Centaur did, at least momentarily, because he paused beside the studio.

"Come on." Stick guided his friend's shoulder back onto the Boulevard. "We need to leave Rhinopolis as soon as possible, remember?" Stick's greatest enjoyment was using someone's weapons against them.

"So this entire island is an art bazaar?" I asked. "There can't be enough business to support all the artists here. Do they live as paupers or does the government support them?"

Centaur had shaken off his craving for art and had returned to MISSION ACCOMPLISH mode. Stick and I had to practically jog to keep up with him. "Most of the art studios are in the center of the island, along the Boulevard. Rhinopolis's most expensive estates are on the island's perimeter, what most people refer to as the Riviera. A majority have private marinas. The Rivierans mingle with the artists. They sustain them by purchasing their paintings and books, and bestowing endowments. The most prestigious Rivierans board the most prominent artists and entertainers. Wearing an expensive necklace isn't as stylish as having your personal soprano entertain your guests."

The Boulevard terminated at the western dock, where another ferry, less full, waited. An additional copper was demanded. It departed after it was about half full. The percent of mutes aboard had greatly increased----more than a quarter of the ferry passengers, including a woman barely a meter tall.

She wore a full length gray dress, with black, pointy shoes. A yellow scarf covered her head. She wore a large thatch backpack, half her size, on her back. She clutched the straps in front of her. How was she able to survive on her own? She was either much tougher than she looked, innately elemental, or imprudent. She didn't even carry a weapon.

As soon as the ferry docked, its passengers disembarked, with an impatience the beginning of a long journey demanded. They remained bunched up the first kay, but slowly separated as walking speeds and motivations became distinct. The quickest was the short woman. I understood now why she was able to survive--- nothing could catch her. Centaur, Stick, and I were about in the middle of the pack. We weren't on our way home, or trying to enjoy the scenery.

"How far do we have to walk?" I wasn't concerned with the length of the journey. I had finally acclimated to the arduous Limboan environment, my on-the-job aerobic and strength conditioning paying off. My concern was not reaching Briarwood--- the town on the other side of the Beetlewoods---before dark. Too many dreadful things happened after the sun dimmed.

"Fifty kays," Centaur replied.

"So we're not going to make it before dark, are we?"

"There are a few inns in the Beetlewoods, about halfway between Rhinopolis and Briarwood. We should reach one of them by dinner time."

"Some make it in one day," Stick uttered. He tone indicated he would have liked to be counted among them.

"Only those who get a pre-dawn start."

"We could push through if we wanted to. The Beetlewoods aren't as feral as the Bluewoods. If we keep to the road and...."

"Why take the risk? Arriving a day earlier won't make a difference."

"What about Osquip?"

"I don't think he'll send anyone this far out for us. If he was that determined we would have already been waylaid." Stick became sullen: another opportunity to face death and test his endurance, lost.

"Are the Beetlewoods safer than the Bluewoods because of their proximity to Rhinopolis?" I asked.

175

"That and their proximity to the Frontier, this part of the Frontier," answered Centaur. "Positive mutes inhabit the west. Their goodwill rubs off on the neutral ones nearby."

Being so close to the Frontier reminded me of Pebble. He was obnoxious at times, what one might call a PISS OFF ARTIST, but he did liven things up. Centaur was stoic, and Stick thought too much of himself. Why did Pebble have to die? Were some people more death prone than others? We had been through so much together since our bonding behind the Beetle's Lair, including Pebble being re-created and returning to us. Maybe he could do it again.

The forest kept its distance from the road. Either the hundreds of feet passing through it every day kept the brush and saplings back, or the forest deliberately diminished itself to put some distance between it and them. It wasn't treated with much respect. Litter was everywhere, another consequence of being so close to a major city: old clothing, damaged equipment, ruptured bags, half-eaten sandwiches....

"Why would someone waste a good piece of food like that?" Stick stopped to examine it.

"You're not going to eat that, are you?" From his tone, Centaur wasn't sure.

"Just curious. You can tell a lot from the food someone, or thing, leaves behind. Lipstick traces means a woman probably dropped it. Its freshness indicates how long it has been lying there. Its contents, what type of person he or she is."

"So what did you discover?"

"The person was a vegetarian, with an average sized male mouth."

"An arbol?" I conjectured. "Aren't positive mutes supposed to be kind---to everything---to all animals, vegetables, and minerals?"

"Morality is relative, and often situational," said Centaur. "If a person believes killing an animal is for its own good, he might consider himself to be extremely moral. An extreme case would be someone killing another person to benefit society: an assassination of a dictator or a child abuser. It's unlikely the sandwich came from an arbol. They are stewards of their environment. They would never trash it. If an arbol dropped the sandwich it was because something had startled him, enough for him to forget to pick it back up."

Stick studied the area beside the trash. "Nope. No signs of a struggle. From the freshness of the sandwich there probably wasn't time for the scene of the potential disturbance to be contaminated."

"So the sandwich was probably just dropped by someone too lazy to pick it up?" I asked.

"Yep." Stick continued to examine the sandwich.

"You ARE thinking about eating it," stated Centaur.

Stick jumped back up. "If it wasn't for the alfalfa sprouts I might have. I have my standards. Once the highway clears something will come by to claim it, something with a less discriminating palate. Alfalfa. Blah."

We traveled a couple of kays more, peacefully for the most part, until Stick blurted out, "This must be the most boring road in Limbo. Why does it have to be so strait and level?"

"We could make our own path," Centaur suggested. "If you're willing to forego the safety a well-travelled road provides. It would also take twice as long."

"Blah."

We stayed on the Briarwood Highway. No deviations in the terrain, but above us, clouds began to appear, dark and ominous. Thunder was heard. I was beginning to believe the weather never changed. If the sun was stationary, why couldn't it be sunny every day? Large raindrops began to fall, one to the right, then one to the left, then one in front. The pitter-patter intensified, become a sheet of water within seconds.

"Blah."

Having no rain gear we sought natural protection, rushing into the forest to hide under a tree. We were careful to stay within sight of one another and the road.

I heard a sound coming from inside the tree I stood under. I clutched the trunk as I put my ear against it to investigate. A beetle the size of a medium-sized dog crashed through the bark and grasped my head in its over-sized mandibles. The pressure was intense. I felt that any second my head might implode. I cried out as soon as the beetle lunged for me. It wasn't necessary.

My companions came running when the beetle emerged. Stick was first to reach me. He stabbed the beetle in the middle of its back, creating a loud crunch, followed by a squishing sound. Centaur hit it in nearly the same spot. His battle axe sliced it down the middle. It stopped moving, my head still in its post-mortem grasp. Centaur set his weapon down and grabbed the mandibles, one jaw in each hand. With a strain that caused sweat to bead and blood vessels to be raised, the mandibles were slowly pried apart. Stick cautiously removed my head, being careful he didn't tear any flesh in his urgency to free me.

Even with Stick's delicate removal, my head felt raw in a couple of places. It also felt damp and sticky. I reached to examine it. I looked down at my hands. They looked like they belonged to a small child that had attempted to spread strawberry jelly on a piece of toast.

Centaur removed the healing rod from his pack.

"They're just scratches," I pleaded. I wasn't known for my nobility. Maybe my companions' unselfishness was rubbing off on me. Or maybe I was just a man, who like most men, refused to go to the doctor.

"Possibly, but you may also have internal bleeding. I'm giving you a shot." Centaur squeezed the rod's trigger, transmitting a burst of energy. My skin absorbed the blast first, functioning as a shield. Then the massaging, tingling feeling began to soak in, like lotion. My cuts healed over, and the throbbing in my head lessened, then ceased.

"So that's why this is called the Beetlewoods," I remarked.

"That's one of the more mild varieties," said Centaur. "The rhino beetle has a pair of vertical horns on its forehead. It's larger than a crop beetle, and more fierce. It's always in a bad mood, and it doesn't care who it takes it out on. There's also the stink beetle. It's just 125 sims long, but it expels a noxious gas from its ass. The expulsion is so loud it causes temporary deafness to anyone nearby."

"It has stopped raining," said Stick. "Maybe we can still make it to an inn before dark."

We walked back to the road, but were tackled from above before we could make it. Eight green arms pinned me down. The improved health the healing stone provided renewed my spirit. With vigor I flung my attacker away. The spider smashed into a tree, rupturing its abdomen.

My companions weren't faring as well. Stick looked unconscious, as a spider stuck a tube into his back. Centaur was still active, but fighting off two of them. I struck Stick's opponent first. The jarring jerked the spider off Stick. Before it could recover, I gave it a second whack with my blade that finished it.

Centaur had dispatched one attacker. The other climbed a tree and vanished in the foliage. I grabbed Pebble's bow that had become mine, and cocked an arrow. I watched for the spider to re-emerge. "Don't bother," said Centaur. "I don't think it will attack us again unless it has reinforcements. Spiders don't normally attack humans. They were probably confused by the rain and thunder."

We rushed to Stick's side. He was still breathing, but it was shallow. Centaur injected both a healing and a curing charge into him. He recovered, but still looked weak. "Blah."

"Another healing charge?" I asked. "He must have lost a lot of blood."

"I'll be okay." Stick pushed himself up. "After a hot meal, some sleep...and the companionship of a.... I was going to say arbol, but I don't think I have the energy for her, not for a couple of days."

# Chapter 28

# DINNER

Shortly before dusk we arrived at one of the inns between Rhinopolis and Briarwood. It was not only the smallest inn I had seen on Limbo, it was the most run down. Moss grew on its wooden shingles. A middle-aged man sat on a rocking chair on the front porch. "Pick you out a good bunk," he said in his deep, raspy voice. "Only one other traveler here now, but it will fill up by sundim."

The inn consisted of two rooms: an eat-in kitchen and a bunkhouse. Eleven double-stacked beds were evenly spaced in the 20 by 15 meter room. A large, hairy, dirty man, with a full beard and patched clothing, snored on a lower bunk in one corner. We choose the opposite corner. Centaur and Stick picked lower bunks. I took the bed over Centaur's. We placed our packs and supplemental weapons on the beds, retaining our primary weapons, money, and armor.

We returned to the front porch. Centaur opened the communal wallet. "How much do we owe you?"

"Three coppers each. The protection is free." The innkeeper tapped his axe against the wood planked porch. It looked more like a tool for chopping wood than a weapon for battle. Centaur paid the man a silver. "I don't give change. I'm not a bank."

"What's for dinner this evening?" asked Stick.

"It depends on what you catch. The only charge for using the kitchen is giving its owner a portion."

"I could use a little target practice," said Stick. "Without our art, one of us needs to double up on his duties."

"I'll go with you," I said, not wishing to be alone with the disheveled man or the old coot. "Will you be okay here, Centaur?"

"Just make sure the dinner that's brought back isn't you."

There were many narrow trails leading away from the inn. We chose a trail on the same side of the road as the inn, judging the infinitesimally closer proximity to civilization would make it safer. "What do you think we might catch?" I asked.

"Ticks, poison ivy," Stick replied without a hint of amusement in his voice. "There probably isn't a game animal within five kays of here. If you were a deer or a rabbit would you stick around with a dozen people hunting you every day?"

"Then why are we out here?"

"I need the target practice. Maybe we'll find some squirrels or raccoons."

We heard, then saw birds, but no mammals. We shot at a couple of wild turkeys, me with my bow, and Stick with his crossbow. We both missed. Better under these circumstances than when we were in danger.

"You hear that?" asked Stick.

"Wind? Is it another storm?"

"It's running water. A creek is nearby. Animals frequent ponds and streams. If we're going to find anything by dusk, it'll be there."

We found the creek as the sun began to dim. White-accented water cascaded over stones and collected in pools. I scanned the area, looking first across the creek, then upstream, then finally down it. "I don't see any animals. Shouldn't we head back before it gets too dark to see?"

"Let's wait another couple of minutes. Dusk and dawn are the most popular times for animals to come out."

We waited on a rock overlooking a deep pool. We had a great view of the immediate area, but our prey probably had just as good a view of us. Something struck Stick, stuck to him, then yanked him into the pool. Two long, narrow, rubbery strands were also flung at me. One struck a rock, and was quickly snapped back. The other hit my leg, attaching. I was pulled to the cliff's edge before I was able to find a handhold. I had just enough strength to counter the tension in the line. I couldn't pull myself up, but at least I wasn't being dragged down. With my free hand I removed my dagger from its scabbard and struck outward, slicing the strand in two. The sudden absence of counter-pull thrust me backwards. I almost fell off the outcropping as I slid down. Catching a handhold again, I halted my descent, then pulled myself up. The remnant strand was still attached to me. It looked like a tongue.

I peered into the pool. Stick was beneath its surface. His armor must be too heavy for him to free himself from the water. I thought about leaping in after him, but what good would both of us drowning do? Stick's hands were thrashing frantically. Two frogs, both nearly as large as he, jumped out of the water, landing on the far shore. One of them was bleeding from its mouth. Seconds later they leaped simultaneously 20 meters upstream into the next pool. They submerged from sight. A third frog was still attacking. It and Stick both remained underwater. I waited helplessly for a miracle.

Stick's head burst from the water. He gasped for breath, then dropped back down. A moment later he pulled himself onto the bank beneath the outcropping. I reoriented myself to observe the outcome. Stick dragged the frog by a leg. He flung it halfway up the bank. Water dripped through his armor down his legs. I descended the outcropping then slid down the bank. "Dinner is served," spoke Stick through gasped breaths.

"Do you need a healing stone?"

He put up a single finger. I reached into my wallet for a

stone.  Stick waved me off.  I returned the stone, finally comprehending.

On our journey back to the inn, Stick told his tale, as we dragged the frog, each of us clutching a back leg that was longer than its body.  "It tried to swallow me whole.  With my armor on, and probably even without it, I was too big.  It sought to leave, like its companions.  I held it back.  I wasn't going to endure being dunked without something in return.  It attempted to free itself by kicking away, but I was determined.  All I had available was a dagger.  My crossbow fell into the water and was lost to me, and my sword sheathed.  In my attempt to retrieve it I would have lost the frog.  I caused some significant brain damage before the frog expired."

"Shouldn't we have searched for your crossbow?"

"How far can you see?"  It was almost pitch black.  It was no longer raining, but it was cloudy, blocking the perpetual full moon.  "It looks like you're the one who will need the target practice, at least until we get to Briarwood tomorrow."

"Cut it up at least 100 meters away from the inn," said the innkeeper still in his rocking chair.  "We don't want any scavengers."

We dragged the carcass back into the forest.  We dissected it in minutes, not wanting to be in darkness with fresh meat any longer than we had to.

We returned, each with a hind leg.  The innkeeper for once wasn't on the porch.  The odor of meat cooking wafted from the inn's doorway.  We placed the frog legs on the cooking grill beside the other bits of meat, all much smaller---a rabbit, a raven, two squirrels.

There were considerably more people in the inn than when we left to go hunting.  Half the bunks were full now, and from the number of people in the dining area, the remaining bunks were probably rented out.  Excitement began to build when we entered with the meat. From what was on the grill, the people waiting to eat expected just a bite or two each, enough maybe to supplement their trail rations, not to replace them. Yes, Stick and I had to share, or there would have been a riot. Hearing the increase in noise, some of those resting joined the party, including the hairy man. He still looked half asleep.

The small bits of meat became appetizers, placed on two platters, one on each of the two tables in the dining room/kitchen.

Centaur joined the gathering, looking like he just woke up. "I would have guessed it was you two creating all this ruckus."

"So you don't want any dinner?" asked Stick.

"I didn't say that."

It took nearly an hour for the frog legs to cook through. As they did, the excitement built. Most of the men in the room were freight-haulers. I was surprised that some of them had beasts of burden. "Wasn't it taboo to enslave a creature that may have been your friend in a past life?"

"Generally, but a new philosophy---that we retain our intelligence when we're re-created---has been gaining acceptance, particularly near the Frontier. Domesticating animals therefore does not enslave."

"Who determines how stupid an animal has to be before it's not possible to have been human in a prior life? There are some dreadfully dumb humans and some extremely bright animals."

"I imagine it's a personal choice," Stick broke-in. "Aren't we the ultimate conscience of our actions? Exterior motivators have limitations. It's primarily up to us to create lasting change--- physical, mental, and moral. Nothing someone else can say is as devastating as self-condemnation."

There were four freight-haulers who followed the new philosophy. They tied their oxen to posts beside the inn. If the innkeeper wanted to retain his business, limited as it was, he had to change with the times. The carts the oxen pulled were also beside the inn, as were the carts some of the self-sufficient freight-haulers pulled. There was a noticeable difference in the size of the two varieties of carts. Freight-haulers without carts carried goods on their backs. Muscles developed differently from pulling than from carrying. It was easy to distinguish between the two types of men.

"What are the consequences of killing an intelligent animal?" I continued. "Is it treated like murder? Is the person locked up or fined? Without permanent death capital punishment isn't equitable compensation, or even possible."

"Hunting any non-humanoid is acceptable," Centaur answered. "One doesn't worry too much about extinguishing a life accidentally when the consequences aren't dire. Slavery is much more frowned upon than murder. Have you noticed that none of the freight-haulers ride their oxen? Riding is considered more demeaning than using animals as beasts of burden. I've heard of people riding privately, but even they would feel ashamed if caught. There are some things you just don't do in public."

"I'm surprised how trusting these freight-haulers are with one another. They have all committed crimes. That's why they're here. Their goods aren't locked up. They don't even watch them."

"Freight-haulers understand the potential for thievery, so they have a pact of solidarity, similar to the Human Pact of mutual protection against demons. They promise to look after one another, be it someone taking an apple from a cart, or a goblin charging with a club."

Stick's voice echoed through the room. "I think they're done. LET'S EAT!" The frog legs did taste like chicken. The freight-haulers were exceedingly complimentary. They weren't used to such fine fare en route.

As the meat became scarce and bellies became full, two of the strangest men I had ever seen entered the dining area from the bunkhouse. They wore brown capes with deep hoods that completely covered their heads. Beneath their capes they wore a green robe, tied at the waist by a plain leather belt. Their leather boots were twice as large as mine. Each carried a staff, looking more gnarled and natural than those bought at a weaponry. While they picked at the scraps, they either kept their staves in one hand, or beside them. Facial features couldn't be determined, the depth of their hoods obscuring their contents. They had large pointed noses, that was obvious, and their eyes looked yellow, but that could have been a reflection off the inner lining of their cowls. They didn't speak, either to the inn's other patrons, or to each other. The only time they emitted any sound was when one of them tried to snatch a morsel from his companion. A high-pitched, annoyed grunt caused the hand to return empty. They returned to the bunk room in their awkward BEING CAREFUL WHERE THEY STEPPED saunter.

The hairy man and the innkeeper were the only two up---in addition to Centaur, Stick, and me---when those two strange men returned to the bunkhouse. There were three freight-haulers still up when they entered the dining area, but were frightened away by their strange nature and appearance. The hairy man never fully woke-up. He returned to his bunk a couple of minutes after the strange men did.

Stick whispered to the innkeeper, "Have you ever seen anything so strange?"

"At least those two have two feet and a head." He walked over to his bed in the corner of the room and appeared to instantaneously fall asleep.

We also headed off to bed. The bunks were not as miserable as one may have thought by looking at them. The straw still smelled fresh, and it wasn't too lumpy. Pillows and a blanket were provided. It took awhile for me to fall asleep, being inundated with the numerous sounds twenty men make.

# Chapter 29

# KIDNAPPED

I woke in the middle of the night. I thought I heard something, but whatever it was, the sound didn't return. I had to pee. It wasn't an emergency, but if I didn't do it now I would have to later, probably when I was sleepier. The inn had facilities, but they were outdoors. Couldn't the innkeeper have supplied us with chamber pots? Not for the three coppers a person he charged.

I stepped down, being careful not to step on Centaur. He wasn't in his bunk. Maybe he also had to pee. That's what I heard: him leaving.

I knocked on the outhouse door. No answer. Maybe Centaur had already returned to the inn. He hadn't.

I woke Stick, being careful I didn't make too much noise. The swordsman instantly held a dagger tightly to my throat. He dropped it back into its scabbard just as quickly when he saw who it was. I pointed to Centaur's bunk.

"Did you check outside?" he whispered.

"He wasn't in sight of the inn," I whispered back.

Shock erupted on Stick's face. I turned in the direction he was looking. The two hooded men were also missing.

We put on our armor as quickly and as silently as possible---which wasn't much of either. Surprisingly, the only person to wake was the hairy man. In a deep, calm voice he said, "Time is of the essence. If I knew this area better, I would know how much danger your friend was in. You must prepare yourself. It may be too late."

He seemed to know what he was talking about. We gave

him implicit permission to lead us. He didn't take any weapons with him. He apparently didn't have any. Our confidence in him waned.

The innkeeper was in the kitchen. He was adding the last piece to his full plate. Our mouths dropped. It was 1000 gold to purchase that quality of armor. More amazing was the two-handed sword he withdrew from a metal case padded with red velvet. A platinum octagon in the shape of an hourglass was emblazoned on the blade. It was trimmed in gold. "An Octagonal Knight," Stick choked out.

"The last five years more or less retired," the innkeeper replied. "I believe those two who kidnapped your companion are falicans. I didn't think they were that bold. Their memories of my more, shall we say adventurous lifestyle, must have faded."

"It has been a generation, Knight," spoke the hairy man.

"A revival or a last hurrah, Braeburn?"

"That's still to be determined."

Kidnapping Centaur apparently was the falicans' only goal. They had left his weapons and the communal wallet. Stick snatched the leather pouch from the mattress, where it had lay hidden beneath Centaur.

The last thing I grabbed was a lantern and a flint to light it.

We left the inn, the hairy man leading. Stick and I were out of our league. We allowed ourselves to be led without argument. Time was of the essence if we wanted Centaur returned to us unharmed. We traveled by moonlight---the moon was still concealed in clouds, but not as severely---momentarily shunning the lantern. If the things we followed became aware of our encroachment they might cut their losses, literally.

"Mutes are not what we stereotype them to be," spoke the innkeeper. "They were once human. Many of them retain their morality. Some have weakened moralities. Others, stronger. There are mutes that will help, if given the opportunity."

Braeburn discarded his ragged clothing. His hairy hide became even hairier. His face elongated. His feet grew claws. He slumped down as his body bulked out. Braeburn had transformed into the most feral of bears: a grizzly. Stick and I retreated a step. A smirk from the animal may have been an attempt to reassure, but instead it added a sinister element. A wild animal with a sly intelligence wasn't a mild combination.

"Now he'll be able to track the falicans," said the innkeeper.

A quarter of intense bushwhacking brought us to a hilly area. Many of the hills were rocky, some having indentations, possibly entrances to caves.

Braeburn stopped. He grunted something to the innkeeper, who relayed the information. "There is a labyrinth beneath us. It can be entered from two locations. The more active one is in front of us."

"Why would they want to kidnap Centaur?" I asked. "And just Centaur?"

"One person was probably all they could manage. It's a good sign your friend was the one taken. If they wanted dinner, they likely would have taken the weakest looking of my guests--- perhaps even me." He displayed a wicked grin, nearly as frightening as the grizzly's. "For the falicans to choose who they did, they probably have different plans for him."

"Slavery?" suggested Stick.

"Possibly. For the falicans to live in Neutrality, it's unlikely they're inherently evil. Apathetic to your friend's plight perhaps, but not cruel."

"What's our plan?" I asked, concerned we didn't have the firepower to defeat an entire...flock?

"Every enemy can be defeated. The key is finding their weaknesses, while taking advantage of your strengths. Surprise will be our greatest advantage, so it's best we don't barge in through their front door. If we can sneak in the back way, we might be able to free your friend before they learn he has escaped. Worst case scenario, we just have to fight our way out." From the manner in which he said it, it sounded like just another hoop to jump through, persistence accomplishing the feat more than talent. It likely meant at least one of us needing a healing stone before the evening was over. Was getting injured so common on Limbo that recovery became routine?

Braeburn grunted something. "We need to return to the forest," translated the innkeeper. While safely hidden behind foliage, we saw a bird flying towards the cave. It was wearing a green robe and carried an irregular staff in its human arms. I struggled picturing it wearing a cape, hood, and boots. How did they do it? They looked a little odd, but....

The innkeeper, sensing my thoughts, said, "Some mutes have an innate ability to deceive. Those staves they carry are conduits."

"If they had such abilities wouldn't they have done a better job of concealing their natural form? They may not have looked like birds, but they didn't appear entirely human either."

"A poor disguise is better than no disguise. Their abilities might be minimal, but they were sufficient to accomplish their mission."

"Not entirely, if we free Centaur," said Stick.

We walked around the hill to the other side. Another entry was seen. It wasn't as large as the first, barely wide enough for Braeburn to fit through.

The bear led, followed by the innkeeper, me, then finally Stick. It smelled really bad in there. White gunk covered the floor. I lit the lantern. It flared brightly, then de-intensified, but not enough. I turned a knob, which lowered the wick, diminishing the illumination.

Tarps fluttering in the breeze erupted above us. Hundreds of bats released themselves from their inverted perches and swarmed. Their frenzied shadows danced on the cavern walls and ceiling. I had to escape the madness. I ran into a passage, still carrying the lantern. My companions followed their only source of light. The chaos began to fade, but not entirely. One of the bats had followed us.

I tripped over something ankle high. The bat circled above me like a vulture. A cord lassoed it, then dragged it away, beyond the illumination the tipped over lantern provided. I picked myself up, lantern still in hand. The illumination increased enough to reveal a crab-like animal tearing apart the bat with one claw, as it stuffed its mouth with the other.

"We must go around," the innkeeper declared.

"I think we can take it," countered Stick.

"That isn't the point. An Octagonal Knight cannot attack the righteous. The crab has done us no harm."

"It tripped me," I said.

"It has trained you to move more carefully. We must go around."

We climbed onto a shelf above the crab, cautiously watching it as we passed, as it watched us with its two stalk eyes. It backed up a meter, wanting as little to do with us as we did with it.

High pitched grunts like those emitted from the hooded men began to be heard in the distance. Now aware what they were, they did sound like squawks. We were getting close. The gallery narrowed.

The floor beside Stick rose. It leaned back, like a snake on the precipice of attacking. Stick struck first. "NO!" the innkeeper pleaded in a whispered shriek. But it was too late. Stick's two-handed sword chipped off a fist-sized chunk off the gray slab of stone. The edge of the weapon, where it made contact, showed rust. Three additional strokes dismantled the monster, but in doing so destroyed the sword. It fell to the ground in pieces, piling into a corroded mass. Stick threw the hilt of his sword down and withdrew his short sword from its scabbard.

"Allow me next time," said the innkeeper. His opportunity came a moment later. His sword not only didn't rust, it sliced through the stone like a knife through butter.

"It's enchanted," Stick whispered to me. "It's worth as much

191

as his armor."

"You didn't think their back door would be undefended did you?"

Braeburn stopped. It began to get cold. The floor in front of him looked like the stone and dirt behind him, but its texture was as rubbery as clay. The temperature continued to drop. The bear backed away. The floor was covered wall to wall with that stuff, but for only four meters. "We could leap across," Stick suggested.

"Braeburn feels that it might leap up at us, like that last thing did," said the innkeeper. "There is only so much heat loss a person can take. A direct hit will likely freeze a person to death."

"Maybe we can burn it," I suggested.

"Let me see that lantern," spoke Stick. I handed it to him, but hesitantly. He wasn't really going to throw our only light source at that stuff, was he?

Stick opened the lantern's oil reservoir. He dipped the rag he used to clean his sword into it. He sealed the reservoir, then dangled the dripping cloth over the lantern's flame. It caught fire, instantly. He flung it towards the stuff on the floor, an instant before the flames reached his hand. Not soon enough. As he shook his hand, the brown goo tripled in size.

"If heat makes it grow," said the innkeeper, "cold should shrink it."

I opened my water flask and flung its contents onto the floor. Nothing happened except me getting colder, due to my increased proximity to the creature.

"It's not cold enough," said the innkeeper.

Stick fished through the communal wallet. He swallowed a stone. "GET OUT OF THE WAY!" He raised his arms, pointing them in the direction of the creature. A white wave shot from his fingertips into the creature. It shrunk to its original size, then crusted over, looking like something kept in the freezer too long.

Stick leapt over it. We followed his example, not willing to risk contact. "Is it dead?" I asked "Or hibernating?"

"Let's hope we're not around to find out," said the innkeeper.

Braeburn paused again. He grunted to the innkeeper unhappily. "We made too much noise back there. Two falicans are approaching to investigate. We need to be prepared."

We stopped in a medium-sized cavern. There were boulders to hide behind. Braeburn and the innkeeper choose ones on the far side of the cavern. I choose one farther away. I had my bow cocked with an additional arrow beside me. No longer having a crossbow, Stick crouched behind a boulder about halfway between me and the others, his short sword ready. His primary job was to guard me, backing up Braeburn and the innkeeper, if needed.

The falicans walked sternly into the cavern, firmly clutching their staves. Having the only ranged weapon, I was first to attack. The initial arrow hit, grazing one of the falicans in the side. The second arrow wasn't released quickly enough. The falican not hit raised a hand. An invisible force struck me in the chest, knocking the wind out of me.

The distraction allowed Braeburn and the innkeeper to attack from both sides at near point blank range. The Octagonal Knight's enchanted sword ripped through the robe and armor of his opponent, dispatching the falican instantly.

Braeburn's attack took longer, but was just as deadly. The falican's staff slid off his massive bear hide. One claw struck the creature and attached, then the other. Braeburn squeezed it to death.

Stick frowned. "You two didn't leave anyone for me."

"I'm sure you'll get your ration before the day is done," said the innkeeper. "You okay?" He looked at me.

"Bruised ribs at worst," I replied. "Nothing to waste a healing stone on."

"I believe our advantage of surprise has returned. We need to push if we don't want to lose it again."

It wasn't that much farther to the falicans' lair. One

additional brief skirmish was all it took to conquer them. A second energy pulse struck, this time hitting Braeburn. To show his displeasure, he stood on his hind legs and growled. The remaining five falicans cringed in a corner. One of them recovered enough to grab the innkeeper by an arm, in an attempt to electrocute him. Octagonal Knights must be resistant to certain attacks, because he barely flinched. The innkeeper didn't have to strike back. The falican's expression of unconditional surprise, then defeat, terminated the battle.

Centaur was found sleeping in a corner, drugged to keep him in line. He was confused when woken, but capable of walking. He kept muttering something about it not being fair to be sent to bed without dessert.

The innkeeper spoke to the surviving falicans briefly, in their language. They bowed to him, gave him a sack full of something, then bowed once more.

"They won't kidnap anyone from the inn again," stated the innkeeper. After we were safely out of the cave complex he summarized his conversation with them. "They were extremely apologetic. Your friend wasn't going to be harmed. They needed a little help around their house after their mother died. Centaur was chosen because he was the largest. Larger meant being able to do more. Their mother was larger, and she did more. I reminded them of their mother. That's what all that bowing was about. As a self imposed punishment, they gave us this sack of coins." The innkeeper threw it on the ground for us to examine. Copper, silver, even gold, coins, hundreds of them, tumbled out.

"So Centaur's discomfort didn't come without compensation." Stick looked at his short sword with disgust. He had already spent the money---mentally. Maybe after replacing his sword and crossbow there would even be enough left over for a nice meal: dinner in Briarwood.

"Once treasure comes into an Octagonal Knight's possession it must be dispersed, to the people needing it the most." Stick's mouth dropped. How quickly found money disappeared, especially after it was already spent. "It's customary for it to be taken to the Octagonal Prism first, but since I'm about as far from it as one can possibly be I'll have to use my own judgment. I'll start with those self-powered freight-haulers. They have an arduous job that rarely gets the respect it deserves."

"I've been wondering about something," I said. "I thought Limboans were sterile. How could the falicans have children?"

"Mother and father are terms mutes sometimes use for people who have spent a longer time in a similarly altered form. Aunt and uncle are also used. Or granny or grandpa if a person has been in that form a particularly long time."

Upon returning to his clothes, Braeburn transformed back into a hairy man. "Invigorating."

# Chapter 30

## OCTAGONAL KNIGHT

We ate a hearty breakfast before heading to Briarwood. The freight-haulers hit the road at dawn, about the time the falicans' lair was reached, so it was a peaceful and quiet endeavor. The innkeeper was melancholy. "I guess I'm going to have to wait until today's group arrives to distribute the wealth. But not all is lost. I haven't felt so alive in years. The physical and emotional exertion has re-invigorated me. Maybe it's time I returned to a more active role in the order."

His enthusiasm carried over to breakfast. He shared fresh

fruit he had been saving in his root cellar. "Some travelers barter instead of paying with coin. The apples and pears came from the foothills of the Platinum Mountains, the raspberries and strawberries from the Berry Peninsula, the oranges and grapefruit from the Sun Coast." He also placed bread and cheese on the table they shared in the dining room. "The cheese comes from Spring Valley. Its proximity to Gulag gives me an excuse to wander through its idyllic fields and groves at least once every pilgrimage to the Octagonal Prism." He became melancholy again.

Stick was as a positive person, but even he was becoming depressed. The dourness needed to be abated. "You've displayed some impressive fighting skills. How does one become an Octagonal Knight? Is there an academy?"

The innkeeper's eyes sparkled. One corner of his mouth curled. He didn't want to fully commit to bliss, his emotions being so precarious that morning. "Training is on the job."

"So anyone who wishes to can become an Octagonal Knight, if they have the ability, and desire?"

"The Octagonal Order limits their numbers, preferring quality over quantity. Eight is the number of dual-axis moralities, primary and secondary."

"Why not nine?" I asked. "Isn't neutrality a morality?"

"It's inert. Adding a zero to the front of a number doesn't change its value." That sounded too much like what people thought of people like me: balanced in physical, intellectual, and emotional attributes.

"So the only way someone can become an Octagonal Knight is when there's an opening?" asked Stick. "When a Knight retires or dies?"

"Exactly. For an Octagonal Knight, they are synonymous. Before he can retire he must be defeated, by the hand of his successor."

"So anyone who kills an Octagonal Knight takes his title, his armor, his power, and his respect and admiration?"

"Only if the Octagonal Knight accepts a challenge."

I was confused. "So if an Octagonal Knight dies for some reason other than losing a challenge, he remains an Octagonal Knight when he is re-created? It must be cumbersome at times for a Knight to reclaim his armor and weapons."

"That's if an Octagonal Knight is re-created. If he never dies he can't be re-created."

"But you said he must be killed by his successor."

"I said defeated. At the brink of death an Octagonal Knight's essence is transported to the Octagonal Prism, as is his armor and weaponry. The Prism assists in the replenishing of flesh around his essence. An Octagonal Knight must remain pure, to have never been re-created. The first time he experiences death is when a challenger defeats him."

"So if I wanted to be an Octagonal Knight," asked Stick, "I couldn't have been re-created?"

"Once a man has been touched by Gaea he forfeits his potential acceptance into the Octagonal Order. You see how difficult it is then to become an Octagonal Knight. An individual not only has to have the good fortunate of a Knight accepting his challenge, he has to defeat him. Those young enough to never been re-created usually don't have the experience to do so. But those miniscule few who do are richly rewarded. Not only do they take possession of the platinum arms and armor, acquire the title of the 3$^{rd}$ or 7$^{th}$ Knight, and adopt all the respect and fear that's attached to it, they are privileged to become DEFENDERS OF THE PEOPLE."

The conversation was successful in stimulating Centaur out of his slumbered stupor. "I can't imagine anyone no longer wanting to be an Octagonal Knight."

"Even a noble life becomes tedious after awhile. Escape from eternal excitement becomes desirable. But does taking a vacation from it mean having to give it up? Perhaps it does. Weary Knights often seek a fight, hoping they can find their harbinger of doom and salvation. Does anyone wish to challenge me?"

After the food was consumed, it was time to leave the Octagonal Knight to his deliberations. "Thank you for rescuing me," said Centaur. The innkeeper, for he was as much that now as he was a DEFENDER OF THE PEOPLE, nodded. Braeburn bowed deeply. A vision popped into my head, of a bear clawing the ground.

"And for the food." To Stick, pampering his belly WAS saving his life. Another nod from the innkeeper.

Packs were placed on backs and feet began to move. Still within sight of the inn, but just barely, Braeburn caught up with us. "May I tag along? It's time for me to return home. I live just inside the Frontier."

"We would be honored," said Centaur. "Thank you again for liberating me from the falicans."

"They are a bit misguided, but not evil. They just needed to be taught to be more respectful." And squeezing one of them to death must have been the lesson.

Midday, nine large wolves crossed the road in front of us. They stopped in the middle, blocking our way. Centaur, Stick, and I unsheathed our weapons. Before we were able to approach them, Braeburn, still in his human form, ran up to them, growling. They ran off, kicking dirt up behind them. "Infants---and toddlers---die more often from mental mistakes, than from physical ones," he said after we caught up to him. "One doesn't have to fight to prevail. Choosing to not engage is often the best course."

"But sometimes one has to fight," Stick stated.

"Yes, sometimes we are forced to fight, when the two sides are evenly matched and neither side wishes to back down, or when one side has something to prove, even when it has the potential for providing its downfall."

"Sometime things don't go your way, no matter what you do." I knew as soon as he saw the innkeeper fighting, Stick would want to become an Octagonal Knight. But he couldn't, could he? He had been re-created once, just once, but once was one time too many to become an Octagonal Knight. "But if one works hard, most obstacles can be overcome"

"But we'll never earn perfection."

"Did someone mention me?" spoke the ethereal voice of our intermittent companion. Lynn leapt into the road in front of us. I had subconsciously deleted her from our company. Aware it wasn't wise to discard assistance, from anyone, in any form, I allowed my brief ill-feelings to dissipate.

"Pebble died again," stated Centaur glumly.

"We feel he has been completely transformed this time," I said, "and has been re-created far from here. Another of your predictions has come true."

"Where have you been?" asked Stick.

"Dryads are known for charming handsome young men, and using them as chattel, until they get bored with them, which releases their hold. I thought it would be entertaining to charm one of them. Truffle was catnip in my paws. She fell completely in love with me. She stroked me and washed me---cat style of course---and fed me exotic dishes on the table as she ate on the floor. I left her just moments ago. I must return to her shortly, so I can gradually wean her of her devotion. But how can one wean a heavy heart? I'll return after you leave Briarwood." The lynx vanished back into the forest.

"I didn't know cats could be so romantic," said Braeburn.

"Let's hope she finds the cat of her dreams soon," said Centaur. "To be battle ready I need to be able to keep my food down."

# Chapter 31

# SHRIEK

Briarwood, having the same population and geography as Bluewood City, looked similar, but was more lively, both in the number of people who came and went, and in the passion those people performed their daily routines. We were near the Frontier, the part of it that was inundated with chaos. Ideas were exchanged on every topic. No opinion was too extreme. The village appeared to be less taken care of than Bluewood City. Its streets were full of litter and in ill-repair, and some of its citizens should have been in jail for the mischief they were creating. Was one city better than another, or just different?

I was surprised when no one met us at the village boundary. "Don't they want to collect their protection fee?"

Braeburn answered. "Some settlements have militias. A sales tax pays for Briarwood's minimal expenses."

We shared a room at the MUSKY FOOT, an inn with an active night life. Entertainers performed on stage in the great room for tips. Everyone in Briarwood was an aspiring actor or singer, the village merely the springboard for their career. One day they hoped to entertain paying patrons on the stages of Sunset City or Rhinopolis, or Gulag. A majority of the entertainers were dancers, how the inn got its name.

It was a treat to see a woman on Limbo, more so a beautiful one. The dancer currently on stage didn't have the best this, or the best that, but when all of her attributes were combined she looked striking. She looked familiar. Maybe that's what caught my eye.

But who could she be? Was it someone I knew before my incarceration? It had to be. I had been on Limbo just a week.

The crowd cheered when the dancer left the stage. I dropped a silver into her bowl, on top of coppers. I felt guilty about it, considering it was half the amount we spent for our room, but it was so rare when I splurged. I wasn't the only one enchanted with her. Two men followed her out the door.

"You should follow her, too," suggested Stick.

"For the amount you donated, you could have had dessert in Rhinopolis," stated Centaur.

But I didn't leave the inn. I wasn't very bold when it came to women, and I definitely didn't want to fight for her.

A woman shrieked. NO, NOT HER! We rushed outside. The woman had been stabbed to death. A pool of blood grew beside her. If I went outside when she did, I might have been able to save her. Then I remembered where I saw her. She was the woman who had been killed by the wild dogs. How did she get ahead of me? She must have been constantly traveling after she was re-created. Or was she already on a short path to becoming a mute? Sometimes a person was re-created somewhere for no particular reason. Twice I had almost saved her. If I only reacted a little quicker.

I had enough of the night's entertainment. My friends followed me back to the room we rented, to console me, but it was also an excuse for rugged men to give in to their weariness. How many days had it been since we had a good night's sleep?

# Chapter 32

# NAILS

We woke refreshed, having slept three hours undisturbed. There were no night watches, no forced marches, no attacks in the middle of the night, no kidnappings.

I yawned. "Maybe we should spend an extra day in Briarwood."

"We can't lay up now," Stick pleaded. He had slept soundly like the rest of us, but as soon as the moon began to brighten, he leapt out of bed and bounced from one place to another. The only way a person could have forced him to sit back down was to lasso him, and that was only if the rope was strong enough. A switch had been turned on and couldn't be turned off until the timer expired, seven or so hours later.

"One does not hibernate before eating." Braeburn began the night in his bed, but by morning he was curled on the circular area rug in the center of the room in bear form. He looked embarrassed, like he was caught doing something he shouldn't have been doing. He returned to human form immediately, but having a naked man curled on your floor was nearly as bad as having a bear there. Braeburn stretched as he worked his way to an erect position.

On our way out of town I searched---visually---for the body of the woman who had been killed the night before, compulsion overwhelming revulsion. Her corpse was gone. Some things in Briarwood were cleaned up. The ground where she laid appeared groomed. There was no sign of blood, or even a struggle. I wondered if I would see her a third time. Would she greet me from the middle of the Copper Forest? Good for me, but that meant she was mutated out of humanity. Someone that lovely didn't deserve to be cursed like that. But being beautiful didn't necessarily make someone a good person. That was the fallacy with fairy tales. Characters were either heroes or villains, and the stories always ended the way you thought they would. On Limbo people didn't live happily ever after.

With a forced, but affable pace, we headed west, towards Wilson. The town was just inside the Frontier, the last human controlled settlement before the Copper Forest. "You'll reach Wilson by dark, assuming you don't have too many delays," said Braeburn.

"You, not we?" Centaur questioned.

"Did you forget? I'll be leaving you once we enter the Frontier. I've enjoyed the companionship, but my home beckons. I've been away too long."

"So it's true," said Stick. "Mutes get homesick."

"I heard it's more like a drug withdrawal," said Centaur.

"Maybe somewhere in between. It's not physically painful to be away, but emotionally…. It's like you're in love, newly in love, and you find it difficult to be away from that special someone. The unrelenting desire builds. I've heard of some of the Changed becoming so distraught their bodies can't handle the strain. They die from the anguish. I think it's more likely they died from committing suicide."

"Won't that hurt them more in the long run?" I asked. "Won't becoming more mutated make the Longing stronger?"

"It doesn't work that way. Once a person becomes changed enough to be re-created in the Frontier he becomes inflicted with the Longing. Being around someone with a cold if you already have a cold won't make your cold worse. The Longing does vary from person to person, but the severity of mutations generally doesn't affect the degree. When one of the Changed dies they usually retain their morality, which means they are re-created in the Frontier, which alleviates the Longing."

The terrain to the west of the Beetlewoods consisted of dry straw-grass and sage. If we had gone north to Sunset City, humidity would have set in already, the terrain transforming into swamp by the time the town was reached. Instead, we began to see large boulders, carelessly scattered across the eternal field. Marmots, monstrous yellow-bellied rodents, squeaked their disapproval, our passage forcing them to abandon their sun spa to scorn the interlopers.

A stone plain extended for kays before us. Boulders continued. The landscape looked like a game board. Cairns---rocks stacked on top of one another---guided us.

Our first delay---of the day---occurred there. A scuttling sound, like a dog's nails across a floor, was followed by an acrid smell. Nothing was seen yet, but that wasn't surprising, considering the cover the boulders created.

"It's safer to wait them out." Braeburn halted, abruptly. "They'll come to us." He transformed into a bear before we were able to ask what THEY were.

"Four corners defense," Centaur commanded. Without debate Stick and I did what we were told. Without consultation Braeburn took Pebble's usual position. It, apparently, wasn't the first time he was under siege. We drew our weapons and raised our shields. The proximity of the boulders made it improbable to release an arrow before whatever was making that sound was upon us.

The scuttling intensified, vibrating the stone beneath us. The sound echoed across the game board, swirling around the rocky monoliths, making it difficult to ascertain which direction it came. The scraping slaps began to drill their way into our cores, like water dripping, or nails on a chalk board.

They finally appeared, startling us, even with us anticipating their arrival. The anticipation had been as frightening as the actual confrontation, maybe more so. The unknown we couldn't control. Helplessness was mortifying. We now knew what to expect. We didn't like what we saw, but we had at least a foundation from which to prepare.

There were three of them---two meters long, six legs, two pincers, a beak-like mouth, and one long flexible tail with a dagger at its tip. "Their most dangerous attack will come from their tail," said Centaur. "While they mesmerize you with their claws and their movement, their tails snake around and sneak in an attack. The point secretes venom that will cause the area struck to swell upon contact. The swelling spreads as your veins feel like they're on fire. In less than a minute your heart is consumed. You die, but your body continues to transform. Eventually your flesh becomes tender in the marinade of your own juices. Then they feast."

We watched them vigilantly, readying ourselves for a strike. There was no margin for error. If one of us went down, we might all go down. A pillar displaced could topple an entire building. A flank unprotected could create the wedge needed to split us apart.

The positioning intensified. A leg moving a meter caused an arm to move an identical distance. A sword extended was countered by the twisting of a torso, or the raising of a claw.

One side flinched too dramatically, and the brawl was on, a chaotic every man or monster for him or itself battle to end all battles. I was concerned for Braeburn. He didn't have expensive protection like the rest of us. It didn't matter. Experienced reflexes did as much for him as our armor did for us. And we needed it. All of us, Centaur, Stick, and I, were hit at least once, our armor deflecting blows, including ones from stingers. After one of the scorpions was struck down---in the madness of battle, I wasn't even sure by whom---the other two quickly followed, like dominoes. Their defense had been as precarious as ours. One member out meant their offense, and defense, was reduced by a third. They were overwhelmed.

The bitter odor of their venom was what I remembered

most from the event.  Whenever I ate or smelled something bitter, I remembered those over-sized scorpions on that rocky plain.

# Chapter 33

# SPECTRAL

Shortly after resuming our journey we saw the Western Sea. The turquoise, florescent water miraculously darkened, almost to black, whenever a cloud blocked out the sun.  Then just as miraculously began to glow as the cloud moved away.  Two worlds beckoned on the whims of water vapor.

The road meandered through transforming terrain.  Dry straw became coastal saw-grass.  Hills became dunes, some bald, some scattered with vegetation.  The Copper Highway paralleled the coastline atop a bluff.  At times, the saltwater slapped against the bluff.  At other times, its energy expired on salt and pepper beaches.

"The shore will become rocky with boulders and cliffs when you reach the Copper Coast," Braeburn declared.  Once the danger was alleviated he had returned to his human form.  I had a feeling if there weren't humans to communicate with he would have remained a bear.  There was a peacefulness he exuded as an animal he didn't as a human.  He appeared to be unsettled when he was a man.  He looked uncomfortable, not in any pain, more like being at a party where he didn't know anyone.

"What form were you in when you were first re-created in the Frontier?" Stick asked him.  "Did you learn to transform, or did you transform in an attempt to return to your original form?"

"The latter. I've heard of both occurring, but usually the animal form comes first."

"You just think about becoming a bear or a man and you change?" asked Centaur.

"Something like that, but if I think about it too much a block is formed and it doesn't happen. It's much easier to transform into a bear. That's now my natural form. If I just let myself go, trying not to think human thoughts, I'll become hairy and bulk out almost instantly."

"Like last night," I said.

"My intention was to return to human form before anyone woke. Bears like their sleep."

"You mentioned HUMAN THOUGHTS," said Centaur. "Aren't all our thoughts human? Even you must have human thoughts while you're human."

"Some thoughts are universal, others remind us we are human, so unique that only a human would think them. Thought patterns are as distinctive as finger prints or scribbling out our name."

"So for you to transform into a bear in your sleep you must dream as a bear," I conjectured.

"At times. Other times I dream as a man. Sometime the two become confused."

"You don't partially transform then, do you?" asked Stick.

"No, though some changelings do, even when they're awake. If one set of thought patterns isn't substantially stronger than the other, to displace them, the form I am currently in retains."

"What does a bear think about? Do you find female bears attractive? If a beautiful human woman walked naked in front of you, would you just yawn?"

"It depends on how hungry I was." Sensing our uncertainty, he added, "I haven't eaten anyone---human or animal---since I was re-created in the Frontier.

"I have memories of my alternate form. Flashes of thoughts. Instead of seeing spectral images, I think spectral thoughts."

"What does a bear think about? Everything I've read says animals think about primary needs: food, safety, procreation if they're in heat."

"Females go into heat. Males of most species are always in the mood. That's why dogs rub up against your leg. They aren't bright enough to know it's not a female dog. Actually, I don't know what a bear thinks, because when I'm in bear form I'm influenced by human thoughts, as am I bombarded by bear thoughts while in human form. I can tell you how my thoughts differ in my two forms. When I'm a bear life becomes simpler. I rarely think about what will happen tomorrow, and never what will happen a year from now. I don't worry as often. If I have a full belly and a place that's not too hot or too cold to lie down I'm generally content."

"So as we continue to evolve we become less happy?" I hypothesized.

"Becoming wealthier doesn't make us happier," stated Centaur. "Why should it be different with intelligence?"

"The trees have it right."

"What did you say?"

"Oh, just something I heard awhile back."

# Chapter 33

## ROAR

A herd of sea lions clustered on a narrow strip of beach. Being Limbo, they actually looked like lions, the front half of them. Their lower torsos looked more like walruses. The males had manes the texture and color of seaweed. What they had most in common with the land felines was their roar. And roaring seemed to occupy most of their daily activities, from what we heard.

We couldn't see what they were roaring at, initially, the bluff concealing the direction they were facing. A paw swung at something. It didn't reach its intended victim, stopping mid-motion. The entire pride attacked. A reptilian head emerged, then claws and a tail. We hurried around a bend in the coastline so we might see part of the battle before it was over. Two more lions stiffened where they stood. Seven were still moving, two of them for just a moment. Their bloody bodies toppled over. A yellowish liquid drained from their mouths. Six great lizards, twice as long as the sea lions, also lay dead, their bodies sliced and torn in dozens of places. The marine cats licked one another's wounds, including the two that had fallen. The three frozen were ignored. After five minutes of washing and comforting, the remaining male placed a paw on each of the fallen. The four females dropped to their haunches. The sorrowful roar emitted from the upturned head of the male skimmed the surface of the sea, meandered through the saw-grass, ultimately penetrating the worthiest part of our souls.

"Will the three frozen revive?" I asked Braeburn.

"Possibly. Paralysis differs from one species to another.

Sometimes the muscles are only affected and loosen within the hour. Those victims recover completely. Sometimes the cells solidify. A majority of the time the state is temporary. When they finally soften, the victim usually doesn't survive the shock. Those that retain their solidity have become petrified, their cells transformed to stone through eternity."

"They didn't look like they changed to stone," said Stick, "so they may recover."

"Does ignoring them mean they no longer exist? Or just not at this moment?"

"Wouldn't they have said good-bye if they believed they weren't returning?" I suggested.

"Are you proposing spending the afternoon here to find out?" asked Centaur.

I wasn't, so we resumed our journey. Another couple of hours and we'll be in Wilson. Another bed. Another prepared meal. Then what? How many days after that would we be on our own? Camping. Cooking our own food. Living off the land when our rations ran out. Should I have stayed in Bluewood? Too late now to change my mind.

# Chapter 35

# FRONTIERS

I expected something special when we arrived at the Frontier. A rainbow, perhaps? Or a unicorn sentinel. There was a stone marker. Chiseled into it were two symbols: an addition sign, and a starburst. "Shouldn't there be a gate or something?"

"Moral boundaries are more mental than physically," said Braeburn. "The Changed can pass from the Frontier to Neutrality at will. The Longing draws us back, eventually. If it wasn't for the Longing those negatively inclined would be able to terrorize the entire world, instead of just its fringes."

"So there are worse things than falicans and scorpions?"

"And better."

"Is the boundary separating the Frontier from Neutrality stable?"

"It's an approximation. Politics are involved. Most settlements don't wish to be viewed as too extreme. A few prefer the notoriety."

"With no one dying and people continuing to be sentenced here, most of them mutating, won't the Frontier eventually fill up? Shouldn't the boundary be moving inward to compensate?"

"It has---in the east, where the negative Changed live. Some call that area the IMMORAL BULGE.

"It's time for us to split ways. My home is southwest of here. Wilson is due west. Continue to follow the road. May your journey be short. If you push, you can make it to Wilson in an hour."

We waved as Braeburn veered from the road. Ever since we entered the Frontier, I noticed a change in him. He became more at peace, but also more distant. We were no longer what was important to him. Family and country beckoned, and maybe the god of his creation and re-creation. He felt secure and invincible. He had returned to the womb. A hundred meters away he ripped away his clothes. A larger, much hairier creation appeared. He lowered his head, clutching his clothes in his mouth, then began to run. He was out of sight before we resumed our strides.

I expected to feel something unpleasant when I entered the Frontier: indigestion perhaps or insects crawling over me. Instead, if felt like I was sinking into a warm bath, a soothing of my emotions instead of my muscles. The effect was certainly more psychological than physical. Being male I was too insecure to express my feelings, so I never learned if Centaur and Stick felt the same.

# Chapter 36

# RIBBONS

Wilson was smaller than Briarwood, about one-third its population, but it looked even smaller. Briarwood was lively, markedly so. Wilson was excessively tame, in an attempt to contain the chaos surrounding it. Chaos had a tendency to expand. Order organized, condensed. Towns were primarily built by humans for human occupation, but humans were a minority in Wilson. The humans that were present had tense looks on their faces, like teachers at the end of the day. Wilson's mutants took delight in the humans' uptightness. They taunted and played practical jokes. We felt uncomfortable being there, but we didn't wish to abandon a soft bed, likely the last we'll enjoy for many weeks.

The innkeeper of the WASTED WHALE was excited to book a room full of humans. "Arbols are the worst. Those monkeys re-arrange the furniture. Sometimes I can hear their perverted ruckus. Trogs are better. Their stout hides aren't as nimble. The only time they get on my nerves is when they chant. I fear Satan will come up through my floor to take them home every time they begin one of their pagan rituals."

From the window in our room we saw a half-dozen fishing boats in the harbor, and nearly as many catamarans. The latter were occupied by mer, a less tame variety of the ones we saw in Rhinopolis. They were more aquatic looking, with green-tinted skin instead of blue. Their gills and webbed feet weren't the only things they exposed. They were nude, except for a small loin cloth. The females' chests were pierced, with colorful ribbons hanging from silver rings. It was too much for me. I sought a shower, on the cool side.

Every time we came within sight of the innkeeper, he wanted to talk to us. I felt he should have paid us to stay in his inn.

"I think I'm going to do some exploring," Stick stated. All three of us were affected by the sight of the mer women, but Stick's method of coping was more direct than either Centaur's or mine.

"The mer put on a good display," said Centaur, "but when you try to make a transaction the product isn't available. Chaotic mutes like to play games. If a person misconstrues the rules of the game, sometimes the game ends unpleasantly. An ambassadorial excursion may delay us. This time tomorrow we'll be entering the Copper Forest."

"Okay," Stick replied begrudgingly. Now it was his turn to take a cold shower.

Like the night before, we turned in early. The two large bowls of seafood gumbo each of us had may have had something to do with that.

I dreamed of the woman who had been killed twice within meters of me. I must have combined thoughts of her and the mer, because I had to take another shower in the morning.

# Chapter 37

# AMBITIONS

We left the Wasted Whale early in the morning.  We woke simultaneously, a quarter before dawn.  We were done with sleep, having more important things to do.

"Please stay," the innkeeper pleaded.  "For every night you pay I'll let you stay the next free."

"Maybe some other time."  Centaur kept on walking.

"Could you throw in a free breakfast?" asked Stick.

"Come on."  Centaur's tone was as effective as grabbing him by the arm.  Stick became more focused on leaving, but not completely.  He hadn't been as ambitious as Centaur in wanting an early start.  He had paused every couple of steps while crossing the inn's great room.  He was looking for something.  A few steps from the exit he finally spotted it.  He leapt at the remnants of a drumstick of questionable origin and cleanliness.

"THAT MIGHT MAKE YOU SICK!"

"But not for a couple of hours."

I was last to leave.  It wasn't that my stomach led me around, like Stick.  The further back I was the longer I delayed the unpleasantness the Copper Forest represented.  I knew I would reach it eventually, but that didn't eradicate those precious seconds I procrastinated.  I used to be the type of person that wanted to get discomfort over with, quickly.  That was before I lived in a place where the undesired never ceased.  Hurrying permitted more opportunities for unpleasantness.

The innkeeper continued to follow us, still clinging to a

thread of hope. I felt stalked. My residual seconds of contentment were being annihilated. I had to confront the man. "If you don't like it here why don't you move?"

"This is my home. I shouldn't be the one to leave. Why can't people just stay where they are?"

"So, you're saying that you have always lived in Wilson?"

"I live here now."

"And you expect no one else to relocate since you stopped moving?"

"Everyone will be happier if they lived with their own kind. Why can't demons stay in the Frontier?"

"Wilson's in the Frontier."

"Cities don't count. I meant in the real Frontier, in the Wilds. That's where demons are supposed to live. Only those still civilized, those retaining their humanity, should live in the cities."

"We're on the way to the Wilds. We'll make the savages there aware of your concerns."

"Would you?" The innkeeper smiled, then headed back towards the inn. He had followed us to the edge of the village.

Why did I feel so protective of the mutes? I didn't fear them the way the innkeeper did, but I wasn't excited to be in their prescience either. Was I a hypocrite? Did knowing someone who was a mute make a difference? I didn't want to be one of those people who spoke about being friends with a mute every time he met a group of them.

"It looks like your friends are gone, Stick." Centaur stopped at a bluff outside the village. It overlooked the harbor. It was finally light enough to see that far, but just barely. The four mer catamarans were no longer moored. They had either left earlier in the morning or sometime during the night. Stick saluted the ocean. "Something as exotic as a mermaid is enticing, but nothing good will come of it, in the long run. Would you be happy having a relationship with someone with gills?"

"I'd be willing to try. We still have that water breathing

rod."

"But what happens when her prince turns back into a landlubber? Don't mer dry out on land? If they don't submerse themselves every hour or so their skin looks worse than Pebble's before his last re-creation. If they stay out longer than that they eventually dehydrate, to death. You wouldn't want that on your conscience, would you? There is no guarantee your potential lady friend will be re-created as a mer. You wouldn't want to deny her the freedom of living in the fluidity of the sea."

"I wasn't thinking about a lifetime commitment. There are some things you can do in water that you can't do in air, or so I've imagined."

"No, it's better you don't get involved at all. An individual mer might be willing to do some inter-species experimenting, but her people as a whole wouldn't be so welcoming to the relationship. You wouldn't want to be responsible for starting a race war, would you?"

Stick sighed. From the raising of an eyebrow, and a glancing towards the sky, then the harbor, he was in fact weighing the pleasure he would receive from such an encounter with the potential doom of the local community. Stick sighed again. "Maybe another day."

Now that Wilson, and the mer, were behind us we could focus on the termination of our quest. How exactly were we going to pry an emerald pearl from tree dwelling mutants? We still hadn't come up with a concrete plan.

"It will just work itself out," Stick asserted.

"No, we need a plan," Centaur insisted.

"Then what is it? Maybe I could woo an arbol princess."

"I thought you decided having a romance with a mute wasn't a good an idea."

"You were the one who decided that. I begrudgingly went along with it. An arbol is different than a mer. They don't have gills or live in the water."

"They do live in trees. I don't think you would enjoy falling out of one. If you become too enamored you might not be paying enough attention to your surroundings."

"I can multi-task. I'll be willing to take one for the team."

The road continued up the coastline, the terrain looking very much like it did the day before. We saw no one, and I mean NO ONE, west of Wilson. Who in their right-mind would chose to travel through the Frontier? But we should have seen freight-haulers. There were a few human settlements in the Frontier, and the less-mutated traded goods. Where was everyone? Did freight only travel by sea in this part of Limbo? Was the terrain so harsh foot travel was unreliable?

Clouds covered half the sky, parts of them looking dark and thunderous. "If I find my mate today it'll be a gorgeous day," spoke a voice in my head. "Predictions about myself are usually muddled."

"Do you intentionally reward us by leaving for an extended period of time?" asked Centaur. "Or do you have an additional excuse for your delay?"

Lynn appeared in the saw-grass beside the road. Her expression was a mixture of glee and embarrassment. "Life is a complicated combination of choices and uncontrollable circumstance. The dryad wasn't as helpless as my pride forced me to believe. Her powers of seduction were as strong as mine. I was trapped within her tree, chained by my own desires. She fed and petted, and had this warmth about her, both physically and emotionally, that attracted me to her like a magnet to metal. Whenever she left me alone the intensity of my feelings lessened. At one such depression, thoughts of my future mate snuck in. I ran, my four legs becoming a hundred, until her attraction was safely behind, many kays away."

"Have you had any more predictions about us?" I asked.

"Always. Most people have idle thoughts. I have idle predictions. As with the former, the latter is often immaterial.

Surprises for all, before the sun dims.  Major transformations of ambitions."

More questions to be asked?  Yes, but not directly to Lynn, but to ourselves.  What was going to happen later in the day that would change my life?  What could change my goals?

Time passed quickly when one was occupied, and we continued to be occupied with our thoughts.  Every time something got sorted out something new to ponder would take its place.  There were too many unknowns, too many possibilities.

We saw the Copper Forest many kays before we reached it.  It glowed:  copper-colored trunks shining with a metallic glean through cedar-like foliage.  Mature trees were hundreds of meters tall.

We paused at the boundary of the odd looking trees.  It felt like we were trespassing.  We didn't belong there, no more than those within belonged in our world.  Would physical laws we took for granted work there?  Would apples drop down?  Would yellow and blue combine to form green?

Lynn led.  Appropriate under the circumstances.  She was a mute and we were entering the heart of the Western Frontier.  She walked slowly, her paws stepping high, not quite sure where and if they should fall.  In single file we followed, I first, having the closest connection to the lynx, then Stick, then Centaur, returning to his duty as proc now that we were all healthy.

I thought once we entered the forest my fears would be exorcized.  The forest would begin to appear as normal as the Beetlewoods, or the Bluewoods.  Strange to think of those hazardous woodlands being control environments.  The Copper Forest never settled into a familiar setting.  There was definitely something odd about the trees, and the bushes, and the needled floor.  Whenever a ray of light penetrated the canopy, which it did often now that the clouds had completely dissipated, it didn't simply brighten the forest floor when it hit, not in a vanilla fashion.  A full spectrum of colors splattered like oil atop water.  The colors eventually combined to white, but there was a brief, brilliant delay. The sounds of the forest were also different. The randomness of chirps, squeaks, and squawks were replaced with precise combinations of sounds: melodies, rhythms, operas, entire symphonies. Supplemental sensual stimuli were tweaked, but less easily describable. A massaging step. A fragrant odor. An uncomfortable feeling of well being, more so than when I first entered the Frontier. I caught glimpses of the abnormal, but never concretely. Insects with the faces of men and women. Draks. Horses with the upper torso of a man. Trees that moved. Arbols. Men waste-high. And cats that appeared and disappeared on a whim.

One such feline reclined on a limb where moments before there had been a branch. The copper-colored cat with dark-green stripes grew, becoming twice its original size. It flicked its tail. Lynn became mesmerized. "Sometimes the clarity of my predictions astonishes even me." The copper cat fell onto its side, revealing it was indeed male. His two powerful forelimbs stretched out, more than ninety degrees apart, the massive paws at their tips clenched. Lynn growled deeply in her throat, then mewed mournfully at a high pitch. The copper cat sat up on its haunches. It stared intensely and wondrously at Lynn. She said softly and distantly, as if she was in a trance, "My ambitions have also transformed. I won't see you again until the Sun Coast." Lynn mewed painfully one last time before she leapt onto the branch to face her suitor. Both cats vanished, replaced by two twisted, interconnected branches.

Stick was first to break free of the petrifaction of our psyches. "Maybe I shouldn't woo an arbol princess after all. If my mind becomes that muddled I will definitely fall out of a tree."

# Chapter 38

## ARBOLS

The road slowly veered from the coast. The sea could still be seen, but intermittently, whenever there were gaps in the foliage. There were more capes and coves. Fewer beaches. The shore was more picturesque, but less accessible. The onslaught of waves against rocks was spectacular, even from a distance. Finally, no sea at all. The coniferous forest became more dense, and loftier. The tops of the trees could no longer be seen.

Abruptly they appeared, angels from heaven, their emerald wings guiding them to us, but with bows instead of harps. There were dozens of them, one soft-cushioned needle landing to the next more securely boxing us in. Their wings folded upon landing, the green leather flaps obscured by the garment they were attached to. We didn't attempt a rebuttal. We conspicuously lowered our weapons, then sheathed them.

One of the arbols walked up to us. She didn't look remarkably strong, or agile, or tall. She didn't appear to be more intelligent than those around her. She didn't exude charisma or superiority. The only thing that distinguished her from her peers was the slim copper choker around her neck. It was of a simple design, bought for a silver at any market. "I've been chosen to address you," she spoke with unequivocal, non-condescending confidence. "Follow us, to find what you seek." She walked into the forest, appearing to wander aimlessly through the copper-hued woods. There was no trail.

We stood motionless. Then we stood some more. I became

concerned.  The chosen had walked far enough into the wilds to no longer be seen.  We would have certainly lost her if it wasn't for the train of arbols following her.

"If we're going, we need to leave now," Centaur blurted out.

"I guess it's why we're here," Stick seconded without much enthusiasm.

It was kind of out of our league, wasn't it?  Fighting insects and birds wasn't the same as challenging someone who could drop from the sky and flawlessly blend into the forest.

It took barely a minute for me to become lost.  If we hoped to leave the Copper Forest we had better be on good terms with the arbols.  The forest was homogenous, except for the occasional meadow that was nearly as dark as the clusters of trees.  Even if the tall trees didn't create deep shadows, we were far from the stationary sun.

The monotony ended when we entered a village.  The ground cover looked the same.  That couldn't be said for what was just meters above it.  Major limbs, bare of branches, three meters in diameter, were connected to neighboring limbs.  It was impossible to determine where one limb ended and another began.  Or was it one vast tree?  Maybe the limbs were grafted.  Natural or artificial, the interlocking limbs were an engineering marvel.  Numerous platforms were scattered among the sub-canopy, some railed, others more precarious.  Hundreds of arbols worked, and played, and relaxed, on those decks that varied in size from two meters across to nearly fifty, the larger ones enveloping the massive ten meter diameter trunks.  I didn't see any bridges or ladders between the platforms.  My mind became more at ease when I saw an arbol walk from a platform into a tree and disappear.  The trees must be hollow.

What the arbols considered PLAY would have gotten a human arrested, or killed.  Nothing appeared to be taboo or deemed too dangerous.  If one wanted a physical relationship with another person, or two or three, they did so in public view, often just a platform away from where others participated in more wholesome activities: primarily sharing heroic anecdotes and playing tag, the latter consisting of fleeing precariously close to the edge of a platform. Their agility, in all endeavors, was amazing.

"You still want to woo an arbol princess?" asked Centaur.

"Even I don't have that much of a death wish. Even if I was able to maintain my balance well enough to not fall, I don't think my body could endure the strain. As you might have noticed, arbols are more limber than humans. Their entire bodies must be double-jointed."

A handful of arbols glided down to us. The one with two copper chokers spoke to us. "I have been chosen to guide the arbols this cycle. The emerald pearl is yours if you are able to claim it."

It should have surprised me, the arbols being aware of our mission. But it didn't. Nothing surprised me much anymore. They may have been able to read our minds, but the explanation was likely more mundane. We couldn't have been the first to attempt the acquisition of such a valuable artifact.

"You give it freely?" asked Centaur.

"We do not hold the pearl."

"Then it isn't in the city?" asked Stick.

"The pearl is near and distant."

"Are we to look blindly, then?" I was becoming impatient. We had been through too much to be delayed by these GAMES. "Will you at least give us a clue to its location?"

"Seventy-five will guide you."

We glanced around, hoping to see something numbered: trees, limbs, platforms---something. Nothing.

"We appear to be speaking the same language," stated Centaur, "but we don't seem to be communicating."

"The problem is we're not asking the proper questions," spoke Stick. "The direct approach is often the best. Better yet, asking questions leaves too much to interpretation, leading to vague replies, intentional or not.  PLEASE LEAD US TO THE PEARL."

"One of you will be guided to the entrance of the Arboreal Labyrinth when he is ready."

"I'll go," Stick volunteered.

"I should be the one to go," Centaur countered.  "I'm the strongest, the most sturdy.  I'm more likely to survive."

That angel on my shoulder must have knocked off the devil on my other shoulder, because I said, "No, I should go."

Stick immediately responded. "Centaur and I are both more...."

"Would fine swordsmanship or great strength been enough to overpower the arbols if they were unfriendly?  Intangibles will be required to acquire the pearl.  I survived a hornet and a drak, alone.  Most people consider the balanced cursed.  But we're also considered to be lucky.  Luck was as crucial a factor for us arriving here as agility or brawn, or experience."

Solving the problem for us, the chosen said, "Two of you have prior commitments."

"But---," we replied simultaneously.

Four equines, horses with the upper torso of a man, trotted towards us.  They were broad of chest and wickedly joyous in demeanor.  They stopped ten meters short of us.  Each carried a bow, cocked with an arrow.  "Come," spoke one of them.  We didn't have to ask who they were referring.  Centaur went grimly toward them, probably believing sacrificing himself would protect Stick and me.  What did he do again to earn his name?  The equines surrounded him, one at each corner.  He walked off, his head held high.  If he was going to the gallows, he was going to do so with class.

Was I going to be next?  A warrior in full plate appeared.  He held a two-handed sword emblazoned with a concave platinum and gold octagon.  "I believe this is my battle," said Stick.  "I may not become an Octagonal Knight, but I can at least determine if I can better one.  Can I borrow some of your luck, Hornet?"  The

Octagonal Knight turned and walked away upon Stick's approach. A battle among warriors was a private affair.

"Lead me," I said to the chosen. "I am as ready as I will ever be."

# Chapter 39

## COUNTERED IN KIND

My guide strolled, her movement uncluttered by obligation, serenity tempered with playfulness. She wandered aimlessly through the boles, stopping beside a tree that looked no different than the numerous others we passed. Nothing was remarkable about it, until she pressed her palm against the trunk, opening a door I wasn't aware existed. The door perfectly matched the trunk, as if a slice of the tree was cut out and replaced. The hinges were roots.

Within the trunk was a circular room 10 meters in diameter. Dozens of vines filled the room. Every few seconds an arbol---there were three of them---would bring one up their face, becoming transfixed as they looked through its hollow end.

"What are they doing?" I asked.

"Observing."

The chosen climbed a ladder. I followed directly behind, wishing I wasn't wearing armor. It was no longer a mystery why the arbols had never been conquered. Those attacking would be worn out before they reached the heart of the city.

We passed through the room above us. Five arbols sat at an

irregularly-shaped wooden table discussing something in a language I couldn't comprehend. It was very musical, organic in nature, reminiscent of water dripping, or a light breeze rustling leaves. The table was an extension of the floor, rising up from the wood, forming an undercut plateau.

Another room. This one vacant, with a corridor leading away from it. We continued climbing.

"Exactly how far up are we going?"

"Near the middle, to the twelfth level." I was concerned I wasn't going to make it. I was already sweating and out of breath. But somehow I did make it. For myself, perhaps, but more so to impress the arbols. If a salvager couldn't climb some steps, what did that say for common townsfolk? For every unchanged that believed mutes were brutes, there must have been a mute that believed the unchanged weak.

We stopped in a room slightly smaller than the one we began our climb. A single arbol stood in front of the entrance to a tunnel. She said, "I have been chosen to guard the entrance to the Arboreal Labyrinth today."

"I've been wondering. Everyone seems to be chosen to do something. How is one chosen?"

"The only method that's truly unbiased," the arbol chosen to be mayor replied. "Randomly. A dart is dropped on a platform of name plates arranged spirally, selecting someone for a specific duty."

"Don't those names in the center get chosen more often?"

"Once a person has been chosen, their name is moved to the perimeter, at the end of the spiral, moving everyone else closer to the center."

The arbol chosen to guard the Arboreal Labyrinth said, "Each wrong decision will be countered with nature. Each action countered in kind. May the Arboreal Labyrinth guard what needs to be retained, release what has been earned. Enter, relinquishing freedom until termination."

My friends were in at least as bad a predicament as I. "Here I go." The tunnel was wooden, but had the sheen and strength of steel. It glowed. From the sunlight, perhaps. More likely, from some internal energy. It pulsated with life, warming, and comforting. It was alive, but more so. It may have been part of the plant kingdom, but not exclusively so.

I came to a fork. I went right, deciding I would always take the right fork, so I wouldn't become lost. I came to another fork. I must have chosen correctly. The next tunnel terminated at a room, without visible means of egress. I couldn't have found the pearl already.

I felt a draft, from no discernable direction. It intensified, churning around me. I attempted to fight my way back to the tunnel, but was held in place by the conflicting air currents. My hair danced above me, thousands of narrow worms crawling through invisible earth. Pieces of my armor pulled away. The wind continued to intensify as I increased my resolve to escape. My armor was breaking apart, pieces of metal and strips of leather rotated about me like satellites. My dagger was also pulled free. And my backpack. I withdrew my sword, using it to deflect objects. The sword was pulling free from my hand. I couldn't take it anymore. I curled into a fetal position on the floor. The winds immediately died down, followed by the thud and dings of my armor and weapons falling to the floor. I stood up hesitantly. There was no wind at all. I looked around, hoping to see the emerald pearl magically appear. I couldn't be that lucky. I wasn't. I retrieved my dagger and sword. The armor I left, not having the time, skill, or patience to reconstruct it.

I returned to the tunnel, being careful to turn right at the fork, so I wouldn't return to the beginning prematurely. The guardian insinuated I could only leave the labyrinth by achieving my goal or by dying.

I came to another fork. I chose right again. There had to be as many wrong left turns as wrong right turns. I couldn't afford to

226

become lost, and I would if I randomly chose which fork to take.

I entered a room similar to the last. I braced myself: I saw no emerald pearl. Water seeped into the room through the walls. It was up to my knees in less than a minute. "What was keeping the water from pouring out through the tunnel?" I wasn't going to allow the trap to achieve its full effect this time. I darted towards the tunnel. I bounced back, like I had hit a trampoline. I tumbled into the water, momentarily gagging when my head went under. I pushed myself back up, first with my hands, then with my legs. The water was up to my waist now. I could only keep my head above water so long. What could I do? Carve my way out? I was confident the arbols wouldn't allow me to do that. What tools did I have, other than my weapons? The water was up to my chest. I took off my pack. I searched through it. THE UNDERWATER BREATHING ROD! I injected myself with it, instantly growing gills. I smiled as the water rose past them. A couple of minutes after the water filled the room, it receded. I shook away the excess liquid from my clothes, then walked confidently into the tunnel.

I continued with my strategy. I went right again at the next fork. Instead of arriving at a room, I came to another fork. How can I bypass the elements of earth and fire? I didn't want to be buried alive or burned to death. What clue was I given? Seventy-five? How did that relate to the Arboreal Labyrinth? I had two choices at each fork. Two choices repeated. Why did that sound familiar? Computers. Binary code. What would 75 be in base 2? Two to the sixth power was 64. Thirty-two added to that was 96. Too much. Sixteen was also too much. Adding eight would make the sum 72. Adding 4 would be too much. Adding 2 would make the sum 74. And adding 1 would make it 75. In base 2 the number would be written as 1001011. Ones for lefts, and zeroes for rights: LRRLRLL. That's not right. What if lefts became zeros and right ones? RLLRLRR. Yes, the first four choices match. I should go left at the next fork. I experimented. ANOTHER FORK APPEARED INSTEAD OF A ROOM!

I followed the sequence to its conclusion.  My last selection brought me into a room with a wooden column.  It was engraved with a life-size arbol woman carrying a sword and a small green sphere.  The sword was not part of the engraving.  It was a real weapon, embedded in the wood.  As was the sphere.  With my sword raised in one hand and my dagger in the other, I entered the room.  The wooden arbol dropped out of the column.  With equal parts malice and chagrin, she moved towards me, sword thrust before her.

If I didn't do something immediately I was doomed.  She wasn't a hornet, or an ant, or a beetle.  And I wasn't the strongest man, or the greatest swordsman, or the best archer.  What did the guardian say?  Each action countered in kind?  Raising my weapons and bringing them forward represented an attack, so the wooden arbol was preparing to attack.  What was it I wanted the arbol to do?  Give me the pearl.  OF COURSE!  I handed the arbol my sword.  She handed me hers.  After sighing deeply, I handed her my hornet dagger.  I had become attached to it, but not too attached to risk the failure of our mission.  She handed me the green sphere and returned to the column, which she became part of again, my sword and dagger embedded in the wood.

With reverence I examined the green sphere.  Finally.  After hundreds of kays, above and below ground, numerous battles and injuries---and deaths.  The sphere was metallic.  So it wasn't an emerald.  But if someone was willing to pay hundreds of gold for it, it might as well be.  It looked familiar.  Nothing I've seen on Limbo.  In a museum.  An assortment of them, in different colors.  THE EMERALD PEARL WAS PART OF A TRANSPORT PORTAL!  One of those portable ones field agents used, self-destructing after a single use, so it wouldn't be left behind.  If I could find the other spheres….

*** This concludes Book 1 of the Limbo Chronicles.  ***

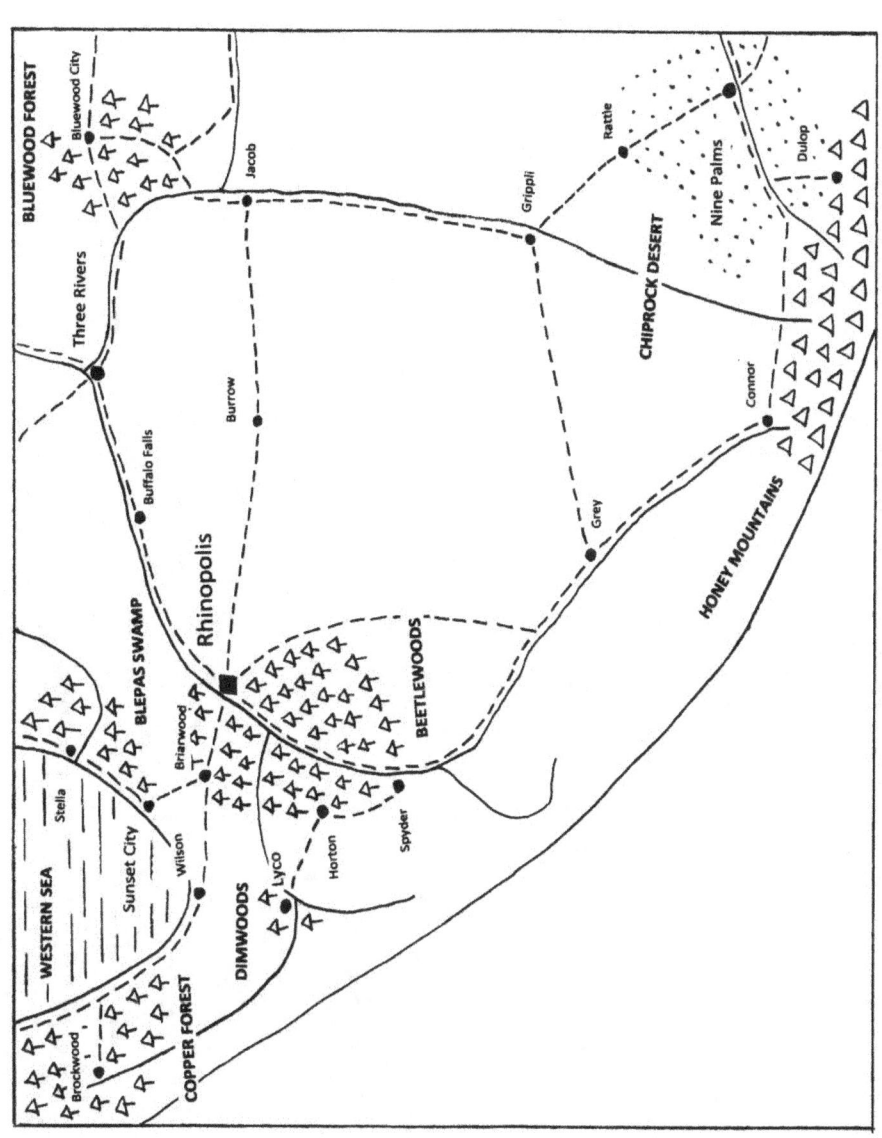

www.ingramcontent.com/pod-product-compliance
Lightning Source LLC
Chambersburg PA
CBHW050734230626
47052CB00002BA/186